The Cry of the Innocents

iv

The Cry of the Innocents

Paul W. Lentz, Jr.

Ty Ty Press, Peachtree City, Georgia

www.PaulLentzAuthor.com

Copyright 2017 Paul W. Lentz, Jr.

Cover Art by J.R.C. Dyer, jrcdyer.com

ISBN-13: 978-0692985199 (Ty Ty Press)
ISBN-10: 0692985190

10 9 8 7 6 5 4 3 2

Dedication

This story is dedicated to the millions of Jews, Gypsies, Homosexuals, Disabled Persons, and Others named "Undesirable" and murdered by the Nazis during the Holocaust. We must never forget them.

Other books by the author:

"On Ty Ty Creek: Sweet Potato Pie, Moonshine, and other Southern Traditions"

"The Stuff of Life"

"Holy Fire"

Upcoming books:

"Enemy Planet: The House of Wolf"
("The Stuff of Life, Book II)
Fall 2018

"Enemy Planet: Son of Wolf"
("The Stuff of Life, Book III)
Late 2018

"Three Planets" (Working Title)
("The Stuff of Life, Book IV)
2019

Books are available on Amazon.com.
https://www.amazon.com/author/paullentz
All royalties go directly to the
Friends of the Peachtree City Library.

For information on
upcoming books check
www.PaulLentzAuthor.com

TABLE OF CONTENTS

Jessie Long Tree

Jessie Long Tree lies beside a yucca bush. One of the yucca's sharp spines pierces his right arm, but he does not feel it. He does not see the sun that bakes his flesh. His eyes are gone and the empty sockets stare at nothing. He does not breathe; his heart pumps no blood for his liver and kidneys to clean. His lungs, heart, kidneys, and liver are not present. His chest and tummy are a gaping emptiness framed by ragged flesh and mangled bone.

Spencer Hansen

Spencer Hansen pushes the rolling bucket a few feet down the service hallway of the Glen Canyon Medical Spa, dips his mop into the bucket, wrings it out, and swabs another strip of tile. He puts down a yellow *Caution-Cuidado* cone, and prepares to move the bucket.

Through a window, he sees an ambulance pull into the rear portico. Two black SUVs with darkened windows lead; two more follow. Men in black suits with curly wires from their collars to their ears jump from the SUVs. They turn away from the ambulance. One raises his wrist to his mouth and speaks. *Secret Service?* Spencer wonders. *Dr. Standart told me I might see important patients – guests, they call them – but Secret Service?* He watches the rear of the ambulance open and people in white scrubs lift a gurney and allow its wheels to unfold. The people in white roll the gurney toward the door, led by two men in black.

The door from the portico into the hallway opens about 20 yards from Spencer.

A man in black sees Spencer, who has the presence of mind to resume mopping. The man rushes toward Spencer, grabs his ID badge, and compares the photo to Spencer's face. He pats down Spencer. "Stand still. Do not speak. Do not make sudden moves."

Spencer is afraid even to nod, but squeaks out, "Yes, sir." Dr. Standart also told him everyone at the spa is "sir" or "ma'am," and that he is to be polite.

Spencer watches the people in white scrubs wheel the gurney toward a patient wing. As soon as the men in black disappear and Spencer's shaking stops, he continues mopping.

Two hours later, he has reached a patient wing. He is busy mopping when a door opens. A nurse steps into the hall, sees Spencer, and gestures. "Come in here. Bring your mop."

"Yes, sir," Spencer says. *I want to be a doctor, so I applied to be a nurse's assistant, but janitor – orderly they call it – was the only job open. Oh, well. It's a job. And I only have to work here for three months until school starts in September.*

Spencer rolls the bucket into Suite 9. This is the first time he has been in a patient's room. Except for the tile floor, the hospital bed, and the connections on the wall for oxygen and suction, it looks more like a resort hotel than a hospital. The walls are like a purple-gray. White crown molding and window frames match the stark white of the floor. White, except where a yellow puddle with lumps lies next to the bed. The nurse gestures to the puddle. Spencer tackles it with his mop. As he works, he sneaks a look at the patient. It is a middle-aged man. Spencer is startled when the man's eyes meet his. The whites of his eyes are yellow. *Jaundiced,* Spencer thinks, and blushes when the man smiles.

"The puddle," the nurse says. Spencer ducks his head. The next time he rinses the mop, he looks away from the bed and nearly drops the mop when he sees four of the men in black. Two hold assault rifles. All of them watch Spencer. The one who accosted Spencer in the hallway earlier speaks. "*Rajet minh.*" The other three relax.

Jumpin' Gerbils! That's not English and this is the guy they just brought in. The men, they look Middle-Eastern, not like Secret Service. What have I gotten into?

When he finishes with the puddle, Spencer looks to the nurse for approval. Before the nurse speaks, the patient does. Spencer understands the man's heavily accented words. "Thank you, young man. Come closer, please."

Spencer looks first at the men with guns then at the nurse. The nurse seems to be in charge. He nods. "Do it."

4

Spencer steps to the side of the bed. The patient pats him on the shoulder. "You are a kind young man, and an honorable one. Service to the sick is a blessing." When Spencer does not flinch at the man's touch or his stare, the patient pats Spencer's cheek before dropping his arm and looking away.

"That will be all," the nurse says.

Spencer is sure he has mopped every hallway in the spa and has emptied and refilled the bucket at least twenty times when his pager goes off. The message is to report to Dr. Standart, the Medical Director. Spencer changes the brown scrubs he is wearing for a clean set, and hurries toward the Administration Wing. The doctor's secretary ushers Spencer into the director's office.

"Spencer, you know who I am."

It is not a question, but Spencer answers, "Yes, sir."

"You remember the contract in which you agreed not to talk about any guest, including those you might recognize as celebrities, politicians, or other important people. You agreed not to speak to a guest unless he or she spoke, first."

"Yes, sir."

"Good lad. Keep that in mind when you hear what I'm about to say. Your cleanup job, this morning, earned a lot of points – with the guest and therefore with me. The Emir wants you—"

"I didn't mean to say that," the director interrupts his own words. "I just broke one of my own rules."

Emboldened by the man's manner and words, Spencer grins and then says, "I won't tell if you won't tell."

Dr. Standart chuckles. "You will do well here, Spencer. The guest in Room 9 will undergo treatment in two days. He wants you to be part of his care team afterwards. We tested you for TB before we hired you. You must get some additional tests – blood, urine, and feces. Before you go into his room, you will be scrubbed and gowned. Let me see your hands."

Spencer steps closer to the desk and holds out his hands.

"Good, fingernails trimmed and clean. Nurse Emile Grassier, who you saw in the patient's room, will show you how to scrub before you go into the room. You will do exactly what he, any other nurse, and all doctors tell you. That and nothing more. Do you understand? Good. You will work an 8:00 AM to 6:00 PM shift every day for at least two weeks. We will pay overtime. Is that agreeable?"

Spencer's mind is quick to realize how much more interesting his job might be, not to mention how much money the overtime will bring. "Yes, sir."

"Report to the lab for the tests. They are waiting for you. Take tomorrow off, and report to Nurse Grassier at the nurses' dressing room at 8:00 AM, on Wednesday. And thank you, Spencer. The Emir is a very important guest, and it is incumbent upon all of us to keep him happy."

The lab technician greets Spencer and takes him from the anteroom into the laboratory, itself.

"I hear you will be on a care team," the tech says. "You might want to see more of the testing than just watching me stick a needle in your arm…" He pushes a needle into a vein in Spencer's arm as he speaks. The needle attaches to a cup about a half-inch in diameter and an inch long.

"… and pushing these sample tubes into the cup. They have a vacuum in them, and are color-coded. Some have coagulants, some anticoagulants, some nothing but vacuum." The tech describes the tubes as he pushes them into the cup.

"We call them vampires. Red vampires, green vampires, blue vampires, gold vampires. We don't say the vampire part in front of guests." He fills four more tubes. Then, he hands Spencer a sample cup and an envelope that holds a Popsicle stick and a folded piece of cardboard.

"Pee in the cup and try your hardest to poop. Before you flush, take a sample of poo with the Popsicle stick, and put it inside the cardboard. If you can't do that today, do it tomorrow at home and bring me the envelope." He points toward a restroom.

When Spencer returns, the tech holds out a long swab. "Open your mouth."

Spencer complies. The tech scrapes the inside of Spencer's cheek and puts the swab in a test tube, which he seals. "DNA sample," he says. "Routine."

"Where is the DNA sequenced?" Spencer asks.

"Right here … come on, I'll show you."

The tech leads Spencer into another room. On a table is something that looks like a microwave oven on steroids – a box three feet wide, at least that tall, and two feet deep. Like a microwave, there is a window on the front. There's no touch panel, but rather a computer terminal, mouse, and keyboard.

"It will take two days to do this. Not as long as it used to since we got a sixty-four-banger capillary electrophoresis machine. It's all automated. *Set it and forget it.*"

"Will I get to see …?" Spencer asks.

"Oh, sure. Check back. Give me a few days. When you have time, I'll show you how it works."

After thanking the tech, Spencer leaves the lab and bicycles to his apartment.

≈≈≈≈≈

On Wednesday morning, Nurse Grassier meets Spencer at the nurses' dressing room. "Step one, shower. These sponges are impregnated with antibacterial soap. Use it on your hair and all of your body. Spread your legs wide and don't overlook the inter-gluteal cleft and perineum. Those are—"

"I know what they are, sir." Spencer blushes. *I blush too easily. It's the price I pay for being a Norwegian blond. Blushing, and being teased about it all the time.*

The nurse nods. "You know medical terms?"

7

"Yes, sir. I'm going to be a doctor, some day."

Nurse Grassier laughs. "You know the story about the nurse who died? At the Pearly Gates, St. Peter asked where the nurse wanted to be in heaven and the nurse said, 'Anywhere except where there is a doctor.'

"St. Peter took the nurse to a beautiful cloud. The nurse pointed to a figure in whites, with a stethoscope hanging from his pocket. 'That looks like a doctor and I asked for no doctors.'

"St. Peter said, 'He's not a doctor; he's God. He just thinks he's a doctor.'"

"That's a good story," Spencer says. "Does that mean we can't be friends?"

"Friends? Not that easily or that soon. Colleagues, yes. And I'll not tease you too much about wanting to be a doctor."

≈≈≈≈≈

At 1:00 PM the next day the Emir returns from the recovery room. A team of orderlies and nurses rolls him into Room 9. Spencer is one of six people who lift the sheet – and the Emir – from the gurney and onto the bed. Then the team moves four tubes connected to the patient.

"This one's a morphine drip, for pain," Grassier says. "It's a simple catheter into a vein on his arm. On the other arm is a peripherally inserted central catheter or PIC line, which we'll use, later. You still following all those words?"

"Yes, sir. A PIC line is a catheter, which runs from his arm through the subclavian vein to the superior vena cava and within centimeters of the right atrium. A PIC line is like a power-port, except usually in the arm and only temporary, while a power port is normally in the chest or abdomen and can be used for years. Power ports and PIC lines are used for powerful drugs, especially chemotherapy."

"The others?"

8

Spencer looks at the bags. "This one is saline – salt water for hydration. The orange one hanging out from under the sheet is a Foley urinary catheter. The other one, from under the sheet, I don't know. And the last hanging one doesn't have anything on it but a bar code."

"Very good, Spencer." Grassier picks up a gadget from the bedside table. It looks like a thick, heavy cell phone covered with a thin film of clear plastic. Grassier makes sure Spencer is watching when he raises the gadget to the bar code, presses a button, and scans the bar code. He looks at a display window on the gadget. "This bottle is human immunoglobulin to fight infection. First thing we will do is to hook this line to a pump to regulate the drip and plug it into the PIC line."

Hopping Higgs. That bottle must hold 30 cc of immunoglobulin. When Mother had hepatitis, they only gave each one in the family a one-cc shot. In the gluteus maximus. What happened that the Emir needs so much more than that?

Only minutes later, a nurse comes in with another bag, which is hooked to the second side of the pump to feed a second PIC line. Spencer reads the label on the bag. *Muromonab-CD3 dil Saline. Something diluted in saline. I've got to remember that name so I can look it up.*

Grassier reads numbers from the chart. The second nurse compares them with numbers on the bag. Grassier hooks the line from the bag to the pump, then punches a keypad on the pump to insert the numbers and the rate of flow.

After hooking up everything, Grassier gives Spencer a lesson on the pump. "This funny looking on top of the pump is a wifi antenna." He points to the ceiling. "And so is that. the copper combs are where we can attach a second pump."

Spencer sees in the ceiling a V-shaped antenna about four inches long projecting from a dull gray box. "Who is monitoring this?"

"Pharmacy and medical records. And billing."

Spencer is puzzled. *I understand why a regular hospital would want to keep track of every drop of every drug for billing, but the people who come here are paying tens of thousands for face-lifts and liposuction. Does the spa really nickel-and dime them for their drugs?*

Spencer is overwhelmed by all the information and instructions Grassier gives him. In the confusion, he does not ask about the second line that comes from under the sheet and is hooked to an opaque bottle.

Grassier dismisses Spencer at 6:00 PM. Spencer doesn't stop to change from his scrubs, but returns to his apartment to shower and eat something. Re-heated frozen pizza is tonight's choice. He sets his alarm clock and climbs into bed before remembering to Google *muromonab*. He grabs his iPad and types in the name. The top result is UNOS, the United Network for Organ Sharing. That is surprising. Then Spencer reads further. *Immunosuppressant. Keeps the body from rejecting a transplant. It stops the action of T-cells, which would otherwise attack a transplanted organ. Normally administered by injection. That's weird. The Emir is getting it diluted in saline. Why are they giving him that? Just what did they do to him?*

On the second day as a member of the Emir's care team, Spencer is holding a urinal bottle for the Emir, who insisted they remove the Foley urinary catheter. Spencer looks up, waiting for the Emir to signal he is finished peeing. He meets the Emir's eyes. *They're white. He's not jaundiced. The anti-rejection drugs, sterile procedures, and now, no jaundice. OMG – Oh, my Gerbils – he got a liver transplant. That second bag is a surgical drain.*

≈≈≈≈≈

Spencer finds it easy to be part of the Emir's care team. The other members of the team treat him with respect, even though as the lowest person on the pay scale he gets many of the nastier jobs, and handling bedpans seems to be a critical part of Spencer's duties. Even then, the Emir takes it in stride. *I'm not sure I could ever face someone who held a bedpan under my butt while I pooped*, Spencer thinks. *But the Emir seems able to separate that from whatever else he thinks of me. Mostly, he wants me where he can see me. I think he's gay, or at least appreciates—*

"Spencer? Would you…?" A nurse asks for help hanging a new bag of saline, interrupting Spencer's thoughts.

Four weeks later, the Emir is sufficiently recovered to leave the spa. Grassier and another nurse will accompany him to his home. The Emir hints he would like Spencer to join them, but Spencer demurs. "I will begin school soon to become a doctor. I would rather be a doctor should you need me someday." The Emir gestures, and one of the men with guns hands Spencer an envelope. "Open later," the man says.

Spencer puts the envelope in a pocket of his scrubs and thanks the Emir for the opportunity to serve him. "I have learned a great deal about the practice of medicine. I have learned many things I would not learn in medical school, and I thank you for that."

≈≈≈≈≈

Spencer whistles when he opens the envelope. It holds hundred-dollar bills. The money is welcome. The five thousand dollars will pay tuition for two semesters at the community college. *If the guy is rich enough to come to the US for a liver transplant, I guess he's rich enough to tip the help,* Spencer thinks.

≈≈≈≈≈

Spencer is once again mopping halls and scrubbing toilets when he spots Nurse Grassier. "You're back," Spencer says.

"Hey, Spencer. Yes. Three days now. Come on, let's get a coffee and I'll tell you all about it."

"I'm not supposed—"

"Not supposed to fraternize with the *professional staff?* Don't sweat it. Dr. Standart is playing golf with the warden."

"The warden?"

"Sam Red Horse, warden of U.P.S. #9 – the state prison across the river."

Spencer pushes his bucket and mop into a janitor's closet and follows Grassier to the nurses' break room. Grassier makes them both coffee from a cup-at-a-time machine and gestures Spencer to a table.

"Thank you … Nurse Grassier," Spencer says, not sure how to address the man.

"Emile," Grassier replies. "Unless a doctor or administrator is around, it's 'Emile.'"

"Thank you, Emile. How was your trip?"

Grassier tells Spencer about flying from the local airport to New York, where the plane was refueled, then to Morocco for more fuel, then to Riyadh, Saudi Arabia. "The Emir … the patient slept most of the way. We kept a nurse on duty, but the rest of us could sleep in real beds, not just reclining seats. There was a chef who cooked real food, not just reheated stuff.

"Somebody in white robes with one of those rope things that hold a white scarf on his head met us. Everyone bowed to him. The ropes were gold-colored, and we found out he was the crown prince, and the patient was his uncle.

"They took the patient, with a doctor and one nurse, in an ambulance and the rest of us in black SUVs." He chuckles. "Chevrolet Tahoes, with tinted windows. Just like the Secret Service uses."

Grassier stops to drink some of his coffee, and then describes the patient's quarters, the staff's quarters, the servants, and all the Emir's people did for the medical staff. "It was a two-week vacation for most of us."

"That's pretty amazing," Spencer says. "I was wondering, though, where they got the liver."

Grassier looks hard at Spencer. "You shouldn't even think about that, you know." Then he relaxes. "I assisted yesterday on a kidney transplant, and saw the donor in the recovery room. Couldn't tell much about him but one thing was odd."

Spencer raises his eyebrows.

"Remember, you're not supposed to talk about this. He was wearing one of those electronic things around his ankle, like he was under house arrest or something."

≈≈≈≈≈

Labor Day is Spencer's last workday at the Spa. He expects an easy day, since many people will be on holiday. The summons to Dr. Standart's office surprises him.

"Spencer, this is your last day. I understand you will study to become a doctor, and wish you luck."

"Thank you, Dr. Standart."

"Please, since this is your last day at work, call me Todd. We may be colleagues, some day. I think you will make a fine doctor. You know we are not part of the community college's in-service program because of the risk to our patients' privacy. However, I have sent an email to Dr. Deschene at the Navajo Western Regional Hospital. I hope he will contact you through the college."

"Thank you, sir. Thank you, very much."

Spencer spends that night with his thoughts and more re-heated pizza. Tomorrow will be his first day at the community college. That thought weighs on him. The envelope of cash weighs on him.

Is it a thank-you gift or a bribe? The Emir didn't have a facelift or liposuction; he had a liver transplant. I know the spa is not licensed for transplant surgery. Wonder where the liver came from? Or lobe. I'd forgotten that. They can take just a lobe of someone's liver and transplant it into someone else, and it will re-grow a liver. Wonder if that's what they did. Still, where would a lobe come from?

≈≈≈≈≈

A few miles away, while Spencer is thinking about his future, Dr. Deschene, the pathologist at the Navajo Regional Hospital, is reading Standart's email. *Smarmy bastard,* Deschene thinks of Dr. Standart. *But he is a harsh taskmaster. If he goes to the trouble of recommending someone, they're probably very good.* Deschene picks up the phone and calls his golfing buddy, the provost of the community college.

14

Jessie Long Tree

The scavengers, so nicknamed by those who are not members, think of themselves differently. They are Reapers, not scavengers. They are men and woman who seek the isolated, the lonely, those without homes and without a future, those who congregate in the neighborhoods around bus stations and Salvation Army shelters. These teams ignore the elderly, the obvious drunks, and those whose eyes, pustules, and slack mouths mark them as drug addicts. They search for the young, those disenfranchised by their families, those hoping to make their way to the Promised Land of California.

The bus station in Gallup, New Mexico is the territory of the Tonaleah Reapers, one of the most successful and therefore richest of the scavenger gangs. When the Moenkopi Reapers gang tries to horn in on the bus station, the Tonaleah Reapers wage a silent war. Three of the Moenkopi become organ donors or medical research subjects. Three of the Tonaleah Reapers are injured, but not seriously enough to end their lives. After that, the other gangs leave the Tonaleah Reapers and the bus station alone.

A month after that battle, a Tonaleah Reaper spots a youth, Navajo by appearance, walking toward the bus station. At one moment, he appears determined. At the next, he seems afraid. The Reaper understands. The boy is running away from home, away from the reservation. He will not need much encouragement to follow the Reaper.

The Reaper decides on his approach. He walks toward the boy and holds out his hand. "Can you spare a couple of dollars so I can get some food?"

Those words startle the boy just enough he stops walking. "Um, I don't have much and it's got to last a long time. I'm sorry … isn't there somewhere? A Sallie? A shelter?"

"Nah, the Sallies don't come down here. Territory's too rough for them. The OTCC runs the only shelter … " Seeing the puzzlement on the Navajo boy's face, the Reaper adds, "The One True Christian Church. Heavy-duty fundamentalists. You don't want to mix with them, no matter how hungry you are."

The Reaper pauses as if in thought. "There is a guy who runs a youth hostel," he says. "They say you can get a meal and a kip for the night."

"At what price?" the Navajo boy asks. He is old enough to have heard stories of men whose promises come with conditions. "What does he ask for?"

"Nothing," assures the Reaper. "Except it's only for one night."

Somehow, that lowers the Navajo boy's concern just enough. "I am Jessie Long Tree. Will you take me to this place?"

The Reaper is right. Jessie's stay at the hostel is only one night, although he does not wake the next morning. The drugs in his supper plus an injection at 3:00 AM make sure of that.

≈≈≈≈≈

Henry Belka's knuckles are white on the steering wheel of the tall, white Mercedes van. He is driving carefully and keeping to the speed limit. *I can't be stopped with what's in the back …*

Henry picked up the body at the Glen Canyon Spa and is on his way back to the Peaceful Rest Mortuary when his cell phone buzzes. Henry takes a quick look at the screen and finds a place to turn off. He pulls into the parking lot of the local Sprawl-Mart and reads the text message. What he sees is frightening.

Why would the State Mortuary Board pull a no-notice inspection today, of all days? Damn Mr. Hilflinger, anyway. He keeps cutting corners. I know one of these days he's gonna get caught. Henry sits in the van allowing the cool air from the vents to dry his sweat. *I can't drive around all day with a body in the back, especially not one like that. I can't go to the mortuary, and I sure can't go back to the spa.* A plan forms in Henry's mind.

Forty minutes later, he has crossed the river. He pulls the van into the side yard of his home. Thirty minutes after that, he has saddled his horse. The horse shies at the body bag as if knowing what it holds, but Henry calms the animal and slings the bag across the horse's withers just forward of the saddle. An hour later, Henry unzips the bag and dumps the body. Despite the rough treatment, the body rests on its back. The arms are at its side; legs, outstretched. Henry does not notice that the sharp leaf of a yucca bush penetrates one arm. *Animals will take care of this. Won't be nothin' left after tonight. Come Coyote, come! Come Raven! It's suppertime.*

Henry returns to his home, showers, and heads to the mortuary. He stops at a quick-lube place and has the oil changed in the van. The receipt and Henry's claim to have had lunch at a sit-down diner should explain his long absence.

≈≈≈≈≈

Henry slides a cardboard coffin over the rollers and into the already-hot oven, closes the door, and monitors the progress of the cremation. When the cremation is complete, Henry turns down the gas and scrapes the still white-hot cremains into a bin under the oven. After the bones – all that remains – have cooled, they pass under a magnet to remove ferrous metal before Henry dumps them into a high-speed, industrial-strength blender, which reduces them to powder.

He is about to roll another body into the oven when Mr. Hilflinger comes in. "Where were you? Did you get the body? Where is it?"

At first, Henry's boss is livid at Henry's answer. After yelling at Henry for a while, Hilflinger calms down, and agrees. "It's too late, now, and too risky to retrieve the body. Let the animals have it. And wash that body bag with bleach. There'd better not be a trace of DNA left."

Dr. Nastas Deschene

The Tuesday after Labor Day is the first day of Spencer's first year at the Folio Community College. The college consists of five brick buildings on a plot of land at the southeast corner of US Highway 85 and State Route 74 south of Folio. Unlike the grammar school, middle school, and high school, there is no landscaping except two pots of cactus flanking the doorway of the administration building, and a planter of now-dead *Aizoaceae*, what most people call *ice plant,* at the base of the sign at the entrance.

Parking is at a premium, and Spencer is glad he rode his bicycle over the dirt trail from his apartment to the campus. He is also glad he found an apartment only a mile from the college even though when the wind is from the northwest he occasionally gets a whiff of the sewage plant.

Spencer and at least three hundred other new students crowd the halls. After waiting in line for an hour, he gets a class schedule and his first in-service assignment. The Admissions Counselor tells him that Dr. Deschene called the school and asked for Spencer.

"You have impressed someone important," she says. "Your in-service is with Dr. Deschene at the Navajo Regional Hospital. You understand you will have classes in the morning and in-service in the afternoon. You must provide your own transportation."

Spencer is doubly glad he rode his bike. Parking at the hospital is worse than at the college, but the hospital is only two miles from the college. *I'll get plenty of exercise. I hope the winter won't be too cold. I'd better bring a jacket, though.* Spencer knows the air of the high desert cools quickly after sunset.

The Admissions Counselor's voice drones on, explaining things Spencer has read in the handbook. He tries to pay attention on the off chance she will say something he doesn't already know.

Dr. Standart must have written the letter he promised. I wasn't sure he would. He made a promise and kept it. I must remember that, and I must remember my promise to him to keep in touch. I'll have to intern at a teaching hospital someday, but that's a long time from now. Afterwards? Maybe a position at the spa.

Spencer thinks of his mother's insistence he write thank-you notes for gifts. When the scout troop disfellowshipped him, his devout Mormon parents made it clear he was no longer welcome in their home. They did not completely abandon him, but put money into an account each month. It is enough to pay for his apartment and important expenses, but they expect him to work to pay for his education. Spencer fears the money will stop when he turns twenty-one.

Spencer writes a thank-you note to Dr. Standart. In his mind, he composes a similar note to his parents, but he neither writes it nor posts it. There is no reason to do so. His parents have returned, unopened, all his cards and letters.

≈≈≈≈≈

On the Wednesday after Labor Day, at 1:00 PM, Spencer waits in Dr. Deschene's outer office. He is wearing his best clothes although they are none too good. Instead of ragged blue jeans and a faded T-shirt, he wears a polo-style shirt and khaki trousers with an ironed crease. Plain, white trainers replace sandals. He showered earlier that morning and applied an antiperspirant, which he is sure has worn off.

The secretary's intercom buzzes. He leads Spencer into Dr. Deschene's office. Dr. Deschene stands to greet Spencer and steps around the desk to shake his hand. Although Spencer is tall, he has to look up to the doctor, who is at least six inches taller than he.

20

Tallest Navajo I've ever seen, Spencer thinks. There is no doubt Dr. Deschene is Navajo. Black hair, pulled back into a ponytail. Eyes that seem to look through Spencer and the wall behind him. An aquiline nose, like the great Cheyenne war chief, "Hook Nose," completes the image.

"You are interested in pathology," Dr. Deschene says after they sit at a bay window. The window looks over the grounds of the hospital. A careful selection of drought-tolerant plants plus judicious watering makes the hospital, like the Glen Canyon schools and the Glen Canyon Country Club, an oasis of green.

Spencer reflects on his early training as a scout. Despite being disfellowshipped from the troop and his family, he still holds to some of those teachings. *I owe him the truth.* "Sir, I am interested in medicine. I want to be a doctor, a surgeon. Dr. Standart offered a letter of introduction. I spent the summer mopping floors at the Glen Canyon Medical Spa. I would much rather learn about pathology than be stuck as a gopher anywhere else. On my honor, I will do my best to be a worthy student."

Dr. Deschene is briefly surprised. No student has offered such a clear explanation and commitment about his or her reasons for wanting an in-service. Dr. Deschene believes his mission in life is to mentor apprentices. This young man – maybe he will never be a pathologist or, like Dr. Deschene, a forensic anthropologist – but in Dr. Deschene's opinion he will become one heck of a doctor.

"Then welcome, son," Dr. Deschene says. "On my honor, I will do my best to be a worthy mentor."

On his honor? He recognized the scout oath and responded with it. I must tell him—

Dr. Deschene interrupts Spencer's thought. "Come on, now. Chief Joseph White Eagle is waiting for us in the laboratory. You'll get to see a real autopsy on your first day."

≈≈≈≈≈

Dr. Deschene leads Spencer to a dressing room. Spencer strips and picks up one of the antibacterial sponges. Dr. Deschene turns and sees that Spencer is naked. "Um, Spencer, we don't shower. Sorry. I should have explained. Just scrubs, mask, and gloves. Mostly, to protect street clothing from what we'll be examining – and us from the odd pathogen. You'll find coverings for your shoes in that drawer. They're all the same size, usually too big."

Spencer's blush is brighter by at least a thousand watts than the lighting in the dressing room.

The pathology lab is cold. A body, covered by a sheet, lies on a stainless steel table. Above the table are both bright lights and observation windows.

"Joseph White Eagle, Chief of the Navajo Nation Police," Dr. Deschene says, pointing to the observation window. Spencer sees a man wearing a uniform and standing at the window. His eyes rest on Spencer's face.

"A new student," Dr. Deschene says. "His first forensic autopsy. Perhaps he will see something we old men do not." The chief nods, and Spencer realizes the microphone above the autopsy table is carrying Dr. Deschene's words to the observation room.

Dr. Deschene begins with a complete external examination while speaking into the microphone for later transcription.

"This is a forensic autopsy conducted at the request of the Chief of the Navajo Nation Police. Conducting the autopsy is Dr. Nastas Deschene, MD. Assisting is Mr. Spencer Hansen. Observing is Chief Joseph White Eagle. I have weighed and photographed the body.

"The body of a male approximately twenty years of age presents. By appearance, he is likely Navajo … his weight of 60 kilograms is below average but not abnormal … scars are consistent with recent abdominal surgery … no other scars are present … the tattoo of an eagle covers the right scapula … feet and hands are swollen … there is a white powder on the skin of the chest." Dr. Deschene uses a sterile scraper to put a sample of the powder into a test tube, which he seals and sets aside.

Dr. Deschene sees that Spencer is not reluctant to help handle the body and turn it so he can examine both back and front. Spencer lifts the body while Dr. D puts a rubber block under it. "We position the block midway in the thoracic region," he says for Spencer's benefit. "This makes the chest protrude forward and the arms and neck fall back, making the next step easier."

Spencer nods.

Dr. Deschene takes a scalpel. "I will use this to make an incision from each shoulder – the acromia – meeting just below the sternum and continuing down to the pubis." He sees Spencer flinch as the scalpel descends over the belly and curves around the belly button, toward the pubis. *Not unexpected*, Deschene thinks.

Deschene uses a long, heavy knife to cut away cartilage and pulls back the skin and underlying tissue to expose the rib cage and abdominal cavity. "He is young enough I can use the same knife to cut through the sternoclavicular joint and the costal cartilage." He does so and removes the sternum and the bands of cartilage. "If he had been older, the cartilage might have calcified, and I would have used an electric saw."

Spencer hands Dr. Deschene spreaders and clamps to hold the rib cage open. Dr. Deschene talks Spencer and Chief White Eagle through the removal of the larynx and esophagus. He cuts arteries and ligaments. He cuts attachments to the spinal cord, bladder, and rectum and – with Spencer's help – removes the thoracic and abdominal organs as a unit.

"The right kidney is absent, and there is evidence of recent surgical intervention," Dr. Deschene says into the microphone.

Spencer seems a little queasy, but helps Dr. Deschene weigh, examine, and take samples from all the organs.

Dr. Deschene then directs Spencer to move the rubber block and place it under the neck. Spencer moves with speed and precision.

Dr. Deschene sees Spencer is fighting to keep himself from throwing up when Dr. Deschene cuts across the skull, from one ear to the other and around the back. *Gives a whole new meaning to scalping,* Spencer thinks before his tummy settles down. For a moment.

The smoke from the bone saw is more pungent than any of the other smells, and Spencer's stomach heaves. Dr. Deschene notices and turns on an exhaust fan. Fresh air comes from vents, and Spencer's tummy settles down again.

Dr. Deschene severs the brain from the cranial nerves and the spinal cord and removes it. "No visible abnormality of the brain," he says, and the autopsy is at an end. Except for the cleanup.

"We will return the organs and pack the cavity with surgical sponges. I will start to close the main incision using a baseball stitch. You will finish it, if you would like to."

Spencer nods. His tummy has stopped complaining. "Just show me what to do, sir."

After cleaning up, which does include a shower, Dr. Deschene and Spencer return to the doctor's office where Chief Joe is waiting. He does not speak, but his entire demeanor says, *Well?*

"Several indicators of end-stage kidney disease – the swollen hands and feet, the white powder on his skin. Did he complain of anything – Restless leg syndrome? Changes in sleeping habits? Changes in appetite or urination?"

"No idea, Doctor. He lived alone in one of the abandoned trailers. His grandmother found him when she went to check on him. Given the condition of the body, I figure he'd been dead for about two days."

"Very good guess, Chief. Perhaps three days, now. Do you want to switch jobs? I've always wanted to run around in a car with red and blue lights. I'll know more when the toxicology reports come back. Oh, please meet Spencer Hansen. He's a student at the community college doing an in-service. This was his first autopsy. You did very well, Spencer."

"Thank you, sir. But, except for the bone saw, it wasn't much worse than holding a bed pan while someone … um … poops."

"Spencer! We're doctors. We say *defecate*."

After the chief leaves, Dr. Deschene gestures for Spencer to sit in a chair at the bay window. "Spencer, I am sorry about what happened in the dressing room. It was my fault. I should have explained that we don't shower until after the autopsy. Many of my students have experienced much worse teasing at the hands of the older technicians. I will make it clear you have passed your initiation without, however, telling them what it was. Will that be satisfactory?"

Spencer is still floating in the air somewhere above the hospital. *He said we were doctors.* "Yes sir. And thank you, sir. This has been an amazing first day."

"It's not quite over. You need to stop by HR – Human Resources – what we used to call "personnel" before they got too big for their britches. They'll need an INS Form 9, and a W-whatever-it-is for income tax withholding, and—"

"Income tax, sir? I'm going to be paid?"

"It's not much better than minimum wage, Spencer. And, trust me. You'll earn it. You will work at least 30 hours each week, so you're considered full-time and will get your health insurance covered. They'll make you an ID badge, which you need to wear above the waist and visible at all times. Except when scrubbed."

Spencer floats down the hallway toward the HR office. *He said we were doctors, and I'm going to get paid.*

~~~~~

The toxicology report on the organs, blood, and powder from the skin arrives five weeks later, and confirms that the single, remaining kidney had failed. Dr. Deschene calls Chief Joe and puts the call on the speakerphone so Spencer can take part.

"The problem is, Doc," the chief says, "I can't find any record of where his first kidney was removed. His grandmother said he came into some money about six months ago, enough to buy a new truck, but never said where it came from."

"He sold a kidney on the black market," Spencer says.

Dr. Deschene stares at Spencer. "It fits the facts," he says. "Not enough information to pursue at the moment, but a damn good hypothesis, Spencer."

Dr. Deschene turns to the phone. "Joe, I'll have everything faxed to you this afternoon. Please, if you run into anything else even remotely like this, let me know."

"I will," Chief Joe says. "Walk in beauty."

"Walk in beauty, Joe," Dr. Deschene replies, and cuts the phone connection.

≈≈≈≈≈

The morning crowd at the coffee shop in Folio thins out by 9:00 AM. The early coffee-and-pastry crowd has stoked up with caffeine and sugar, and left. Spencer has no class until 10:00 AM, and sits with a cup of green tea. He studies an anatomy book, propped open on the table.

"Yá'át'ééh, Spencer."

Spencer looks up to see Tommy Chee. "May I join you?" the boy asks.

"Yá'át'ééh, TomTom! Sure. I haven't seen you in three years. You were twelve. You've grown up. And you shouldn't be talking to me."

"Thirteen, when you left. I'm sixteen now." Tommy sits. "And it's okay for us to talk. I've been disfellowshipped, too."

"Jumpin' Gerbils, TomTom, what for?"

"Same as you. I wasn't reverent enough. I got the trustworthy, loyal, helpful, and other stuff okay, but I couldn't believe the religious stuff."

Tommy takes a sip of the coffee he brought to the table. "You know, you're the only Bilagáana I didn't mind calling me *TomTom*. The boys at school … it was a joke for them.

"I remember my first day at the Anglo school. I had just got there when other students – Bilagáana – discovered my name and made fun of it. 'Tommy. Like Tom-Tom,' one said and the others beat their hands on their thighs in a 4/4 rhythm and chanted, 'TOM tom tom tom, TOM tom tom tom.' It's something they learned from the cowboy movies, the ones filmed in Monument Valley, the ones that create stereotypes of Indians.

"I tried to smile, to grin, like I was part of the joke. It didn't work. They walked away from me, still chanting and laughing.

"They weren't just mocking me, but were mocking our most sacred traditions – the four winds, the four corners of the earth, the four colors, the four sacred mountains, the four seasons, all the things that come in fours and make us The People.

"You called me TomTom, but never when others were around, and you never snickered or laughed."

Spencer looks at the kid, now grown up, who was in the scout troop that had disfellowshipped Spencer when he questioned the church's claim American Indians were of Jewish ancestry. DNA tests proved they weren't, but the church leaders still claimed it to be true – and expected Spencer to believe it.

"No, TomTom. Never in public. I guess …" Spencer hesitates and blushes. "I guess it was a private name. You were young and I was your patrol leader. They expected me to be a big brother to you. I figured, I guessed, if I had a real little brother, I would have a nickname for him, a private one, just between us."

Spencer's blush doesn't go away. "I kind of hoped that you might come up with a private name for me, but I was disfellowshipped before that could happen."

"You and I are not the only ones, Spencer. There are ten of us, now, plus you. You were the first. We get together, hang together, and do a lot of talking, and stuff. Some of us have jobs; some are still looking. You know them all. Maybe, we can find a secret name for you."

Spencer doesn't question the difference between a private name and a secret name. It doesn't seem important at the moment. "How did you know I would be here?"

Tommy laughs. "My uncle – Chief Joe – told me he saw you, and that you were a student. Everybody knows this is the biggest student hang out."

Tommy and Spencer talk for an hour, catching up on years apart. Tommy names the other boys who have been disfellowshipped. "We do more than just hang together. We have created a kiva society where we learn the old ways of our people, the creation stories, the stories of the gods. Two of the older boys are working with Shamans and Dancers to learn the chants and ceremonies. It's secret, 'cause some of us are Navajo and some are Hopituh Shi-nu-mu. The elders of both nations would not approve of a mixed kiva. You can't tell anyone."

"No, of course not, Tommy. I promise."

Tommy has been holding his breath. He lets it out with a deep sigh. "Thank you. That was the last test, your promise and your trust. Do you understand what that means?"

Spencer thinks for a moment. TomTom is still a boy, three years younger than Spencer. Between sixteen and nineteen are more years than three. In a flash, Spencer understands. Tommy is offering more than trust. He is offering Spencer – a Bilagáana, a non-Indian Caucasian – entry into the society that surrounds him.

"I understand," Spencer says. "Trust is not easily earned, but can be broken in an instant by a single word. You offered your trust when you told me about your kiva. Now, I return that trust with my oath, not just a promise. I swear on my life to keep the secret of your kiva."

"Good." Tommy smiles. "If you agree, we will initiate you this weekend."

Spencer realizes then what Tommy means by a secret name. "TomTom, I would like that very much."

~~~~~

After another week of classes and in-service, Spencer plans to sleep late on Saturday before tackling his homework. He wakes when his phone chimes with a text message from Tommy.

<<meet at coffee shop main street tuba city 630 pm>>

Tuba City? That's at least an hour, maybe hour-and-thirty drive from Folio. I have plenty of homework, but all weekend to do it, Spencer thinks. *I can make the time.*

Tommy is waiting for Spencer outside the coffee shop. Tommy grabs a roll bar and jumps into Spencer's jeep without opening the door. "Drive south on 244."

Spencer follows Tommy's instructions and turns west on Path of Harmony Road toward the Three Wise Men, an iconic rock formation. It is one of many similar formations throughout the west, so-named by Bilagáana based on one of their myths. Spencer knows the Navajo have another name that translates to "tourist trap." A few miles later, Tommy directs him to turn onto a dirt track that leads to an isolated trailer, one of many that dot the reservation.

The sun has disappeared behind the western mountains. The sky darkena and the air is cool. The growing dusk makes it easy to see the flames of a fire burning in the yard. Shadowy figures move between Spencer and the fire.

By the time Spencer and Tommy reach the fire, the figures sit in a circle. "Sit, please." Tommy gestures to the circle. Spencer sits and looks around. The fire is bright enough for him to recognize the young men, all of whom were in his scout troop. Now, according to Tommy, they are all disfellowshipped.

"You know their old names," Tommy says. "Tonight, you will learn their new names and you will receive a new name." He sits beside Spencer.

One of the young men speaks. "The E'e'aahjigo Kiva is assembled. I am Cha'tima, the Caller and I call the kiva to judge Spencer Hansen. Who speaks for him?" One boy holds a drum between his knees and begins a soft four-four beat with the accent on the first beat.

Tommy Chee stands. "I am Ata'halne', *He Who Interrupts*, and I speak for Spencer Hansen who was my leader, teacher, and friend. He has honor, and we have need of him."

A second boy stands. Spencer recognizes him as one of the Hopi from the scout troop. "I am Cheveyo, *Spirit Warrior*. I owe my spirit and my courage to Spencer Hansen, whose courage and example led us all to the path we follow."

Spencer is glad for the red glare from the fire, for he knows he is blushing.

One after another, each of the young men speaks, offering praise to Spencer. Ahiga, *He Fights*; Gaagii, *Raven*; and Hok'ee, *Abandoned*. Spencer is in tears when he hears Hok'ee's story. Two years ago, Hok'ee followed Spencer's example and declared loyalty and belief to the old ways of the Diné, and rejected the Bilagáana religion. At age fourteen, not only was he disfellowshipped, his family cast him from their home. He now lives with two of the other boys in the trailer that is the backdrop for their ceremony.

The others speak. Niyol, *Wind*; Ahote, *Restless One*; and Chuchip, *Deer Spirit*.

The drum goes silent and Cheveyo stands. "All have spoken well, but I must ask. Does anyone not want Spencer Hansen to join with the E'e'aahjigo Kiva?"

No one speaks. Cheveyo nods. "Then we must have a name for our new member."

"How about Ashkii?" Someone offers. The others laugh. Even Hok'ee, the youngest laughs. He doesn't laugh often.

"I think you are having fun," Spencer speaks for the first time. "What does that mean?"

"'Boy!' Just 'boy,'" Ata'halne' says. "No, that's not a good name for Spencer."

Gaagii stands. The laughter stops. Gaagii's spirit guide is Raven. Raven is a trickster, a thief, a joker, and sometimes a liar, but Raven can also see the truth in a person, can see into their heart. "He shall be Atsa, Eagle, for he has flown before us and shown us the way."

"It does not require many words to speak the truth," Ata'halne' says, quoting Chief Joseph of the Nez Perce. The words of Chief Joseph settle and seal the question.

Cha'tima lights a bundle of sage. He walks around the circle with an eagle-feather fan, waving the smoke toward each member of the E'e'aahjigo Kiva. The air is still, and a circle of sage smoke and something more envelopes the young men. In the desert, Coyote howls. Above them, Eagle screeches. Raven sits on the eaves of the trailer and lends his voice. A gust of wind blows away the smoke. The ceremony is over. The young men welcome Spencer, now Atsa, with arms clasped, hands near elbows, in the ancient way of the warrior.

≈≈≈≈≈

It has been fifty years since the Catholic Church released the "Decree on the Apostolate of the Laity." As soon as the non-clergy got power, many sought to increase their power. Now, Father Sontag cannot buy a set of vestments without approval from the parishioners who are the Lay Council of the Ignatius Catholic Church.

The Council meets after the last Sunday mass. They give Father Sontag time to change from vestments into the black suit and white clerical collar he wears even on the hottest days. They meet on this Sunday in September in the library of the presbytery. The early Spanish missionary-priests, first Franciscans then Jesuits, had concentrated the local aboriginal population into camps, called *reductions*, and taught them to build not only the church but also a rectory. Following the custom of suppressing aboriginal peoples' religions, they built the church on the ruins of a once-great kiva.

The church, itself, is a one-room, rectangular building 40 feet wide and 120 feet long. Its ceiling is the peaked roof, set on 40-foot high walls. The most remarkable feature is the murals, seven on each side, just below the roofline, depicting the Stations of the Cross. The building fell into ruins in the late 1800s. Bilagáana who thought they were helping the Navajo by offering the Catholic religion to them restored the building and the murals in the 1990s. In 1893, the rectory became a trading post, which moved to Gallup in 1967. After the church was restored, the rectory, which no longer housed an ecclesiastical rector, became a presbytery – a home for the priest.

Father Sontag walks into the library. He sees each member of the Council already has coffee and pours himself a cup. He takes his usual place in a chair beside the fireplace, facing the seven men of the council.

"Good homily, Father." The speaker is the Chairman of the Council. His praise is perfunctory, and he moves to current business. "How is the soup kitchen performing?"

Father Sontag is ready for that question. "It began as expected. The visitors were mostly young mothers with children. There were a few older men, usually drunks, but we persuaded them to return to the Salvation Army. Things were smooth until this week. A gang of four young Navajo seems to have discovered us. Now, they visit every day. They are rowdy and disruptive. The women who serve the meal could not control them. I spoke to them and demanded they behave or not attend. They ignored me. I did not want to call the police."

"Drunk?" The Council Chairman grunts.

"Not drunk, and not on drugs, either. Just hooligans," Father Sontag replies.

"Hooligans, huh? That's the Irish in you coming out, Father." The Chairman catches the eyes of the other six men. They nod. They all have the same thought. This presents an opportunity, not a problem. "We'll look into it, Father."

The hooligans do not come to the soup kitchen the next day, nor the next. Nor ever again. Father Sontag wonders briefly what the Lay Council did and then dismisses the thought.

≈≈≈≈≈

Mr. Karl Hilflinger, owner of the Peaceful Rest Mortuary and Crematorium of Folio, Arizona, opens the door of his Escalade. Even near the end of September, he expects the blast of air, heated to 150 degrees by the high desert sun on the parking lot's blacktop. He does not, however, expect the smell of cooking bacon. He looks at the smokestack of the crematorium. What comes from the stack should be invisible and have no odor. The invisible part is working but … *The scrubbers!* he thinks and rushes into the building.

Henry Belka meets Mr. Hilflinger at the staff entrance to the crematorium. A service hall and a second door secured by an electronic lock hide this door from clients' families. Henry confirms Hilflinger's suspicion. "Sir, the scrubbers failed. I got the alarm in the shop and shut off the gas. The client was a real porker, sir, at least 300 pounds—"

"Henry! Never refer to a client as a – what did you call him? A porker?"

"It was a woman, sir. Sorry sir. But she's only about halfway finished. I reset the circuit breakers, but the scrubbers won't come back on. I don't know what to do."

"Dammit! We can't leave her like that. We can't run without the scrubbers. A company in Truth-or-Consequences made them. I'm not even sure they're still in business. Oh, damn, oh, damn!"

Mr. Hilflinger paces. He opens the access hatch to the cremation oven and blanches. He stares for much longer than is necessary. The image of the partly cremated woman burns into his brain in the first second. He closes the access.

"Henry, you've got to do something. Like you did before, but make sure she won't be found, ever."

"Mr. Hilflinger, that's not in my job description, sir."

"Your job description just changed." Mr. Hilflinger interprets correctly the avarice in Henry's mind from the expression on the man's face. "And your salary. Special job." Mr. Hilflinger cringes. "One thousand dollars. Cash."

Henry nods.

Three hours later, the cremation oven is empty and a body bag is in the trunk of Henry's car. Ten, one-hundred-dollar bills are in his pocket. It is dusk when Henry rides from his home toward the hills. He leads a packhorse on which he secured the body bag. The waning gibbous moon rises at 8:00 PM, and gives him enough light to slide the body from the end of the bag into a clump of sagebrush.

The family of the deceased – the porker – does not suspect the urn they receive contains not the ground-up bones of their grandmother, but those of a sheep, butchered by Henry, who burned the bones in a fire in his back yard before putting them in the heavy-duty, industrial grinder at the mortuary.

≈≈≈≈≈

"Dr. Deschene, thank you for responding to my call." The hospital administrator's words are, in a word, unctuous. He knows Dr. Deschene's qualifications far exceed his own, but finds it comforting, even rewarding, that the man works for him, reports to him, and depends on him for his livelihood and what the administrator thinks of as toys in the pathology laboratory.

"You invited me. It is harmonious that I visit," Dr. Deschene says.

The administrator does not seem to understand what Dr. D says. "It is quite an honor that one of the world's foremost forensic anthropologists would accept a position at an obscure hospital on a Navajo Reservation," the administrator says.

Navajo. Reservation. Dr. D thinks. *He is Navajo, but does not use the words a Diné would use. His thoughts are far afield. He is not a friend. Still, I will listen, for he has great power.*

"I am Navajo," Dr. Deschene says. "This is my place."

The administrator shrugs that off. Dr. Deschene's words have no meaning to the administrator. "People see on television that a body's temperature can tell the time of death. They see a program in which someone discovers a certain insect infesting a corpse and uses that to determine the time of death. An actor in a white lab coat and with a stethoscope around his neck tells them everyone decomposes at different rates. The viewers take all this as fact, when it's a construct of the television producers' imagination."

The administrator gives Dr. Deschene time to think. When he does not speak, the administrator says, "Neither those who produce these programs nor the people who watch them have enough knowledge to deal with these questions, not even to ask the right questions."

He wants me to think he has the knowledge he denies of others, Dr. Deschene thinks. *He is a fool.*

The administrator comes to the point. "It would help the hospital of you were to appear on a television program whose hostess promises to ask the right questions."

The administrator makes it clear to Dr. D he has little choice. While his employment is not in question, the gift from the television station to the hospital's foundation, the money that pays for the equipment he finds essential for autopsies, is at stake. He agrees.

Dr. Deschene rejects demands by the makeup artists at the television studio to spray a bronze coloring on his skin or braid his hair. He walks onto the set, on cue, in chinos and a button-up shirt. His hair flows in a ponytail bound by a plain band of deerskin.

The hostess of the program introduces him and the studio audience applauds to electronic signs.

"Welcome, Nastas Deschene of the Navajo Tribe," the hostess says. She does not stand, but gestures him to a seat next to her.

"So, Mr. Deschene, you have some pretty scary stories to tell us," the hostess says.

"It's Dr. Deschene," he replies. "And *scary?* I think *horrific* was the word I used when I spoke to your people."

'Oooh! Horrific," the hostess says. Electronic signs flash, and the *Ooohs* and *Aaahs* of the audience follow. "What do you mean by that?"

"I mean young people, not only of the Navajo but also others, are being kidnapped and murdered and their organs sold to the ultra-wealthy of the world. Other children as young as twelve, are forced into prostitution and trafficked."

The hostess is a seasoned performer. "You mean, of course, the ultra-wealthy of Russia, the Middle East, China—"

"Those countries, and the United States," he says.

"Surely, you cannot mean this happens in our country," the hostess says.

Dr. D. stands and walks from the set before the star can signal the producer to cut the feed.

"The woman is a fool," Dr. Deschene tells the hospital administrator. "She twice said I lied. I appeared, as agreed. The station and network will pay. Do not ask me to do something like this, again."

~~~~~

A low hubbub of voices echoes from the walls and high ceiling of the Marchant Hotel in Georgetown, DC. Delegates to the American Assembly of Pediatricians greet one another, question the registrars, and congregate at the tables for tea, coffee, breakfast sandwiches, and pastries.

"Excuse me, I'm Susan Calvin with the *Washington Banner*. May I ask you a few questions?"

Dr. Deschene looks up from the conference program he is examining, trying to decide which breakout sessions to attend. None seem interesting. When he sees the woman, he is even happier she interrupted his reading. She is tall, nearly as tall as he. Her pants suit is an expensive cut – professional but feminine. Her hair is beautifully coifed. She wears sensible shoes with low heels. A conference badge, larger than most, declares her to be a journalist. And, she is attractive. Dr. Deschene stands to greet her.

"I am Dr. Deschene, Ms. Calvin. Please, sit. What can I tell you?"

"The speakers list says you are an eminent forensic anthropologist and pathologist, but doesn't explain why you are at a conference of pediatricians."

Dr. Deschene chuckles. Then his face hardens. "It's not widely talked about, but many of the physicians here are concerned about child sex trafficking. That process – recruiting, arranging client encounters, getting the child hooked on drugs – often leads to death. I hope to impress on these doctors the things I have found in forensic autopsies – things that may offer them clues in their regular work. Things they may use to identify child abuse before it is too late."

"I know this exists," Susan says, "but did not know it was so great a problem to draw so much attention."

"Many people don't. In fact, entirely too many people don't. When anyone bothers to think of prostitution, they think of adult women. Their minds cannot accept that children are kidnapped and prostituted, even here in the nation's capital."

"Washington, too?" Susan's voice holds horror and curiosity, perhaps shame, but not the scorn of the television hostess.

"Yes. Interstate 95 is a major artery from the barrios of Miami and the ports of Miami, Ft. Lauderdale, Savannah, and Charleston."

Deschene looks at his watch. "I'm sorry, but I'm supposed to be on the platform in fifteen minutes." He pauses, thinks. "Would you like to meet afterwards? I will call someone with greater expertise and more information."

Susan accepts the invitation. They agree to meet in the cocktail lounge at 4:00 PM. "A little early for cocktails, but we will want to get ahead of the happy hour crowd."

Dr. Deschene is sitting in a booth at the cocktail lounge at 4:00 when Susan arrives. There is an attractive woman seated with him.

Dr. Deschene performs the introductions. "Ms. Calvin, this is Doli Tabaaha." He pronounces the first name, *dough-lee*, not *dolly*.

"She's an advocate whose focus is child sex trafficking. This is Ms. Susan Calvin, a journalist with the *Washington Banner*."

Susan sees a young, attractive woman whose long, black hair, bronze skin, and features suggest she is of aboriginal ancestry. She wears a harvest-gold, tailored business suit that complements her skin-tone. The jacket covers most of a white blouse, leaving a hint of ruffle visible. Her only jewelry is a pin on the jacket's lapel. The pin is a golden tree. Its branches are thin, gold wires that end in clusters of tiny semiprecious stones – yellow, white, blue, green, and purple. The wires, twisted together, form the trunk of the tree.

Susan and Doli shake hands. When all are seated, Dr. Deschene gestures for a waitress. Ms. Calvin, a veteran of many Washington cocktail parties, orders a Tom Collins. Dr. Deschene orders a single-malt scotch, neat, and Ms. Tabaaha asks for tonic water with two limes.

"Your pin is lovely," Susan says to Doli. "And unique. I've never seen anything like it."

"Thank you," Doli says. "I designed it, myself, and a friend created it. The colors are symbolic, from Diné tradition."

"I recognize the turquoise. It offers protection from lightning. The yellow is garnet, but I do not know its meaning." Susan says. "The black must be obsidian, the purple amethyst, and the white, pearl. But pearls are not found in the desert. The amethyst is beautiful, but purple is not one of the four sacred colors."

Doli is impressed and pleased that Susan recognizes her traditions. "You are correct. The pearls substitute for shell. I added amethyst for its beauty, and I thought of the intertwined tree of human life."

"The twisted branches – interconnections," Susan says.

"No one is an island," Dr. Deschene paraphrases John Donne just as the drinks arrive.

"I would like to learn more from you about the colors of your pin," Susan says. "But perhaps we should get to the subject. May I consider this on the record, and may I record?"

"Of course," Doli says. Susan takes a high-end mini memo recorder from her purse and puts it on the table. As soon as Susan starts the recorder, Doli begins her story.

"I work from Fairfax, Virginia. I am a registered lobbyist, but one who does not have the millions of dollars that the *K-Street Crowd* have." Susan nods. She knows *K-Street* is a code word for the lawyers and the lobbyists who write most of the legislation introduced in Congress, and who write it to benefit their paymasters – huge corporations, the ultra-wealthy, and other nations, even enemy nations – but not to benefit the American people.

"My focus is child sex trafficking, which is interstate commerce of the worst kind. Unfortunately, federal law, including the Mann Act, is hard to enforce."

By nine o'clock, after only one drink, a lot of ice water, and a supper of surprisingly good bar food, Susan's head is swimming with frightful stories of women, girls, and boys, some as young as twelve, forced into sexual slavery and then charged with prostitution when arrested. "These are some of the great injustices I fight," Doli concludes.

Susan clutches a paper on which are a dozen internet links.

"The cases you will see are listed in open court records with the child's name redacted. There are many, many others that are sealed," Doli confirms. "There are also a few links – too few – to some legitimate news sources and advocacy groups."

Dr. Deschene has been a mostly silent observer while the two women talked. "Before we break up," he says to Susan, "I'd like to synch our mobile phone numbers, or whatever it is the kids do. Do you know how?"

Susan laughs. It is a melodic laugh and not mocking. "Here, give me your phone."

Doli promises to contact Susan to discuss the colors of her pin and agrees to answer questions Susan may have. Susan is cautious, but accepts Dr. Deschene's offer of a nightcap in his room. "I'm not sure what we'll find in the mini-bar, but the room service here is impeccable," he says.

≈≈≈≈≈

The next morning, when Susan prepares to leaves Dr. Deschene's room, she finds that the hotel's valet has pressed her street clothing and returned it in plastic dry-cleaner bags.

"When did you find time?" She asks Dr. D.

40

"Earlier this morning while you slept. You are so beautiful and looked so peaceful that I could not wake you. My friends say I am not a romantic and while I dispute that charge, my first thought was that you would have to appear at today's session of the conference. The hotel is trustworthy – and discreet."

~~~~~

Four days later, Susan's article appears in the Sunday edition of the *Washington Banner*. Her editor is reluctant, at first, to print the story, but the women on the editorial board stand behind Susan. Early editions of the paper reach the White House at 6:00 AM. Reaction from the White House is swift.

<<@RealUSPOTUS #fakenews from #failingdcbanner not what we want to see Sunday morning>>

Susan's article describes the route taken by victims of the child sex trade. Citing examples, she casts doubt on the efforts of Immigration and Customs Enforcement, saying that ICE agents are too few and too overworked to screen passengers debarking cruise ships. She writes about women and children smuggled into the country as cruise passengers, some promised legitimate work, and then forced to work in sweatshops or as prostitutes.

The article suggests that the millions of dollars of illegal drugs smuggled through the eastern ports is too big a temptation for some agents of the Drug Enforcement Agency, who look the other way when both drugs and human beings are brought into the country. She describes the millions of dollars that flow through the child sex trade, and suggests that Federal laws and law enforcement are weakened deliberately by Congress to keep this money flowing, all the way to the top.

Response to Susan's article is evenly split, and definitely split along party lines. Progressives salute and cheer her. The alt-right, which includes the administration and its supporters, denigrates her. The White House continues its attack upon her.

<<@RealUSPOTUS no truth in #fakenews report of bribes to officials #failingdcbanner now a tabloid>>

Susan is cautious in her article not to identify the lobbying firms or members of Congress – in both the House and the Senate – who receive this money or whose Political Action Committees benefit from anonymous donations. Her caution keeps her from being sued for libel, but does not save her from the anger of those she targeted. The pressure from the K-Street lobbying crowd, the Executive Branch, and the Congress comes in the form of a phone call to the editor from the owner of the newspaper.

The owner is a Non-GMO billionaire, whose agribusiness boasts that none of their products contain genetically modified organisms. He moved to DC and bought the *Banner*. He is known to be an F.O.P. – Friend of the President – and friend of every power player in Congress. He doesn't say who called him. All he says is, "Fire her, and print a retraction."

Ivan Kuznetzov

Ivan Kuznetzov examines the Estonian passport. It passes his inspection. The man who arranged its issue is not only reliable but knows the consequences should it ever be challenged. An Estonian passport is a gold standard, allowing visa-free access to over 150 countries, including the United States. He will have no trouble entering the US or traveling throughout the country. Although Kuznetzov is Russian, his assumed Estonian citizenship will open doors among the American military. The many Estonian islands in the Baltic Sea are important listening posts for monitoring Russian submarine activity and for signals and electronic surveillance of military communications and radar. Kuznetzov's employment with an Estonian start-up electronics company and his mission of seeking investors – people who want to shelter money in an offshore company – will open different doors. There will be other lucrative opportunities.

Kuznetzov buzzes for his aide. "Make the arrangements. I wish to arrive in New York as soon as possible. And send in Ms. Krafft."

"Yes, *Gospoden Kraznachey*," the aide replies using the man's preferred title of "Mister Paymaster." Kuznetzov makes sure that his minions know from whom their paychecks come.

Kuznetzov will fly from Stockholm's Bromma Airport non-stop to New York on American Airlines. It is an eight-hour flight. He will arrive in the early morning, giving him a full day to reset his body clock and make telephone calls. He makes a mental note to buy an American cell phone as soon as he arrives, and wonders if the cash-and-carry electronics stores that were once so ubiquitous on Times Square are still there.

Before he does any of these things, he will consult with Carlotta Krafft.

His staff does not know Ms. Krafft's role, only that Kuznetzov meets with her often. She is an attractive woman of indeterminate age. Most people who see her guess she is in her twenties; a few, her thirties. She has a darker complexion than the Aryan staff that surrounds Kuznetzov. Some whisper she is Romany. Her appearance is exotic enough to make her a member of that people. Although never part of Kuznetzov's official entourage, she always is close no matter how far or how often he travels. The staff knows when she enters Kuznetzov's room, whether office, den, or hotel room, she always closes and locks the door. They draw a natural conclusion from this.

Today, without being asked, Carlotta discards her jacket and sits across his desk from Kuznetzov. She removes a pack of cards from her purse and hands them to him. He shuffles the cards, and returns them to her. "I am embarking on a new and significant undertaking in America," he says.

Carlotta nods, and places the cards, face down, in the Celtic Cross pattern. "This will give a broad understanding of factors affecting the situation, external influences, the best possible outcome, and both immediate and future challenges."

She turns the first card, the one placed horizontally in the center of the cross, revealing the cards to be a Tarot deck. The card she turns is *The Magician*. "Your future is in turmoil and holds both risk and reward. You will need an early success to establish your position and to draw support for your enterprise."

She sets *The Magician* aside and turns the vertical card in the center of the cross. *Eight of Cups*. "You will travel a great distance." She smiles. "We both know that. I made my arrangements, and will meet you in New York in two days."

"What else?" Kuznetzov asks. He looks at his watch.

"This journey will lead to a significant change in your life. You must keep alert to opportunity."

"The moon on the card is blocking the sun," Kuznetzov says. "What does it mean?"

Carlotta stares at the card. "The moon is indifferent. You will receive no help from your colleagues at home, but must strike out on your own." Carlotta continues to turn over the cards, one by one. Kuznetzov grunts. He would get a lot less than help from the Russian Bratva if they knew he was the one who looted their bank accounts in Switzerland. He turns his attention back to Carlotta.

"*The Hanged Man*, head down. In this position, it represents a great unknown. You will need to act with judicious timing."

She turns over the sixth card. *Death*. Kuznetzov takes a deep breath before speaking. "That's my immediate future."

"But it does not mean your death," Carlotta says. "It signifies a great change in your life, one associated with death – but not yours."

"What do you mean?"

"It could be as simple as starting a chain of funeral homes," Carlotta says with little thought.

Kuznetzov blanches. Carlotta does not notice. "We must consider all the cards."

After she has turned the rest of the cards, Carlotta summarizes. "Together, the cards show a long life for you, one with many challenges, opportunities, and successes."

Kuznetzov thanks Carlotta and concludes the ritual by crossing her palm with silver – a British two-pound sterling coin. He makes a mental note to place an order with the Royal Mint to replenish his stock. Carlotta returns his thanks. Besides the coin, Kuznetzov will send her fee and travel expenses to her account in the Bahamas. She hurries to her hotel room, not to pack, but to peer into her crystal ball. The appearance of Death always bothers her, no matter how much she reassures Kuznetzov.

~~~~~

Unified Prison System Unit Nine is surrounded by desolation in Rough Rock County across the river from Folio, Arizona. U.P.S. #9 is one of hundreds of prisons operated by for-profit prison companies in America. The conservative party that controlled the state government for decades gave Unified the contracts to build and operate ten high-security prisons. Number Nine is home to four thousand convicts, mostly young men from various Indian tribes convicted of crimes while off the reservation and whose sentencing falls under the jurisdiction of the Sovereign State of Arizona.

Sam Red Horse, the warden of Unit Nine, stares at the "I Love Me" wall behind his desk. The wall is covered with framed certificates and shadow boxes displaying his many military accomplishments, decorations, and awards. They represent things anyone could be proud of, but Sam's eyes are unfocused and all he sees are blurs and imagined opportunities.

The buzz of his cell phone pulls him back to the reality of his office and his position as warden.

"What?" He demands. Anyone calling this number will be a subordinate, someone who owes his or her position to Sam, someone who owes the extra cash in a pay envelope to Sam, someone who has committed enough crimes for Sam to put them away forever.

"Uncle, sir, my Reaper team has three candidates. We restrained them but didn't drug them. We want two hundred thousand for all three."

"Damn it, you know the rules." Sam pauses. The caller is his nephew and entitled to some consideration. "Bring them to Number 9. Are they clean?"

"Very likely, sir."

"Tell the guards to hold them in isolation. I will let them know you are coming. Tell your Reapers they will be paid after we have done the usual tests and found customers."

"Yes, Uncle," the voice replies before Sam cuts the connection.

Pony Boy. My sister's second son. Wants to make himself a place in the family business, Sam thinks. *A problem for me to solve – once he outlives his usefulness.*

Sam calls the senior guard to tell him three prisoners will be arriving. He calls the prison doctor to order testing for drugs and STDs. If the prisoners pass these tests, the doctor will do more extensive blood tests and will collect DNA for analysis.

≈≈≈≈≈

Henry Belka is feeding his horses when his cell phone buzzes. It's Hilflinger. "Yes, sir."

"I need you at work tomorrow, 6:00 AM."

"Another special job?"

"No. A company, a German company, has sent new scrubbers and an installation team. I was lucky to find them. After the EPA regulated emissions of mercury, it's been nearly impossible to find the right equipment. How much mercury can there be in a tooth filling? This company pioneered in England where—"

Hilflinger realizes Henry neither needs to know nor cares. "They will start work tomorrow at 7:00 AM. I need you there to let them in, learn the controls, and watch them. You've already worked 40 hours this week. You'll get time-and-a-half for sitting on your butt. And take them to lunch at Buster's. Give me the receipt and I'll reimburse you."

Henry presses an icon to shut off the call. *A team from Germany? What you reckon that's gonna' cost? Must be some real money changing hands, somewhere. I know the regular cremations ain't making that much. It's got to be the bodies I pick up at the spa. Maybe I need to ask for a raise.*

While Henry is watching the German team and pretending to understand what they are doing, Hilflinger is in his office with a stack of death certificates, which he feeds one at a time into a typewriter. He is using every bit of his experience and imagination to fill in the cause of death. It doesn't matter what he writes. He has a supply of blank forms signed by the Rough Rock County Coroner. After filling out a dozen certificates, he is tempted to write in a diagnosis of "ischemic priapism" – a semi-permanent erection of the penis – but refrains. Ultimately, the diagnosis becomes bacterial meningitis. *Very contagious, bacterial meningitis is. Must have been an outbreak at the prison.* He puts the same diagnosis on the next handful of certificates and makes a mental note to tell the warden about the 'mysterious outbreak.'

≈≈≈≈≈

Kuznetzov summons Carlotta Krafft to his New York hotel room. She doesn't have far to travel. Up one floor on the elevator and a few steps down the hallway. One of Kuznetzov's bodyguards opens the door to the suite, nods to her, and gestures to an inner door. "He's in there."

Carlotta raps the inner door but enters without waiting for a reply. The guards hear the snick of the lock and exchange knowing looks.

"*Dobryoe utro, Gospoden Kraznachey,*" she says, acknowledging him as the Paymaster who deposited ten thousand dollars into her account. "Thank you for your gift."

"There will be another. I will travel to meet the heads of the Bratva in America. The meeting is at a conference center and resort. Here are the details." He hands her a brochure. "I want you there tomorrow. There will be a room in your name."

"*Da, Gospoden.*"

"Now, the cards. You told me, before, I need an early success to establish my position and draw support. That is my goal for this mission. How can I do this?"

Carlotta hands him a thin deck. Kuznetzov understands he holds only the cards of the Major Arcana. They are more powerful than the cards of the Minor Arcana although thought by some to be less precise. On the other hand, Carlotta's prophecies have always been precise and accurate. He shuffles the cards and watches Carlotta place seven cards face down in an Ellipse Spread with the point of the ellipse toward Kuznetzov.

"You remember," Carlotta says, "I use this spread to answer direct questions. Your question is, *How will I accomplish an early success?* Is that correct?" Kuznetzov nods affirmation.

She turns over the first card. *The Hanged Man.* "You have eliminated one of the past ties that were weighing you down and interfering with your plans. This bodes well for your future success."

How does she know I terminated Sokolov? Kuznetzov wonders. *He was dragging down my American enterprises by his demands for money to pay off politicians. I have recruited my own politicians among the young generation of Americans, not the emasculated ancients he controlled.* He gestures for Carlotta to continue.

The second card is *Strength*, a man wearing a halo in the form of the eternal lemnescate and holding a lion by its neck. "You must follow your plans and stand by your convictions. However, you must also be open to offers of trust and alliance."

Kuznetzov understands. Knowing who to trust and with whom to enter alliance will be his most difficult challenge.

The third card, *The World*, is inverted in the Future position. "You have established your goals and they are sound. Success is guaranteed."

That is the answer Kuznetzov wants to hear. He pays little attention to the other cards.

The next morning, Kuznetzov steps into the back seat of a Lincoln Town Car. Although not a limousine, it is stretched to provide extra legroom. A transparent panel separates the driver from her passenger. Kuznetzov is on the phone for the first hour of the trip. At that point, the driver speaks on the intercom.

"*Gospoden Kraznachey*, please do not use the cell phone past this point to avoid triangulation by the National Security Agency. There are few cell towers in this region, and an individual phone would stand out. Also, please remove the battery for the duration of your stay with us. We understand the NSA can locate a phone even when turned off."

Kuznetzov studied summaries of the papers of Edward Snowden, and knows about the American NSA and their technologies. He pops out the battery. Careful not to bend the contacts, he puts the phone and the battery in a plastic bag and then into his briefcase.

The American press nicknamed the Bratva "the Russian Mafia." The irony of crime lords meeting in a cabin in Apalachin, New York, is not lost on Kuznetzov. He studies both crime and espionage. He has expert knowledge of the cooperation between the American military and Mafia Boss Charlie "Lucky" Luciano as well as with Italian Mafia figures during World War II. He knows Apalachin is where more than sixty members of the American Italian-Sicilian Mafia were arrested in 1932. *If only they understood opsec*, Kuznetzov muses. *Operational Security. I trust our host has arranged that. I did not questioned him, but my people confirmed I will be safe. By not doubting him, by opening myself to him, I create trust. More important, I create an obligation. He is in my debt; he owes me.*

The cabin is much more than just a cabin. Sitting on the north bank of the Susquehanna River is a complex of buildings including rustic cabins and a large central building. A sign at the entrance

50

advertises the complex to be the "Harvest Enlightenment Church Retreat Center." Kuznetzov steps from the car and stretches. Despite the extra legroom, he is stiff after the four-hour drive from New York City.

"*Gospoden*, welcome." The man who speaks uses the simple Russian title of *Mister* as if Kuznetzov were royalty. *In truth, I am,* Kuznetzov thinks. *Putin has more power today than the Tsars ever had, and I have more power than Putin.*

"Thank you for your welcome." Kuznetzov watches as young men in livery remove his bags from the trunk. "They don't look like monks," he says.

"No, *Gospoden*. They are sons and nephews. This is a family business. I see you brought golf clubs. We have guest privileges at a course across the river. It is only a ten-minute drive. When convenient, please tell me when you would like a tee-time. You will carry your briefcase?"

"Yes.

The first meeting is that afternoon. Nine regional leaders, the self-styled Council of the American Bratva, stand when Kuznetzov enters the room and takes the seat at the head of the table. *Good, it will be easy to establish dominance of this group*, Kuznetzov thinks. He looks slowly around the table, matching faces with the nameplates in front of each. *Western, South-Central, Southern, Eastern, Midwestern, Central Coast, New England, and two with only city names, Chicago and New York.* There are only three he has not met before, and he is careful to fix their images in his mind.

"Gentlemen, thank you for coming to this religious retreat." Kuznetzov chuckles at his little joke. He knows these men had no choice except to attend, and he remembers something attributed to the American gangster, Alfonse Capone. *You get better results with a smile and a gun than with only a gun.* He feels the tension at the table relax.

Softball; now, hardball. Kuznetzov loves American idioms. So much more colorful than Russian.

"The Russian Council is unhappy with American operations." Tension rises. Now, softball. "We also have new opportunities for the American Brotherhood." Tension lowers.

Keeping the rhythm going, Kuznetzov points to declining revenues from America to Russia. "We operate under Russian Bratva authority and protection – for the moment. They have kept their end of the bargain; they expect us to keep ours." He says this, but he has no intentions of sending money to Russia. He has established his kingdom in America. With the help of these men, he will expand it and sever ties with Russia.

Kuznetzov does not at first mention Sokolov's assassination. These men know Sokolov's death broke the links to their political and judicial protection.

"You think Comrade Sokolov's death is a problem; however, I have already rebuilt my shield of American politicians and judges."

No one fails to grasp Kuznetzov's declaration. He is in control of the politicians and judges who protect the American Bratva. Kuznetzov sees this in their eyes and knows he has won the victory promised by Carlotta's cards.

Hardball. "Comrade Sokolov's death was not natural. He was killed by the American Sicilian-Italian Mafia. We know they are an enemy, but until now, we have each kept to our own side of a dividing line. The Americans have – as they say – crossed the line. We are at war."

Creating an enemy, especially an external enemy, is one of the classic tools of a tyrant, although Kuznetzov does not think of himself as a tyrant. He is confident his way of operating is superior to the old way. He believes he is a leader and not a tyrant and that he knows the best direction his people should take. In that, he is like many tyrants.

Kuznetzov describes one of the new opportunities. "The OPTN – the US government's Organ Procurement and Transplantation Network – lists nearly a hundred thousand people on the waiting list for kidney transplants, fifteen thousand for liver transplants, four thousand for heart transplants. Those numbers are for the United States, only. The number of people waiting for transplants has increased steadily through 2017 while the number of donors and transplants has remained steady at least 80,000 below the number of donors and transplants needed.

"That is the good news.

"America, Canada, Britain, and other countries that believe themselves to be civilized put people on the waiting list for transplants based only on medical necessity. No one in these countries can buy his way higher on the list. For us, that's even better news.

"The best news is the cost of organs on the black market is high. Two hundred fifty thousand dollars for a heart, two hundred thousand for a liver or a single kidney.

"The Chinese have tried to take advantage of this by executing prisoners and offering their organs for sale. The Chinese have failed because too many of the harvested organs are old when they reach the buyer, and too many are infested with parasites.

"Now, think about our client list. The people we sell prostitutes, drugs, weapons, protection, and more. Consider their wealth. Consider the wealth of those who need organs and are not high on the list. A single donor, carefully harvested, can bring as much as a million dollars. At first, this will not be our greatest money-maker, but it has the potential to make us millions."

"*Gospoden Kraznachey,*" the member of the Bratva whose responsibility is New England, interrupts. "The US government carefully regulates organ transplants. Only certain medical centers may perform—"

Kuznetzov slams his fist on the table. "Do you think I do not know these things? Do you think I do not have answers for your objections, including ones you've not even thought of?"

The man who interrupted slinks into this chair. "I'm sorry, *Gospoden.*"

Kuznetzov explains how American institutions and systems will make it possible to bypass the official organ assignment list. The for-profit prison system will offer a source of organs; the many private surgical centers, especially those patronized by the rich and famous, will handle transplants for their clients. Al Gore's wonderful internet, with judicious use of the dark net and end-to-end encryption, will match donors to recipients, schedule organ harvesting, and arrange the transplant surgeries.

"It is common for the ultra-wealthy from all over the world to fly to America for surgery. There is a ready source of clients with millions to spend, but who cannot position themselves higher on safe transplant lists. We will make that opportunity.

"More and more American doctors are forced by their government to put their patients' medical information on-line, using third-party software. My *Dancing Bear* hacker team easily hacks them." Kuznetzov smiles to himself, remembering the team's motto: *The wonder is not how well the bear dances; the wonder is that it dances at all*. In their minds, the bear is the internet and they are the whip-masters who once displayed dancing bears in circuses throughout the Caucuses.

As the afternoon progresses, the American Council's understanding grows. This will bring hard currency to them. They understand their responsibility for recruiting doctors and prison officials by the usual methods – appeals to greed and, where that fails, blackmail or threats to family.

Despite the cool fall weather, two days of golf and detailed planning follow before the conference ends. A van, marked with the logo and name of the church retreat center, takes the nine American councilors to an airport. Before Kuznetzov leaves, he tells Carlotta to meet him in a few days in Folio, Arizona. Kuznetzov returns to New York in the Lincoln Town Car. Three hours after leaving the center, he reinstalls the battery in his phone, plugs the charger into a power port, and begins making calls.

≈≈≈≈≈

In a room resembling a customer service call center in India or Indiana, where tiny cubicles house people with nothing but a phone and a computer terminal, a computer flashes an alert. Near Apalachin, New York, someone used a cell phone registered to an individual with a Romanian passport. Under the existing espionage laws, the NSA analyst may monitor the call. She punches up the recording that was automatically made and plays the call from the beginning.

It's a woman. Not a heavy accent. Don't recognize it. I'll have to get someone on that. Made travel plans from New York to some place called Folio, Arizona. Plane change in Phoenix. Leaving in two days.

The analyst puts a flag on the phone to ensure the system will route all future calls to her. *Probably nothing. Maybe a tourist.* She calls up Folio in the Google Maps program, and then Googles "folio az tourism." *What's there? Tours of the Glen Canyon dam and helicopter flights through the canyon. Lots of expensive resorts. Navajo jewelry. Ah, here's one. A fat-farm. A spa for important and rich people. Offers liposuction and plastic surgery. Not my idea of a tourist destination.*

≈≈≈≈≈

Pony Boy is the childhood nickname of Sam Red Horse's sister's second son. Sam is the only one who still uses it, and the young man suspects Sam doesn't mean it in a family way. The young man is afraid of Sam. However, he is Sam's nephew and according to custom, Sam's responsibility. Pony Boy delivered three young and healthy people to U.P.S. #9. Still offering his nephew the trust – and in Sam's mind, the doubt – owed to relatives, Sam invites the boy to his office.

"You know you will not be paid until we have a client who is satisfied these individuals are not only drug- and virus-free, but also have the right blood type and genetic markers to make a good transplant – or research subject. In any case, you will pay for the blood and genetic tests."

The young man is unaware of the latter stipulations, but understands from his uncle's voice they are not negotiable. If the individuals he and his Reapers presented to Sam are not acceptable, not only would they not be paid, but they would fall into debt. The boy is confident, perhaps over-confident, when he promises his uncle he and his friends will succeed where others have failed.

Sam decides Pony Boy should have a better understanding of the prison. If so, he might – just might – fall in line and be a good soldier. "Come with me," Sam says, and leads the boy from his office. Two guards fall in step behind them.

Sergeant Mona Goth speaks softly into her radio and notifies the control room the warden is "on the move with one guest." The control room follows Pony Boy using the RFID chip in his visitor badge. Sam is the only person in the prison who does not carry an RFID chip.

Their first stop is one of the guard towers on an outer corner of a prison wing.

"The cell bars and the walls of the prison are the first lines of defense against escape," Sam says. "The guard towers are the second. Guards in the towers have night vision equipment and each tower has a UV spotlight."

Sam points to the fence. "Chain-link and barbed wire aren't good enough. That fence is topped with concertina wire with razor blades welded to it. Anybody trying to climb over it will lose enough blood they'll be dead before they take ten steps. The wire is electrified, so it's not likely they'll take any steps."

"There was something in the news about prisoners who cut through to a utility access tunnel ..." Pony Boy begins.

"That was an old prison and the people who built these prisons learned from it. Air ducts, water, sewerage, and electricity are in tunnels too small for even a midget. Besides, they have steel grids welded across them every ten yards. Somebody who tries to crawl in one of them won't go very far. Come on, you need to see where we stored your meat."

Sam takes Pony Boy to Block 11 – the solitary confinement wing. "We keep the high-potential prisoners here until we are sure they are free of disease, including HIV, Hanta, and Zika."

Sam slides aside a strip of opaque plastic to reveal a two-inch thick glass window. Pony Boy peers in to see one of his three captives sitting motionless on a bunk, facing the opposite wall. Light flickers on his face.

"Television?" Pony Boy says. "What's he watching?"

"*Sesame Street?* Reruns of *The Partridge Family?* It hardly matters. He's passed his blood and DNA tests and our background check. No one's going to come looking for him, so he's been treated until we need him."

"Treated?"

"Prefrontal lobotomy. One of the simplest brain surgeries. Not much harder than sticking a knitting needle into the corner of an eye, pushing it into the brain, and stirring it around a bit. Don't want to do too much damage, or he'd not be able to take care of himself. We have a doctor on staff who is an expert."

Pony Boy swallows the bile rising in his throat, and nods. "Why not drugs?"

Sam watches Pony Boy's throat work, and laughs. "Got to you, didn't it? We use drugs. In fact, we're the largest single user of Valium in Arizona. Naturally, our sources are not the open market."

Sam's tone becomes serious. "One of your gifts was unsuitable. Carried the Human Immunodeficiency Virus – HIV. We may get something for him from a drug company wanting to test a new anti-viral. We might get enough to cover the cost of the testing we did. This one," Sam points to the cell door, "This one is golden. We already have a request for his heart. You're gonna be okay, money-wise."

"Thank you, Uncle," Pony Boy says. "And thank you for the tour of your prison, but I would rather you tell me more about what to look for in our next offering."

Maybe the boy has promise, Sam thinks, and escorts him to the visitors' gate of the prison.

Susan Calvin

At the Navajo Western Regional Hospital, Dr. Deschene's secretary announces a visitor. "Ms. Susan Calvin. She says you are expecting her."

Deschene greets Susan in the outer office and invites her to the cafeteria for coffee. "Or lunch. I guess it's noon by your body clock, right? And even though it is hospital food, the cafeteria does a good job. There should be fruit, yogurt, granola, and pastries on the breakfast bar."

Over what is more brunch than lunch, Susan tells Dr. Deschene she was fired from the *Washington Banner*. "I was fortunate. My contract was written ten years ago and included a golden parachute. I received enough severance pay to carry me for several months, and I already have three requests for free-lance work. I would like to begin with a follow up on the article that got me fired."

"I will be happy to help you. I try to follow the issue, especially after hearing Doli when we were in DC."

"Perhaps I could also interview you about forensic anthropology, perhaps some interesting autopsies?"

Dr. Deschene chuckles. "I'm afraid I'm a bit underemployed at the moment. I am working as the pathologist for the hospital and assistant coroner for the Navajo Nation. All the autopsies I do are pretty much routine. At one time, I was an assistant medical examiner for the State of Arizona, and I've done some consulting for the state ME's office, but since I've moved here from Phoenix, it's too far away. You may decide if it's worth your while to talk to me. I won't be offended if you say not."

Dr. Deschene looks at Susan, thinks quickly, and adds, "If everything else fails, we can invite Doli to visit."

At that moment, Spencer walks into the hospital cafeteria. At 10:00 AM, there aren't many people present. He spots Dr. Deschene and goes straight to his table. Spencer holds a roll of paper, perhaps a dozen pages, squeezed tightly. His hand trembles, and he appears agitated.

"Susan, this is my protégé, Spencer Hansen.

"Spencer, this is Ms. Susan Calvin. I met her at a conference in Washington last month. Please, sit with us."

Spencer's smile is huge when Dr. Deschene calls him his protégé. He looks hard at the woman, however, and then sits at the table, leaving an empty seat to separate him from her. "Sir, I think I know this boy." He hands the papers to Dr. Deschene.

"This is an—"

"Yes, sir," Spencer interrupts and glances at Susan. "Please, just read it."

After reading the summary on the first page, Dr. Deschene returns the papers to Spencer. "We will look at these together in my office. Susan, Spencer has presented something that might interest you, if Spencer agrees.

"Spencer, Susan is a journalist and a very good one, who is not afraid to tackle tough and touchy issues. She is also a friend. I would like her to join us. Do you agree?"

Spencer's, "Yes, sir," is muted and not enthusiastic.

≈≈≈≈≈

Spencer's document is an autopsy report. Dr. Deschene asks his secretary to make copies for Susan and himself. Minutes later, he sits at a small table in the pathology laboratory with Susan and Spencer. "We will not be disturbed, here," Dr. Deschene says, and then chuckles. "No one comes in here unless they have to." He reads aloud the summary of the autopsy.

"How well did you know this young man?" he asks Spencer.

"Not very well. I was two years ahead of him in school, and on the varsity footie team – what you Yankees call *soccer*. He was JV."

"Neither of us are Yankees, Spencer." Susan says. She might have chuckled, and her reply is soft.

"For those of us of the Norwegian persuasion, all North Americans are Yankees, except Canadians and Mexicans. And it's still football or footie, not soccer."

Dr. Deschene and Susan grin, but do not chuckle. Glad for even the slight comic relief, the three return to the autopsy report.

The coroner's words raise more questions than they answer.

"The Rough Rock County Coroner reports that two men, amateur rock and mineral collectors, were hiking in the desert west of Marvel Canyon when they found what appeared to be human remains. As soon as they reached a place with a cell phone signal, they called 911. A Rough Rock County Fire Department EMT team took their GPS position and responded. The EMT team confirmed a death. There was evidence the body was an individual reported missing to the Navajo Nation Police a month earlier.

"When the Rough Rock County Coroner examined the body, it was naked except for an orange rubber bracelet on the right wrist. The bracelet contained a computer flash drive; however, the drive held no data. The preliminary report notes no trauma.

"A number of bones are missing and appear to have been removed from the body by animal activity. Thoracic organs and abdominal organs are missing along with the thoracic musculature. The external sex organs are missing.

"The body matches the description of Jessie Long Tree." Dr. Deschene looks up from the report.

"I know him … I guess, I mean, I knew him," Spencer says. "The varsity and JV footie teams scrimmaged, sometimes. The bracelet. He always wore that bracelet. Kept his schoolwork on it since he didn't have a computer at home. And, it looks like his organs were harvested."

"I'm sorry, Spencer, but this is likely your friend." Dr. Deschene looks at Susan, who is composed despite the graphic description of the body. Dr. Deschene continues reading.

"His parents filed a missing person report a month earlier. According to the report, Jessie was a sixteen-year-old Navajo male who attended the high school at Ya-ta-hey. The last contacts with Jessie were cell phone calls made three days before he was reported missing. There's no mention of who he called."

Susan flips through the other pages. "The body was in the desert for some time, yet they did not call a forensic anthropologist – even though you are just across the river."

"Probably because the state wasn't interested," Dr. Deschene says. *Or because the state Medical Examiner wouldn't want to call on me.*

"Just another dead Indian?" Susan says. Her down-turned mouth and the cadence of her words convey her disgust. Neither Dr. D or Spencer are offended.

"Likely."

Spencer and Susan exchange looks, and then both stare at Dr. Deschene. "Spencer, this report neither proves nor disproves your hypothesis of organ harvesting. We need more information."

"We're going to need a lot of help," Susan says. "Um, I hope I'm not rushing in by assuming you want me to help."

Susan's interest in the autopsy wins over Spencer. "I would like that," he says. "And I know where we can get help. My kiva society."

≈≈≈≈≈

The next Saturday night, Spencer looks around the circle formed by the E'e'aahjigo Kiva. The boys and young men bypassed the fences and gates and sit among rubble – the only thing that remains of what once was a great kiva of their ancestors. It is not on the tourist routes. Both the US Park Service and the Navajo Nation have abandoned it. The boys understand their elders' reason. Having served its purpose, the kiva will return to the earth, destroyed by sun, rain, wind, cold, and heat, like Chetro Ketl and the other great houses, pueblos, and kivas at Chaco Canyon and Canyon de Chelly. It is part of the harmony these young men, like their more traditional elders, seek. These boys also seek places of power, and a greater understanding of their heritage. Both Gaagii and Cha'tima are studying their cultures' traditions, preparing to become Shamans.

A small fire burns in the center of the circle. Cha'tima ignites a bundle of sage, and fans the smoke toward the boys. Gaagii recites a chant as Cha'tima walks around the circle to Ata'halne's soft drumbeat. Spencer watches until Cha'tima sits.

Walk in Harmony, Spencer thinks, to settle his mind before he begins. "I'm the newest of you. I'm not the oldest. But you have honored me by adopting me and naming me Atsa. There is something I must tell you.

"We all knew Jessie Long Tree. He—"

"Knew, Atsa?" Ata'halne' interrupts. "Knew? Past tense. Missing for weeks. Is he dead, then?"

"Yes," Spencer says. "A body found in the desert across the river is his. What is disturbing and frightening, I believe he did not die a natural death, but was killed and his eyes, heart, liver, lungs, and kidneys were removed to be sold for organ transplants."

"Come on, Atsa," Ahote says. "Organ harvesting? That's conspiracy theory stuff. Like the guy who picks up a prostitute, takes her to his hotel room, and wakes up the next morning in a bathtub full of ice with a note to call an ambulance, because his kidneys have been cut out."

"No," Spencer says. "That story is not conspiracy theory stuff, it's urban legend stuff. I've done a lot of reading. Stories like that appear often on the internet, all right. There are no gatekeepers on the internet. Anyone can post anything. For sure, organ recovery is much too complicated to happen in a hotel room. But, illegal organ harvesting is real. The National Agency for the Prohibition of Organ Trafficking estimates 35% of kidney transplants, worldwide, are done with black market kidneys. That's something like 7,000 kidneys each year. That doesn't include ones secretly done in Russia, Switzerland, and other places. And, I don't even want to get into the number of prisoners China executes for their organs."

Hok'ee, whose name means *Abandoned*, speaks. His voice is soft and hesitant. The others stop talking and listen closely. "You know my Uncle Hastiin died of liver disease."

The others nod. *Among the Navajo, Hopi, Zuni, Apache and eighteen other nations of the aboriginal peoples of the Four Corners area of North America, liver disease is* code *for cirrhosis of the liver caused by alcoholism.*

Most of their ancestors, hunter-gatherers until the Spaniards contacted them, never settled anywhere long enough to grow the grains that people in Africa, Asia, and Europe fermented to make beer, nor the grapes that other civilizations turned into wine. The gene to produce the enzyme that helped the body break down alcohol was not of any survival value to these wanderers, and was bred out of most of them.

In a perfect counter-example, the Europeans who invaded the Americas were mostly descended from people who could afford to drink beer and wine, liquids whose alcohol made them relatively germ-free compared to the water consumed by the peasants, and had therefore survived to preserve that gene.

"My uncle owned property off the reservation where they found uranium," Hok'ee says. "He made a lot of money selling the mineral rights. Only a few days after he learned his liver was diseased, men came and offered to sell him a replacement liver."

64

"You mean, put him on the list for a liver transplant?" Gaagii says. Gaagii, or *Raven,* suits this boy. His hair, like many of the boys, is black, but his is the blackest. His nose is narrow, straight, and sharp, like the beak of a raven, and not the aquiline nose more common among his people. There is a deep silence while the boys watch Gaagii's face.

"That's not what you mean, is it?" Gaagii whispers.

"No. They were clear they were going around the regular routes for organ transplants. Uncle realized this and refused their offer."

"Your uncle was an honorable man," Gaagii says.

"Where was he diagnosed?" Spencer asks. "The hospital in Farmington or the one in Folio?"

"In Folio, but not at the hospital. At the Glen Canyon Medical Spa."

Somehow, someone found the diagnosis, Spencer thinks. *Someone in the records section selling information? Should I say something to Dr. Standart? How much should I tell him? What can I say without breaking oath with my Kiva?*

"What Hok'ee told us may be related to what I want to say." Spencer describes the discovery of the body of Jessie Long Tree and the condition in which it was found. He tells of the missing information from the autopsy report. "The body was naked. No T-shirt. Jessie always wore a Man United T-shirt."

Spencer tells them about the autopsy of a Navajo who had apparently sold one kidney.

"My guess is that someone, maybe several different someones, is targeting Indians not just to sell their organs or to sell organs to them, but killing us to harvest organs. That is based only on two autopsies – Jessie's and the other one – and what Hok'ee just told us. We need facts to help decide if this guess – what Dr. Deschene calls a hypothesis – can become a theory, or needs to be discarded."

"Atsa," Niyol stands to speak. "Your brothers in Kiva are enrolled Navajo or Hopi. Some of us are adults 'cause we are of age. No one has a college degree – most of us haven't graduated from high school. We were disfellowshipped from a church-sponsored scout troop because we don't believe in god – at least the god of that church. No matter how old we are, to most people we're just kids. What can we do?"

"You are right," Spencer-Atsa says. "But you are also wrong. We have useful skills. We have courage. And, we can find allies." Spencer tells about Dr. Deschene and Susan Calvin.

"I created a problem, though," Spencer says. "When I spoke to Dr. Deschene about getting help, I said it would be from my kiva society. He will suss as soon as he meets you, that you are my kiva, and it has both Navajo and Hopi members."

"And one white-haired Norwegian Indian," Hok'ee says. He laughs. He doesn't do that often.

"Is this doctor an honorable man, and trustworthy?" Cha'tima asks.

"I believe he is. And I think he was a scout. We'll have to tell him we were kicked out."

"Disfellowshipped," Ahiga says. "It sounds a lot better."

"Agreed," Cha'tima says. "Ask if he will keep our secret. If he agrees, we will meet with him. Is this acceptable to everyone?"

The others' silence is their assent.

"Brothers? Before we start investigating, we need some official cover. I want to bring Chief Joe in on this." Ata'halne scans the circle.

The faces of the boys and young men light up with smiles. Joseph White Eagle, the Chief of the Navajo Nation Police, is a conduit to US Federal resources, including the FBI – and he is Ata'halne's uncle. They agree to bring him into the secret of the kiva.

66

Spencer continues his story. "I worked last summer at the Glen Canyon Spa. Dr. Standart, the Director, was very good to me. The leak about Hok'ee's uncle may have come from the spa's records section. May I tell him what Hok'ee told us?"

Discussion is brief, but lively. In the end, Hok'ee makes the decision for them. "It is my uncle, my story. I say Atsa should tell the doctor at the spa what he knows."

~~~~~

Bidziil "Johnny" Two-Horses and Sam Little Crow, both retired from the United States Air Force, sit on the bluffs overlooking the Folio Municipal Airport. They sit comfortably in folding lawn chairs, sheltered from the sun by broad-brimmed hats and long-sleeved shirts. A cooler of food and drink sits between them. As young airmen, they had tough times with alcohol. Their understanding of the reason and learning of their own limits were partly responsible for both achieving senior Non-Commissioned Officer status before retirement. Now, they enjoy a couple of lite beers and a lot of bottled water with their plane watching.

Things have become a little more exciting since the city extended the runway and built a control tower. It happened after a long battle between the Folio City Council and a vocal group of people who claimed to represent the city's taxpayers and said they'd been "taxed enough already." It wasn't much of a secret the tourism industry would benefit most from the new runway and tower. Tourism, meaning the people who offered tours of the dam, rafting on the river, and an occasional visit to the ruined kiva northeast of town. What was less well known was that it would also benefit the Glen Canyon Medical Spa. Since the Spa and tourism, including the many resort hotels and tour companies, were the biggest employers in town, the objections of the "taxed enough already" people were quickly overturned.

Johnny's attention turns to the Folio airport and the air traffic. It is fortunate the prevailing winds are from the north, because the only place suitable for the main runway is a north-south strip of land between the bluffs, the city, and the Colorado River. There is a crosswind runway running east-to-west, but it is used only by single-engine planes with experienced and bold pilots.

"Holy Mother of Salome, that's a 757," Johnny says.

Sam raises his binoculars and spots the winglets. "757-300 Extended Range," he says. "A brand-new one, too. Copy this registration number."

Johnny uses his phone to Google the registration number. "Saudi Arabia," he reports. "Gotta be royalty, in a plane like that."

The plane leaves the runway at the north end, and taxis to the apron. The two men watch a tug connect to the plane's front landing gear and pull it into a hanger on the west side of the airfield. Before the hanger doors close, a convoy arrives – two black SUVs lead and two follow. Between them is a tall, white, Mercedes van. "That will be the ambulance," Johnny says.

Sam nods. "Headed for the Glen Canyon Spa. A face-lift for some Saudi prince – or for one of his wives."

"Or one of his boy-toys."

"That's so damn typical of those rich middle-eastern countries. Offer lousy health care to their people and fly royalty to the US for treatment. I dated a nurse who said she and a team of doctors and nurses and a crate of equipment flew in a private 747 to Qatar once just to give someone a colonoscopy."

Sam shrugs, and enters the date, time, and registration number of the 757 into their logbook.

Johnny pulls two lite beers from the cooler. "Hey, lookee there. At the General Aviation terminal. There's old Thurmond and his helicopter. Looks like he's about to take a bunch of tourist down the canyon. Too bad we can't watch him."

"Yeah, hope he makes it. He must be, how old? Seventy?"

"Seventy, nothing. He taught Wilber and Orville how to fly. He's got to be over a hundred."

~~~~~

Dr. Standart greets Spencer and asks about his studies and in-service assignment. After some small talk, Spencer tells Standart the reason for his visit. Standart's face becomes white and then red as Spencer relates his story. When Spencer finishes, he waits for Dr. Standart to digest the information.

"Spencer, you know we do a lot of good work here. Fitting prosthetics on children maimed by land mines in the Middle East and Africa; facial reconstructive surgery for children who have been burned; and general surgery for Rohingya from Burma and Bangladesh. I refuse to call Burma, *Myanmar.* That country, its government, is a travesty. And to know their leader received a Nobel Peace Prize – for genocide.

"I'm sorry, Spencer. Sometimes my emotions get the better of me. I hope you understand."

"Yes, sir. Just like when one of my friends told me about being cast out from his family. I cried. I was glad for the darkness and the wood smoke from the fire, because they provided both cover and excuse."

"You are a good boy ... I mean, you are a good young man," Dr. Standart says. He mulls the information for a moment, shuffles some unrelated papers on his desk, and stares at a blank computer screen. Finally, he speaks. "Spencer, I am shocked, appalled, disgusted, and angry someone I employ may have used his position in this way. Have I covered all my emotions? Perhaps not. Whether directly or indirectly, someone has released patient information. That is an abomination."

Spencer thinks back to the teachings of his former church. He remembers the list of Biblical abominations he had to memorize. *Cross-dressers – I guess Scotsmen in kilts are doomed to hell.*

Usury – that covers most of the pawn shops around the Res. The eagle, sacred to both the Navajo and the American Bilagáana is an abomination to God. The vulture and osprey. Catfish and shrimp – not that there's a lot of either of those on the Res. The list goes on and on. Why did their god create so many things he hates? Including, it appears, humans.

Dr. Standart's voice draws Spencer from his thoughts. "Will you allow me to investigate? I will punish any miscreants as harshly as the law allows. On the other hand, I want to preserve the Spa's reputation and resources so we may continue our *pro bono* work. I am faced with a dilemma. Do you understand?"

"Yes, sir. And thank you for your trust."

"Thank you for yours," Dr. Standart says.

After Spencer leaves, Dr. Standart spends an hour thinking. *The boy was discrete and loyal enough to bring this to me and not to the authorities. He has considerable potential. More, in fact, than a records clerk on whom I can pin this breach. Not that it was a breach. It was my people who visited the old Indian. Spencer is a long-term investment, but one with great promise and greater potential.*

Sam Red Horse

Ivan Kuznetzov stands at the glass wall of his suite looking at the Glen Canyon Dam and the lake it creates. The Overlook Resort deserves its name. Carlotta checked in two days ago. As soon as she calls, Kuznetzov dismisses his guard and asks her to his suite.

"*Gospoden*," Carlotta greets him when she arrives. "How was your flight?"

"Not good. The fool tried to do it all on his own instead of using a travel agency. We were late getting to Phoenix. If we hadn't bought all the seats on the commuter plane from Phoenix to Folio they would have taken off without us."

Carlotta knows "the fool" does not mean The Jester of the Tarot, but one of Kuznetzov's guards or assistants – the entourage with which he travels.

Kuznetzov dismisses the problem with a wave of his hand. "Tomorrow I will begin to orchestrate the pieces of the puzzle that brought me to this place. I will visit one of those puzzle pieces in his place of power. He will believe I give him the advantage. He is a powerful man, with many people beholden to him. I wish an alliance, but on my terms. What is my best approach?"

"There are many aspects to this question," Carlotta says as she deals the Celtic Cross. "We need more answers than a simple pattern can provide."

Carlotta's reading reveals a man who is both powerful and vain, yet who hides an important and dark part of his past.

He hides his time as a military policeman and an interrogator – a water boarder – at the Abu Ghraib Prison, Kuznetzov thinks. *I will keep that knowledge in reserve.*

He listens carefully to Carlotta's summary. "Let him think he is in control until you wrap him in your web."

≈≈≈≈≈

Ivan Petrov's American passport, social security card, and drivers license identify him as Isaac Peterson. He owns an auto body and paint shop associated with a national chain, but his real business is head of the Arizona Bratva, a second echelon commander under the Lieutenant of the Bratva of the Western US. In this role, he deals with Sam Red Horse, Warden of Arizona Prison System Unit #9.

On orders from Kuznetzov, Peterson has given Kuznetzov's name and phone number to Sam. Peterson is careful to say only that Kuznetzov is someone who can be trusted and wishes to speak to Sam about expanding his business.

Kuznetzov's phone buzzes. Caller ID shows the number given to him by Peterson. "Hello, Mr. Red Horse."

"*Gospoden Kraznachey*," the voice on the phone is neutral. "I understand you prefer that name. We have interests in common. Will you visit me, tomorrow?"

Ivan Kuznetzov understands this man is not being obsequious, but is mocking him by using his preferred title of "Mister Paymaster." He also understands the man believes he is operating from the stronger position. Kuznetzov agrees to a meeting at the prison the next day. He spends much of the afternoon on the phone with Peterson, quizzing him about their business and learning about Sam Red Horse's strengths, weaknesses, and 'hot buttons.'

≈≈≈≈≈

A prison guard meets Kuznetzov at the gate and introduces himself as Chris Schultz. The man does a perfunctory and apologetic search for weapons and gives Kuznetzov a visitor badge

72

to wear on a lanyard around his neck. He does not tell Kuznetzov the badge contains an RFID chip that will allow the prison to track Kuznetzov's movements.

Sam Red Horse greets Kuznetzov with more respect than he showed during the previous day's telephone call. "Mr. Kuznetzov, welcome to Arizona Unified Prison System Number Nine."

Done his homework, Kuznetzov thinks. "Thank you, Mr. Red Horse, but please, call me *Gospoden.* It's my nickname."

Nickname? More of a title, and you wear it like a crown, Sam thinks. "Then will you please, call me Sam? I understand you have a proposition for me."

"You have a large guard force here. Almost an army," Kuznetzov says. "You are very powerful, and you have created a profitable business." Having stroked his host, Kuznetzov adds bait. "You are acting locally when you could act much more broadly."

"I am listening."

Kuznetzov speaks using the language of prison labor – convicts who are part of the nationwide prison industries scam. Sam understands.

"Your laborers come from local police departments and courts. You have only one place to employ them, this prison's workshop. You have no control over the skills of your laborers. There is considerable waste in the operation.

"I believe with the right associates, you could become the focal point for the entire state system. Prisoners would be screened for desired skills with an eye to increasing efficiency and sent here. Your principal customer would become a global distribution point."

Sam sits quietly digesting this information. He understands Kuznetzov is speaking not of the prison industries game that nets Sam a few thousand dollars in kickbacks each year but the organ harvesting operation, which brings in a few score thousand dollars.

Sam takes time to think before he responds. "I spoke to the contractor who arranged this meeting. He said you have the resources to implement, in his words, "whatever he proposes." Sam reflects for a moment. He knows he will give up the home-field advantage. It will be necessary, however, to cede that to Kuznetzov. "Perhaps we should discuss this over lunch. Have you been in Folio long enough to have found a quiet restaurant?"

"Would you be my guest at the Country Club?" Kuznetzov suggests.

Country Club. There's only one – the Glen Canyon Country Club, Sam thinks. *Isaac was right. If this guy is a member, then he's got more than enough money to expand the operation.*

At a quiet table over drinks and lunch, Sam and Kuznetzov reach agreement. The Arizona Bratva controls the corporation which built the ten units of the state's Unified Prison System. The Bratva controls the guards' union, and they provide the wardens for all but #9. Sam's military record and connection with an Arizona state senator are too much for the Bratva, and he gets that job.

"We control the other nine units," Kuznetzov says. "They will do the preliminary screening of prisoners. When we find a suitable person, they will create paperwork necessary for the transfer to Unit 9."

"You, sir, are in a powerful position," Kuznetzov strokes his lunch guest. "For some purposes, a clerk in the records office can be even more powerful."

"You, sir, are very perceptive," Sam Red Horse says, returning the stroke.

Kuznetzov agrees to send someone to install software on Sam's office computer. "The software will provide secure communication among your suppliers – the other nine prisons. There will also be a database of prisoners. The software will work in harmony to provide an ordering system to match world-wide customer needs for organs with prisoners who can provide those organs."

"What if someone stumbles onto that, or discovers it in a state inspection?" Sam asks.

"Most of the software and the databases will not exist on your computer. All you will see are small programs that mimic real programs in the cloud and call on encryption and communication programs. They will connect with servers at secure locations. Those servers hold the databases and software that make the matches."

Kuznetzov does not think it necessary to tell Sam the remote servers also have deep links into the government's Organ Procurement and Transplantation Network database.

"If anyone unauthorized accesses your computer, either through the internet, your prison's intranet, or the terminal in your office, the little software modules will disappear. The real software and data will be safe."

Sam agrees with Kuznetzov's proposals, knowing he has placed himself in a subordinate position. Sam thinks about his "I Love Me" Wall and understands. Despite Sam's awards and commendations, he is not an equal of this man, this Russian.

≈≈≈≈≈

Kuznetzov has captured one puzzle piece – Sam Red Horse. Now, the second piece – the principal customer for Sam's prisoners. He summons Carlotta to his suite.

"Tomorrow, I will meet with an important revenue source, Dr. Standart of the Glen Canyon Medical Spa. His work, both legal and illegal, harvests much money. He has been operating independently. I will ensure he knows to remit a generous portion of his income to the Bratva. I will balance this with offers to send him new customers and to increase his supplies. What is my best approach?"

Carlotta nods. Kuznetzov has asked a specific question. Once again, after Kuznetzov shuffles the Major Arcana, Carlotta deals the Ellipse Spread with the point away from herself.

Kuznetzov pays little attention until she reaches the fourth card, which sits in the "What to do" position. *The Hanged Man, inverted.* The card depicts a man hanging by his feet from a tree limb. The tree and its limb are in the shape of a Tau Cross. The man wears a blue tunic and red tights. His head is limned by a halo. Inverted, it appears he is standing on tiptoe upon the limb and not hanging from it.

"Ah," Carlotta smiles. "This portends a strong future for you. You have turned uncertainty into opportunity. Your enemies will fall before you. Yet, you must be strong and resolute. Then, the people you face and who are petty and weak will fall before your power and resolution like wheat before the reaper."

Kuznetzov thanks her and crosses her palm with silver to guarantee the outcome she sees. When he returns to his room, he makes a substantial addition to her bank account. The money is meaningless to him. It is a trivial part of the Bratva accounts he looted before he left Russia, and his goal is not money. It is power. It is not Russia; it is America.

≈≈≈≈≈

The computer at the NSA analyst's position flashes a warning. She watches the screen and sees the agency's computers create a link between the phone she bookmarked and a bank account when the phone accesses the account. The analyst watches the replay as ten thousand dollars appear in an account in the Bahamas. A little digging, and she finds the account in the Cayman Islands from which the money came. Neither account has any flags on it and both involve foreign banks and nameless foreign account holders. The amount is not large enough to trigger any particular action. The analyst makes a note and moves to the next intercept.

Dr. Standart accepts the envelope from the bicycle messenger and examines it. It is an expensive piece of stationary, cream, with his name written in black ink. The handwriting is impeccable. He opens the envelope and removes a folded notecard with the Cyrillic letters "ИК" embossed. The note, in the same impeccable handwriting, is an invitation to play golf with a *Gospoden Ivan Kuznetzov* on the next day at 8:00 AM at the Glen Canyon Country Club.

The club's membership is small enough for Standart to know there is no member by that name. He calls the membership secretary and asks about this Kuznetzov.

"He's a new member, sir. Joined just a week ago." The secretary pauses. Standart hears computer keys clicking. "He does have a tee time at 8:00 tomorrow morning."

Standart thanks the man and hangs up the phone. *There have been no openings on the membership rolls, and that name was not on the waiting list. He bought someone's membership. That would have cost him at least five million dollars, plus the club's initiation fee. I wonder who gave him my name – and what service he wants from the spa.*

≈≈≈≈≈

The next morning, Standart arrives at the club at 7:30 AM. The pro introduces him to Kuznetzov, but not to the two other members of the foursome. Their golf cart has no clubs. *Bodyguards*, Standart thinks. *He's either very important or thinks he is.*

The game begins with Kuznetzov tossing a tee into the air. It lands pointing more to Standart than Kuznetzov, so Standart tees up. The first hole is a long dogleg left. Standart selects his driver and puts the ball just past the trees that block the view of the hole.

"Good lie," Kuznetzov says. He also uses his driver and puts his ball a few yards past Standart's.

"Excellent shot." Standart says. "Your next shot will be straight for the green. I'll have to try to draw mine."

Kuznetzov watches Dr. Standart carefully during the play. *One can learn a great deal about a man in a game of golf,* Kuznetzov thinks. *It's a lot more than does he surreptitiously improve his lie or step toward the fairway or the rough when he has to drop a lost ball. It's about how he reacts in these and similar situations. It's about his true feeling, his integrity, and his ability to accept challenges.* Kuznetzov watches Dr. Standart and finds him wanting in all those traits, and therefore, acceptable to Kuznetzov's plans.

At first, Kuznetzov keeps the conversation genial, focusing on the course, the weather, the condition of the fairways and the greens, and the placement of the cups on the greens. "You might think," Kuznetzov says, "they want to make the par fives too easy."

Standart, who has been fairly silent to this point, agrees. "There are many members for whom membership is more important than the game. Initiation is a million dollars. The membership fee is a hundred thousand dollars a year, and the greens fees … well, you are the host for this game, and it would be impolite to mention them."

Kuznetzov smiles inwardly. Standart has exposed his curiosity about Kuznetzov and – more important – about money. Whether intentionally or unconsciously, he has opened one of the avenues Kuznetzov will use to bring Standart under his control.

Play continues, with Standart and Kuznetzov keeping pace with one another's score. They are tied when they reach the 18th tee. Kuznetzov has honors from the last hole, and tees up first. His shot fades. The ball lands in a sand trap on the right side of the green.

"Nearly pin high," Kuznetzov says. "But a terrible lie." He chuckles.

Standart's shot is also pin-high, but on the green. If he doesn't three-putt, he's won the game.

Standart stands aside as Kuznetzov enters the sand trap. He carries a sand wedge and a nine-iron. After seeing his lie, he discards the nine-iron and addresses the ball with the wedge. He shifts his weight to dig his feet into the sand, eyes the pin, stares at the ball, says something in Russian, and swings. The ball and a spray of sand land on the green. The ball rolls toward the cup, but stops about ten yards from it.

Standart's putt takes his ball over a slight depression in the green. The ball changes direction as it crosses the depression, and ends up a few inches from Kuznetzov's, but a bit closer to the cup. Standart marks his spot, and removes the ball from the green.

Kuznetzov putts. His ball rolls, seems to pause at the edge of the cup, and drops in. He is now one stroke ahead of Standart.

Standart replaces his ball and putts. His ball stops a foot from the cup. He taps it in and congratulates Kuznetzov on the win. *That was close. I didn't intend to beat a potential client and probably would have done so if I hadn't remembered the depression in the green.*

"A close game, Komrade," Kuznetzov says. "You forced me to concentrate, and I like that. I would like another game, soon, but first, may I invite you to lunch at the club?"

"I would enjoy both another game and lunch," Standart replies.

Standart and Kuznetzov sit at a table in a corner of the dining room. Two of Kuznetzov's bodyguards sit halfway across the room, at a table allowing them to see both entrances to the room and the window-wall overlooking the 18th green.

Kuznetzov orders vodka, ice cold and neat. Standart, knowing Kuznetzov might not want to do business with someone who doesn't drink with him, orders Schnapps, which the bartender knows to serve the same way.

Kuznetzov raises his glass. "*K vashemu zdorov'yu*, to your health. It is how you say in America, right?"

Standart replies, "You are correct, sir." He adds in his native German. "*Für Ihre Gesundheit.*" The two men toss down their drinks.

Lunch is ordered. While waiting for it to be served, Kuznetzov broaches the subject Standart has been waiting for – the motive behind the invitation.

"We have a client in common," Kuznetzov says. "He gave me your name. Ab al Hakim _____. Not too long ago, I sold him an electronic jamming system for his nation's aircraft. I understand you sold him a liver."

Standart nods as if he understands although his mind is in turmoil. He keeps his hands firmly on the tabletop, knowing they would quiver if he lifted them.

"We also hacked your patient records, Doctor. All of them. You were very foolish to put them on a computer connected to the internet. You must correct that."

Now, Standart is utterly afraid. He is unable to speak. The room seems to spin.

"Again, our motives are not what you think. You have a lucrative business. Moreover, you have an ideal situation. A legitimate spa catering to the rich and famous, and therefore able to demand privacy. A licensed surgical center – although not officially licensed for some of the surgeries you perform – and a nearby, ready source of organs."

Kuznetzov pauses to allow Dr. Standart to breathe.

"I will become your partner in this enterprise. No, no. I see your face and I know what it portrays. I do not mean owner or oligarch, but partner. I will provide new sources of organs and new customers for the organs, both at your spa and for sale outside your spa. I have a client list, a long and wealthy one. I have access to fleets of planes and teams of people to transport organs. These

80

organs will be accompanied by paperwork declaring them legitimate. We will make the system work for us."

Standart jumps on Kuznetzov's last statement. "Organs are always claimed by a surgical team from the recipient's hospital. How long do you think it will be before some outside team discovers something wrong? OPTN monitors all offers of organs and maintains the list of people seeking transplants. How long—"

Kuznetzov's laugh interrupts Standart. "You do know the business, Doctor. The surgical teams will have no reason to be suspicious. And I now control OPTN. I have hacked their database and their software. They are quite unaware. It will be I who sets priorities and allocates organs."

Standart relaxes. Their lunch is served, and they address it while Kuznetzov continues his narrative.

"You now take a liver, for example, and discard the rest of the organs and the blood. A waste. Using my contacts, we will sell all the organs. I will show you how to process the blood to extract certain blood products, including human immunoglobulin. Your spa uses it and you must know it sells for nearly $700 per gram. While that may not seem like much, the average patient requires at least 50 grams per week. Other blood products sell for less; however, by making use of the entire body – all the organs, the blood, and bone marrow – a single body can earn us as much as two million dollars."

Standart is stunned. *I'm a piker compared to this man. But, is he for real?*

"Mr. Kuznetzov, what you propose is both illegal and risky. You ask for a partnership but you offer no proof of what you say. Forgive me, but I need a bit more than a game of golf and a lunch."

Kuznetzov laughs again. Other patrons of the dining room turn toward the sound. Some seem annoyed at the interruption. Others seem glad to see someone enjoying himself so much.

"I like you, Todd Standart – and you must call me *Gospoden*. It is my nickname. I like your caution and your courage. Here is how I will establish my bona fides."

"First, I will send you one very wealthy client per week for the next month. They will ensure you know it was I who referred them. Second, I will use my contacts in your state and federal government to speed your spa's application to be licensed for organ transplantation and removal. Third, I will have my people install a computer in your office from which you can access not only the OPTN database – penetrated by our hackers – but also similar databases throughout the world."

Application to be licensed? What application? Dr. Standart thinks before Kuznetzov continues.

"You will identify candidates for transplantation; my people will vet them. We will also refer candidates to you. The database will allow you to find recipients for the organs left after treating one of your clients. And, yes, despite the prohibition against selling organs, we will find buyers, even in the United States. Where we cannot find buyers, we will find legitimate recipients and provide the organs to them. We will not earn as much, but we will not lose money, either. Finally, I have taken over your main source of organs – the prison. A system has been put in place to increase the efficiency of the prison operation."

Before lunch is over, Dr. Standart and Kuznetzov have established if not a contract, at least an understanding.

The E'e'aahjigo Kiva

Before he invites Dr. Deschene to meet his kiva society, Spencer asks for a private meeting. "Dr. Deschene, I lied to you. Not by telling an untruth, but by not speaking the truth."

Spencer stands in front of Dr. Deschene's desk. His arms are at his side; his eyes, downcast.

"What do you mean, Spencer?"

"Do you remember the first day we met? I promised *on my honor* to be a worthy student. You promised *on your honor* to be my teacher. Those words are from the scout oath. I should have told you then I was disfellowshipped – kicked out of my scout troop. I lied by omission. Please, Dr. Deschene, do not — "

"Spencer, say nothing more," Dr. Deschene commands. "I knew you spoke from the scout oath, but I also know you spoke from your heart. I gather, since you told me this meeting is to discuss your kiva, you are not the only one?"

"No, sir. There are others." Spencer realizes this is a time for truth. "They are all disfellowshipped from the scouts and the church."

Dr. Deschene seems to shrink into himself before he responds. When he speaks, his voice fills the room. "Ke' is the word of relationships, the word of mentorship. To you, I am Ke'Deschene, a private name. You may share it with your kiva society, but with no others."

Spencer is relieved and amazed, but he realizes he will need time to understand.

≈≈≈≈≈

The E'e'aahjigo Kiva, Dr. Deschene, and Susan gather in the pathology lab. They do not tell Susan about the kiva society, only that the young men are Spencer's friends. When everyone sits at the small table or leans against a counter or an autopsy table, Dr. Deschene presents the formal and complete autopsy of Jessie Long Tree. "There's a lot of stuff here that may upset you—"

"Sir, we are warriors who will someday face death," Ata'halne' interrupts. "That may be in battle or in this laboratory. We are strong."

Dr. Deschene nods his understanding to the young man and reads from the document.

These are the partially skeletonized remains of a teen male. The remains are identified by a coroner's tag as "John Doe #2017-121.

"Sorry, sir, but does the date 2017 and the number 121 mean there have been 121 John Doe remains so far this year?" Niyol asks.

Deschene looks up and blinks. He seems startled. "Not 121 John Doe autopsies, but 121 autopsies in Rough Rock County."

"Rough Rock County is rural." Niyol looks up from his cell phone. "The largest town – the only town – is Jake's Lake, the county seat, with a population of three thousand."

"There's our first question," Ahiga says. "Why are the numbers so high and are they normal? I mean, historically, and compared to other counties with the same population."

Dr. Deschene nods, and reads. *The weight of the remains is 50 pounds. Hair is black. Eye color and skin color are undetermined. Hair on the head is long, black, and straight, consistent with Indian ancestry. There is no clothing on the body.*

"That's wrong," Chuchip says. "I mean, it may be right, but it's wrong. Jessie always wore trainers and shorts, even in the winter, and he always wore one of his Man United T-shirts. He sure wouldn't be wandering around naked."

84

"Second question," Ahiga says. "What happened to his clothes, especially his T-shirt?"

Dr. Deschene looks over his audience before reading. He nods his approval of their questions.

There is no evidence of medical intervention.

"Does that mean a surgeon didn't remove his organs?" Chuchip asks.

"Not necessarily," Dr. Deschene says. "It is difficult –often impossible – to prove a negative. What it means is, *we don't know*. It is too often the best answer."

Dr. Deschene continues reading the document each member of the E'e'aahjigo Kiva has in his hands.

No evidence was preserved following the autopsy.

"Isn't that unusual?" Ata'halne' interrupts. "Don't they submit samples for toxicology tests? And preserve the organs, or at least samples?"

"Yes," Susan answers. "And that's the next question. Were samples taken and where are they, or why were no samples preserved?"

Dr. Deschene continues. *Both eyes have been removed by animal activity.*

"Animal activity," Susan says. She snorts. "They got it in their heads as soon as they saw the body, and nothing will change their minds. The entire report is going to conclude that animals and not organ harvesters removed Jessie's heart, lungs, liver, and kidneys."

"Are we sure it's Jessie?" Hok'ee asks.

Dr. Deschene shakes his head. "The state wouldn't pay for DNA testing. If they didn't preserve samples, it would be too late to do that."

"And they were sure in a big hurry to cremate the remains," Spencer adds. "But there was the flash-drive bracelet Jessie always wore."

"We'll never be sure," Susan says. "Unless they saved something, and it sounds like they didn't save anything ... blood, flesh, skin, hair ... nothing that might match his family's DNA."

"Why not?" Niyol asks.

"Sloppy police work," Susan says. "As far as Arizona is concerned, Jessie is just another run-away Indian boy on his way to the flesh-pots of Los Angeles or San Diego to sell his body."

"Why do you say two California cities? Aren't Miami, Atlanta, Washington, and New York just as bad?"

"Only because the California cities are closer. Jessie didn't make it that far." Susan takes a deep breath. "I'm sorry for interrupting. Please, continue reading the report."

"There is nothing remarkable about the arms or legs, except the bracelet we already know about. I'll skip that and move to the examination of the skull. If you wish."

"Yes, please," Ahote says. "I know we've all read it, but we need to hear it again and again and again to find the flaws."

Dr. Deschene continues.

There is a fracture in the back of the skull with a dark stain on the interior at that point. Since the cadaver was found lying on its back on stony ground, it is presumed this occurred post-mortem when the body fell.

"Presumed my ... my butt," Spencer says. "Someone hit him hard enough to cause the hemorrhage. The coroner chose to believe he fell, and wasn't hit."

"Doesn't fit his world view," Susan grimaces. "It ignores reality for preconceptions. Go ahead, please."

Dr. Deschene reads.

All internal organs of the chest and abdomen are missing due to animal activity.

Spencer's snort and those of Susan and Niyol do not stop Dr. Deschene, although he does smile – for a grim instant.

86

"That explains why they didn't examine the stomach contents, though. There wasn't a stomach."

"And why the weight was so low," Dr. Deschene adds before he continues to read.

Because of the lack of blood and urine, only brain and tissue samples were sent for toxicology testing. While the screening test for opioids was positive, none were detected using mass spectrometry.

"The lab in Phoenix does toxicology," Spencer says. "Would they have kept any samples?"

"Good question, Spencer," Dr. Deschene says, and then finishes the report.

"How fast would the state lab have done those tests?" Niyol asks.

"Screening? A couple of weeks. Mass spectrometry? They would send it to Denver so … more than a month," Dr. Deschene says.

"Then how can the final autopsy report be dated only five days after Jessie was found?"

"Another good question."

Dr. Deschene concludes the report. *Cause of death: undetermined. Manner of death: undetermined.* "That, by itself, isn't a flag. Somewhere between two and five percent of all deaths are reported as undetermined. However, given all else we've seen, it does raise questions."

"Lot of holes," Spencer says. "Most obvious is the immediate assumption of animal activity."

"The initial report said there was no trauma noted; however, the autopsy found a broken skull and hemorrhaging of the brain, suggesting blunt force trauma."

"Why were other tests not made, especially when there was a conflict in the two tox tests?"

"The autopsy says there's no evidence of medical intervention and then lands solidly on animals. Doesn't anyone believe a bunch of animals could erase any sign of surgical cuts?"

"Jessie had a cell phone. What happened to it?"

The discussion continues. No one notices Spencer taking notes until the HDTV lights up. Spencer consolidates their questions on his laptop. The questions appear on the HDTV.

Autopsy Questions

- Was it Jessie?
- Who were the hikers in the desert? Do they know more than is in the autopsy report?
- What happened to Jessie's Manchester United T-shirt and the rest of his clothes?
- What happened to Jessie's cell phone? Who were the last people he called? Were they interviewed?
- Was the flash-drive in Jessie's bracelet tested by a computer expert who understands data recovery? What happened to the flash drive?
- Is the number of autopsies (Jessie's was Number 121) normal for Rough Rock County?
- Were any samples preserved at the state tox lab?
- How were the tox reports done so quickly?
- What points to collusion between the coroner and organ harvesters?

"The last question is not a good one, Spencer." Susan is frowning. "We've been accusing the coroner of seeing things to support his preconceptions. Your question might cause you to see things to justify your own preconceptions and ignore things that do not support them."

Spencer nods his understanding and deletes the question.

They break out the questions on Spencer's list and assign them to the boys of the kiva, Susan, and Dr. Deschene.

~~~~~

The next afternoon, Tommy Chee, Ata'halne to his kiva, leaves the school building. Other students stand in line for the long, yellow busses. Their heads still turn when Tommy's uncle's gold and white police car stops at the curb where Tommy stands, alone. When he first entered this school, Tommy took pride in the car that bears the shield of the Navajo Nation Police and the word, "Chief" in gold letters on the door. More recently, he wonders. *What does this mean? How do they understand it? Do they think I'm in juvie – Juvenile Hall – released only for school? Does my protector take me away from them? Will that make me more of a target?*

Uncle Joe. His public name is Joseph White Eagle. Joseph has been a name of The People since Chief Joseph of the Nez Perce. To Tommy, Joe is Shiehe'e, *maternal uncle*, or just *Uncle Joe.*

Uncle Joe does not look at the students gathered at the bus stops but at Tommy. "You didn't make many friends, today," he says. Unnecessarily, Tommy thinks. Tommy believes his uncle is prescient even though Uncle Joe says it's all about his experience as a detective and tries to get Tommy to read *Sherlock Holmes* stories.

"Wow, Uncle Joe! How did you suss that?" Tommy demands before folding his arms and retreating into himself, into his world of might-have-been.

Uncle Joe pauses for only an instant. "Could it be the bruise on your left cheek? It's going to be a real shiner."

Tommy doesn't need to bring the bruise to his uncle's attention. It happened when one of the tom-tom crowd, either more bold or more stupid than the rest, lashed out at him. Tommy tries to find a clever response to Uncle Joe, but misses the opportunity.

"You had a fight," Uncle Joe says. "Someone who doesn't like The People."

"More like someone who doesn't like anyone," Tommy equivocates. It's a way to lie without lying, although it's still a lie. Confusing, but useful. "Just a school bully. Nothing I can't handle."

Twenty minutes later, Uncle Joe stops a few meters from his hogan. Hogans are homes for some Navajo. Uncle Joe's is reserved for ceremonies – and a place to get away from the stress of work. It stands beside a modern home of stucco with a red-tiled roof. The house would fit in Phoenix or another Bilagáana city, but the hogan is traditional.

≈≈≈≈≈

"*Shizhé'é Yázhí?*" Tommy stands at the doorway to his uncle's den-office.

"Yes, Nephew?" Uncle Joe responds. He swivels his chair to face Tommy, and gestures for the boy to enter the room.

"I have something important to say. Something more important than a bruise from a school bully, more important than whether I am making friends at a Bilagáana school."

Uncle Joe is much more than Tommy's uncle. He is the man who rescued Tommy when the boy could no longer follow the beliefs of his parents – Joe's elder sister and her husband. Joe is the man who comforted a thirteen-year-old Tommy when he cried because his parents disfellowshipped him in front of the Bishop and the Stake President. He is the man who feeds and clothes Tommy, and who insists he continue to attend the Bilagáana school.

Joe tells Tommy to sit and asks what the boy needs to say.

When Tommy asks, Joe agrees to keep what Tommy says secret, "… unless it conflicts with my oath as a policeman or my oath to my kiva."

Tommy understands what he means. The older oaths must take precedence. "Yes, Uncle."

Tommy tells Joe what he knows about the autopsies, Hok'ee's uncle, and Spencer's suspicions. He tells Joe about his kiva and their desire to solve the mystery – and their need for help.

Uncle Joe ponders what he has heard for several minutes. Tommy has learned he often does that when trying to unravel a knot of thought.

At last, Uncle Joe speaks. "Spencer should not have told you about the autopsy in which he took part. However, I do not believe Dr. Deschene had yet explained confidentiality. I was present at that autopsy. It disturbed me.

"The autopsy of Jessie Long Tree is on the internet. That does not mean it has been officially released.

"I was not aware of the circumstances of Hok'ee's uncle's death. I will help your kiva society although I see something in your eyes telling me you have more to say."

Tommy nods and then explains the nature of the kiva.

When Tommy finishes, Uncle Joe laughs. It is a happy laugh, not a mocking laugh. "A kiva of young men of spirit and wisdom. A kiva of both Navajo and Hopi – and a Bilagáana. Our elders despair that our traditions will be lost. Perhaps the synergy you create will serve better to preserve our traditions than their attempts to teach language and chants in the schools.

"I will keep your secret and offer what help I can."

≈≈≈≈≈

Dr. Deschene hangs up the phone whens Spencer enters the office. "Good news, Spencer. At least, I hope you will see it that way. I may have overstepped our relationship."

"I don't think you could do that, sir."

"I hope you are right. Here is what I have done. I spoke to Dr. Franklin, the provost at the community college. We are old friends. He agrees you're getting all the lab work you need, right here, and that you may do your winter quarter's courses on-line. I will proctor tests. You will still submit papers to your professors. The hospital will continue to employ you, but you will work twice as many hours, and more than twice as hard since you are responsible for both the extra work here, and your schoolwork."

Dr. Deschene chuckles. "Doing double duty will be good training for when you intern at a teaching hospital. You won't get more than a couple of hours of sleep at a time for at least six months.

"Is this satisfactory?"

Spencer takes no time before he answers. "Yes, sir. I know how important the coursework is, but what I'm learning from you is twice as real, and twice as valuable."

≈≈≈≈≈

Joseph White Eagle is puzzled by his nephew's call. Tommy asks his uncle to meet with his kiva at the diner in Tuba City. "And please don't drive your police car."

Joe's H1A-Hummer, with the new high-powered engine and a roof full of antennas is hardly less noticeable than the Crown Vic with integrated light bar he usually drives, but it is unmarked and the grill conceals the red and blue lights. Tommy is waiting outside when Joe arrives. It is just after dark when Tommy escorts Joe to

92

the back room. Plaques and banners of civic groups – Rotary, Lions, Civitan, and others – decorate the walls.

A handful of young men stands when Joe enters. He recognizes three as Tommy's acquaintances. Others are strangers. All are Athabasca – Navajo or Hopi – other than Spencer, who is a tall Bilagáana with white-blond hair and blue eyes. Before Tommy can introduce the others, a waitress wheels in a cart filled with plates of Navajo tacos, iced tea, and water. The boys help her spread the plates and glasses on the table. Joe watches the orchestrated cooperation among the young men. *There is more to them than I see*, he reasons.

When the waitress leaves and everyone stands behind a place at the table, Tommy introduces his friends. He does so using their Kiva names. Joe understands they have honored him by doing this. When Tommy introduces him as "Chief Joseph White Eagle," Joe says, "When we meet in private, I am Shiehe'e, Uncle. It has been my honor to be uncle-father to Ata'halne'. You are his brothers; therefore, I am your uncle. What can your uncle do for you?"

Cha'tima speaks for the E'e'aahjigo Kiva. "You honor us, Shiehe'e. While we eat, we will tell you our story." That is the signal for everyone to sit and begin their supper.

Cha'tima and Niyol take turns telling of being disfellowshipped, and of the creation of the E'e'aahjigo Kiva. Spencer tells of his invitation to join the Kiva and then of the autopsy report of Jessie Long Tree.

"We intend to find out who murdered Jessie, and maybe others," Tommy says. "We ask you here to find out if you can – will – help us."

They devour the Navajo tacos – puffy fry bread topped with beans and ground mutton, shredded cheese, chopped lettuce, tomatoes, and sour cream, then seasoned to each person's taste with red or green sauce. When Atsa completes his story, Joe pushes aside his plate.

"I have a duty as Chief of the Navajo Nation Police. I have a duty to my nephew and to his friends. I do not see a conflict between those duties. However, duty demands I consider the dangers you may face.

"You are warriors who have already faced challenges. You will face more, and you must prepare yourselves. Part of your preparation is to understand what I can and cannot do.

"The Bilagáana FBI, the Drug Enforcement Agency, Homeland Security, and Immigrations and Customs Enforcement have concurrent jurisdiction over many crimes that take place in Navajo and Hopi territory. The State Police of Arizona, New Mexico, Utah, and Colorado have jurisdiction on federal and state roads running through our nations. I know about the discovery of the body of Jessie Long Tree. He was found in the State of Arizona, completely outside my jurisdiction."

He holds up his hand to forestall the complaints he feels are coming. "I will help you." He chuckles. "I have had nearly twenty years to find ways around the tangle of agreements and treaties that created this – this mess. Not only how to work around them but also how to use them to our advantage."

"First, how many of you are at least eighteen years old?"

Seven of the young men, including Spencer, raise their hands.

"How many of those do not have jobs?"

All the hands go down except Ahote's and Niyol's. Joe scans his memory for their names. "Ahote and Niyol, if you agree, I will offer you a place as auxiliary police officers. This will give you official access to information not available to civilians. You will undergo a six-week training course at the Arizona police academy. The Nation will pay for your training and first uniforms. I will assign you a patrol car that has passed its scheduled life."

He chuckles. "That means no high-speed pursuit. In fact, the lights and siren have been removed.

"You will not be armed, and you will not be paid by the Nation but by people who need your services."

He chuckles again. "Most of these are the mega-churches who want you to stop traffic after their Sabbath services so their parishioners can get ahead in line at restaurants and grocery stores. Their preaching of 'keep the Sabbath day holy' does not apply to those who must work on the Sabbath to serve them."

His smile disappears. "During your training, you will be among the Bilagáana. You must be strong. Can you do that?"

The two young men nod although they are not quite sure of what is being asked of them.

"Now," Joe says, "here are things you do not yet know. You follow the old ways. You understand better – despite your young age – concepts of honor and trust than many of the those of your age. I see that tonight. I have seen it in my first nephew, Ata'halne' – who is so aptly named." Tommy blushes. "The public does not know this and it must not be known I have told you."

Joe tells of three young men missing from near Teec Nos Pos. "They were part of a wanna-be gang of four boys whose exploits were limited to harassing younger boys and crashing the soup kitchen of the local Catholic Church. Suddenly, there were no more complaints from the church. At the same time, three of the boys were reported missing. We investigated, and interviewed the fourth boy, Gahtsoh—"

"Rabbit," Ata'halne' interrupts.

"Yes, Ata'halne," Joe says, emphasizing his name. Tommy blushes.

"Gahtsoh did not know what happened to his friends, but he was present when they were taken."

"Taken?" This time, it is Chuchip who interrupts.

"Taken," Joe says. "Gahtsoh suffered from polio because his parents didn't believe in vaccines. He wears braces on both legs. His friends all appear healthy. Gahtsoh reports a group of men wearing ski masks attacked them outside a convenience store and took his three friends. I believe Gahtsoh was not taken because they believed him to be – flawed, an undesirable."

"OMG – Oh My Gerbils," Ahote says. "They took the healthy ones and left the cripple? Organ harvesters."

Joe furrows his brow, but continues his narrative. "Your friend, Jessie, is not the only person reported missing. He is the first one, the only one so far, whose body has been found. We've never found any trace of Gahtsoh's friends."

"They – whoever they are – are finding some way to dispose of the bodies," Ahote says.

"Likely," Joe says. "And that creates another thread to be investigated."

After the meeting, Joe calls Ahote and Niyol to him to plan their swearing in and training. When they have concluded their discussion, Joe asks Ahote, "Why did you say, *Oh my Gerbils?*"

"If I said *Oh my god* I would have to believe in him and I don't, at least not the god of the church that was forced on me by my parents. Neither Yadilyil nor Naestan, none of the Diné gods and goddesses pretends to be both omniscient and omnipotent. I do not want to defame any of the figures immortalized by my ancestors by swearing by their name."

"*Swear not by your George, your garter, nor your crown, for all are profaned, dishonored, or usurped.*" Niyol paraphrases a line from Shakespeare's *King Richard III*. Joe understands, and is pleasantly surprised not only by Niyol, but also Ahote's recognizing the quotation.

96

Spencer Hansen

The average low temperature in Folio in February is 31 degrees. That does not include the wind chill – what the Diné call the *breath of the mountain.* Spencer peddles against the wind to reach the coffee shop. On this early Sunday morning, he is one of few customers. Tomorrow, he will begin the Spring Quarter at the community college. He will take courses on-line, supervised and proctored by Dr. Deschene. He is on his third green-tea slushie when his phone rings. *Dr. Deschene, why would he call?* "Yes, sir. This is Spencer."

"You have boots? Long-johns? Blue jeans without holes in the knees? Winter coat? Hat? Sunglasses? Work gloves? Wear them, tomorrow. We leave from the loading dock at 7:00 AM. Got it?"

"Got it, sir. What's up?"

"You'll learn, tomorrow. I have more calls to make." The phone beeps. Dr. Deschene has ended the call.

That night, Spencer has trouble sleeping. It could have been the caffeine in the green-tea slushies or the questions that tumble in his mind. *Leaving ... for where? From the loading dock ... where will we go? Heavy clothes ... not going to a coffee shop. Somewhere in the desert.* He lies quietly in his bed, trying to think of nothingness. It doesn't work.

At 4:00 AM, Spencer throws off the covers and stands beside his bed. *Enough of not sleeping!* He dresses and then pats the pockets of the shooting vest he wears over his parka. One pocket holds his cell phone; one, a compass and a geological survey quad map; another, a folding knife and what he calls his survival kit – water purification tablets, a space blanket, energy bars, a signal mirror, and fishing line – not for fishing, but for making snares. A web belt holds two canteens and completes the outfit. He reaches the loading dock at 6:15. He is alone.

At 6:45 a man he recognizes as one of Dr. Deschene's techs arrives. The man yawns, and sips from a go-cup of coffee with the logo of one of the drive-throughs. He sees what Spencer is wearing. "Jumpin' jiminy," he says. "Are you going to war or something?"

"*Semper paratus*," Spencer says. "Always prepared."

"That's the frickin' Coast Guard," the guy says. "What are you, a Boy Scout?"

An H1A Hummer drives into the dock and spares Spencer the need and embarrassment of explaining why he is no longer a scout. Spencer sees the forest of antennas on the roof and recognizes Chief Joe's unmarked vehicle. Joe gets out from the left side followed by Dr. Deschene from the right. Dr. Deschene looks around. "You're the only ones here? There should be three others."

Just then, the door of the loading dock opens and three people in jeans, hooded parkas and boots step out. "We're here, doctor. Whoa! Spencer, you look like you're going on safari."

"The rest of you will, too, when we get there. Or, when we get as far as the Hummer can take us – and that's quite a way. After that, we have a four-mile hike," Chief Joe says. "I have canteens and packs with energy bars for you."

Chief Joe drives about fifteen miles south on Coppermine Road before turning east on a dirt track. "Where does this go?" Dr. Deschene calls over the noise of the engine and of the wheels rumbling on washboard dirt and gravel.

"Nowhere," Chief Joe replies. "Loops back to the highway."

After a few more minutes, the chief pulls to the side of the track. "We're on foot, from here. You found your canteens and packs?"

"Are we really stopped?" a tech asks. "I thought my teeth were going to vibrate out."

"Whine, whine, grumble, grumble," another tech says. It's not clear whether he is complaining or teasing his colleague.

"It's the fresh air. Without formaldehyde his entire system has shut down," the third tech says.

Chief Joe and Dr. Deschene pay no attention to the banter. It is good-natured and doesn't stop Spencer and the techs from preparing to walk over the desert varnish that paves this part of the Navajo nation.

Chief Joe holds a Global Positioning System unit. He sights over the top and takes a bearing on a peak to the northeast. He steps off toward the peak, but says nothing. The others shrug their shoulders and follow.

After two hours, the chief puts away the GPS. "Okay, spread out. We're within fifty feet of the reported location. Treat it as a crime scene and follow protocol.

"Spencer, have you ever done a crime scene?" Joe asks.

"No, sir."

"Then stick with me. The trick is to not mess up any evidence even though I don't expect there will be much. *Protocol* means a lot more, having to do with evidence collecting and chain-of-custody. You'll learn it if you're around Dr. Deschene for long."

"It's here!" A tech calls from ten yards to their left. She points to a clump of sagebrush.

The group gathers around a body. At least, around what remains of a body. "What can you tell me about it, Spencer?" Dr. Deschene asks.

"Female, from the hips, although the mammaries and external sex organs are missing. Tattered clothing, perhaps shorts and a blouse. Barefoot. Thoracic and abdominal organs – heart, lungs, spleen, liver, stomach, intestines, gall bladder, pancreas, kidneys missing. Oh, fu— fudge. She was pregnant. It's a baby's skull."

Spencer turns and runs a few yards before throwing up. He is relieved when a tech follows him on the same errand. Spencer is glad for his second canteen when he rinses out his mouth. It takes several minutes before he can continue.

"Chief? Over here. Scat."

"Any idea what animal left it?"

"Feral dog, coyote, maybe. Too big to be a fox."

"What good is that?" a tech asks.

"It may contain human DNA. Maybe we could get a match with the body."

"No way the state lab would do that for free."

Dr. Deschene is listening, and taking mental notes about Spencer, who found the scat and then proposed the analysis. "I have a discretionary budget. I will send samples to a lab if Chief Joe agrees."

The chief agrees and shows Spencer how to collect and log the scat as evidence. "It might surprise you," the chief says, "how much scat ends up in the court room."

Did he make a joke? Spencer wonders.

The rocky ground is way too hard for footprints and a careful sweep of the area reveals no cigarette butts or signed confessions. Chief Joe unrolls a body bag. The techs place the remains in the bag. Spencer, Chief Joe, and two of the techs take the corners of the bag for the walk back to the Hummer.

On Tuesday night, with Dr. Deschene's approval, Spencer invites the E'e'aahjigo Kiva to assemble at the hospital. Chief Joe stands in the back of the room, arms folded. Dr. Deschene speaks with detachment, although Spencer feels his mentor is not as dispassionate as usual.

"This is preliminary. I did only a cursory examination, not a forensic autopsy. That will come later.

"The body of a female, likely exposed to the elements and animal and insect activity for some time, presents as partly mummified. Her thoracic and abdominal organs are not in evidence and there are remains of a fetus.

"Spencer, do you have a reference number?"

"Yes sir. Number 606 since the hospital was established over twenty years ago." Everyone knows Spencer is pointing out the huge discrepancy between the autopsies conducted at the hospital, and the more than 200 conducted by the Rough Rock County Coroner during 2017, alone.

Dr. Deschene continues his summary. "Based on the development of the *pubic symphysis* and the state of the wisdom teeth, she is approximately eighteen years old."

"Although the victim lacks thoracic and abdominal organs, there is not enough evidence to confirm either organ harvesting or animal activity. The remains of clothing argue against organ harvesting. For the record, and pending the results of toxicology, the individual appears to have been in good health and thus a good candidate for organ harvesting."

"Hoppin' Higgs, Dr. D. You didn't say one way or the other on organ harvesting. Why not?" Niyol asks.

"Because ..." Dr. Deschene pauses. "I must be impartial. So must you. Do you understand?"

The members of the Kiva confirm their understanding. No matter how much the evidence impacts them, they must be disinterested.

"There is a difference between *uninterested* and *disinterested*, between *unimpassioned* and *dispassionate*," Dr. Deschene says. "We must be disinterested and dispassionate, ruled by logic and not emotions. We may, and should, have emotions and we should not suppress them."

Dr. Deschene addresses Chief Joe for the first time. "Joe, before the forensic autopsy, I want to do more research. As mummified as she is, there's little danger of further decomposition. I have put her in a drawer."

Chief Joe agrees and asks to be notified of the autopsy results. "You are using a freezer drawer, right? I will work through missing persons reports, but I would have heard something by now, and would have remembered her."

≈≈≈≈≈

"Sir, Chief Joe said *freezer drawer.* I've never thought about the drawers in the morgue. What does that mean?" Spencer asks.

Dr. Deschene's voice becomes what Spencer has learned is his *teaching mode*. "Six drawers in the morgue are ten degrees Centigrade below freezing to prevent further decomposition. In a mortuary, bodies waiting embalming or cremation are at a few degrees above freezing. The drawers in a mortuary only slow decomposition. Four of our drawers are at three degrees above freezing. I use them for someone who will be autopsied within a day or so or to store someone overnight if the autopsy is interrupted.

"Given the condition of this body, the chief is being very cautious by asking her to be frozen. On the other hand, when it comes to preserving evidence, I've learned never to question him."

≈≈≈≈≈

"Taphonomy. The original meaning is the process of fossilization, creating imprints of organisms over millions of years. Now, it also means the process of decay, the study of what happens to human remains exposed to the elements after death." Dr. Deschene is talking as much to himself as to Spencer. He looks up. "Wear nice but sturdy clothes and boots, tomorrow. You'll need a heavy jacket, gloves, hat, plus clothes and things for an overnight stay. Can you get to the airport by 7:00 AM?"

"Yes, sir. Where?" Spencer asks.

"Glen Canyon Charters."

"I mean, where are we going?"

"Surprise."

Spencer has learned not to question Dr. Deschene when he promises a surprise.

The sun is breaking the horizon when Dr. Deschene meets Spencer at the airport with two go-cups of coffee and a bag of donuts. "No in-flight breakfast," he says. "No in-flight restroom, either. But the trip will only be about an hour and a half. We're headed for Grand Junction. Not the main airport, but a private strip."

The plane is a twin-engine, piston-driven, low-wing model. The pilot greets them, makes sure they are buckled in, and takes his seat. Spencer listens to the pilot's conversation with the flight service station and the tower. Most of it makes no sense, but he's happy to learn the weather will be good, and the flight won't be too bumpy. He mentions this to Dr. Deschene, who tells him, "That's the reason I asked for an early morning flight. Before the sun heats the rocks and creates thermals and causes unpredictable turbulence."

They land at an airport – not much more than a runway, two hangers, and a fuel pump – where a car is waiting for them. The driver is a young woman a few years older than Spencer, a former intern of Dr. Deschene, who greets him as if he were an old friend and drives them to what she calls "the body farm."

Body farm, Spencer thinks. *I've read about them. Places where real bodies are dumped and then watched to see how they decay. The things animals and insects do to them. What happens over days, weeks, months – even years. First one was in Tennessee.*

Now, there is a bunch of them, including one in Australia. I didn't know there was one in Colorado.

Dr. Deschene and the woman, Roseanne Bass, explain to Spencer what he will see. "The first body farm was created in Tennessee in 1981 by a forensic anthropologist. There are now five others, including ours.

"The press and Patricia Cornwell who wrote about one, call them body farms. We prefer to call them *outdoor forensic anthropological research centers*. Not much difference, but it sounds better. The purpose is to study decomposition over an extended period, whether outdoors and exposed to the elements, in a shallow grave such as we find all over the Middle East and Mexico, in a fire, or in other circumstances. This one is part of the state university system and we train future forensic anthropologists and cadaver dogs."

"Where do you get the bodies?" Spencer asks.

"Donations. People whose bodies are not suitable for organ donation because of age or disease, but who want to be part of important research," Roseanne says. "Like everyone else, we use drones to photograph the grounds. They make it a little easier. But we still have to get close. The farms have been responsible for a couple of new sciences, including forensic entomology – studies of how insects affect a body left exposed after death.

"Here, in Colorado, we focus on how altitude and microclimates effect bodies. We're the highest and driest of the farms. Research centers, I mean."

Roseanne drives them to the center. She unlocks a gate and locks it behind them. "The location of the center is a closely held secret. Those," she points to poles scattered over the landscape, "hold high-def security cameras that report to the university over a microwave network and fiber optic lines. One center used the

104

internet to carry their signals until they got hacked. Caused quite a stir. Now, we use private links."

"Are you looking for anything specific?" Roseanne asks.

"Two bodies were found in the desert. Eviscerated and desiccated. Mummified."

"Animal activity?"

"That is a large part of the question," Dr. Deschene says.

The talk turns technical. Spencer takes mental notes as he follows Dr. Deschene and his former student through the center. Roseanne points to several specimens. Wire-grid cages cover many of the bodies. "To keep out the animals," Roseanne says. "The ones with window-screen wire? We try to keep insects away from them." She consults a tablet computer with a bar-code scanner, which she uses to identify the remains.

"Here," Dr. Deschene says, "this one looks close."

"What's your elevation and average rainfall?" Roseanne asks. The talk becomes technical, again. Dr. Deschene shows Roseanne photos of the young woman.

"What do you think, Spencer? Based on what you've seen," Dr. Deschene asks.

"About four months exposed," Spencer says. He sounds confident, but inwardly he is quivering with nervousness.

"Based on your photographs, I agree," Roseanne says.

Dr. Deschene puts his imprimatur on their estimates. "I think you are both right." Spencer's tummy stops quivering.

By now, it is nearly dusk. Roseanne takes them to the campus, to guest quarters and, after showers, to supper.

"I can't violate a confidence," she says over their supper of barbecue and beans. "But I got a call from a sheriff who is investigating three bodies similar to yours. May I give him your name and number? It will be up to him to open contact."

Dr. Deschene agrees. "Please tell him I am most anxious to talk."

The next morning, before dawn, Roseanne returns to take them to the airport where their pilot is waiting.

≈≈≈≈≈

Dr. Deschene has been back from Grand Junction only two days when he finds a note on his desk. The sheriff from a town near the Mescalero Apache Reservation has called. The sheriff is happy to get Dr. Deschene's call. "Dr. Bass was all over your reputation, praising you for your work. I've got three mysteries I cannot solve. Young Apache, two male, one female. All apparently healthy and all eviscerated. One is still unidentified and in a freezer in the morgue. Can you visit?"

"Of course. May I bring my protégé? He is both intelligent and trustworthy."

Dr. Deschene and the sheriff reach agreement. Dr. Deschene hangs up the desk phone and picks up his cell phone to call Spencer.

≈≈≈≈≈

It is dark and windy when Spencer arrives at the Folio Municipal Airport. There isn't much going on, and it's easy for him to find their pilot in the ready room. "Dr. Deschene will be here soon. The Tularosa sheriff got us permission to use the private airport at Boles Farm, just south of Tularosa, and will meet us there. Dr. D thinks we'll need about six hours on the ground." Spencer hefts a small duffle bag. "He said to be prepared for an overnight, though."

The pilot puts a transparent ruler on his sectional chart. "It's 400 miles as the crow flies, but we'll have to swing around the White Sands Missile Range. Call it 435 miles. That's two-and-a-half hours flight time not accounting for winds. Adding six hours on the ground will mean an overnight, or a night flight, or I come back and pick you up, tomorrow. Trust me, it's cheaper to pay my supper, breakfast, and motel room than for me to deadhead two trips."

"Deadhead?"

"Fly back here, empty so I can sleep in my own bed, then fly to Boles Farm, tomorrow, empty, to pick you up. As long as I can get a nap, and the weather holds, I can bring us back on a night flight, tonight."

"Way cool!" Spencer says. He has seldom flown, and never at night.

"Not much to see. Not a lot of people on the Res have yard lights, but I can swing over Gallup so you can see what a city looks like at night."

Dr. Deschene arrives on schedule and Spencer briefs him on the options the pilot presented.

"Let's plan on returning, tonight," Dr. Deschene says. "If we spend more time on the ground than expected, or if the weather turns, we'll deal with it when it happens."

He asks the pilot if he needs to pack a bag in case of an overnight stay. "No, Doctor. I keep BOB on the plane."

"Bob?" Spencer's confusion is obvious in his furrowed eyebrows.

"Bug-Out Bag," the pilot says. "Everything I need for an overnight stay or what I might need in case of a forced landing somewhere in the desert – including a couple of mini-bottles of Scotch."

The flight to Tularosa is uneventful except for a little turbulence. Spencer is in the copilot's seat. The pilot shows him how to send their estimated arrival time to the sheriff through an aeronautical radio service.

"You have a lot of radios," Spencer says. "I counted seven antennas."

"Yep, used to fly with nothing but a whiskey compass."

"Huh?"

"The thing on top of the instrument panel. The compass part is in alcohol to damp its movements, so we call it a whiskey compass. Then we went to DF. That's direction finding radio, and then VOR – Very High Frequency Omni Range – and DME – Distance Measuring Equipment – for navigation. I still have them all. Nowadays, it's mostly GPS. I hang on to the DF 'cause it let's me listen to music."

With that, the pilot tunes to an AM radio station in Gallup playing jazz.

The sheriff and a woman in a long skirt and sunbonnet are waiting when the plane lands. The sheriff introduces the woman. "This is Missus Boles. She's invited your pilot to lunch and a nap in her home. You'll have to ride there in a wagon."

Behind the sheriff's white and blue patrol car is a buckboard wagon with two horses standing patiently, perhaps because of the feedbags hooked to their faces.

"Mrs. Boles, thank you, and I accept your kind invitation," the pilot says.

"Dr. Deschene, Mr. Hansen, I'll take you to my office, if you please."

When they reach the sheriff's office, he takes them into a small conference room where a woman is waiting. Her Air Force uniform surprises Dr. Deschene and Spencer.

"This is Dr. Semi," the sheriff says. "Major Semi is a surgeon, and I trust her more than anyone else at the Luke Hospital."

"Gentlemen, my uniform does not mean either the Air Force endorses my opinions or I have permission from my superiors to be here. However, I have learned in matters of great importance, it is often easier to get forgiveness than to get permission."

She smiles. "Dr. Deschene, I have read every journal article you published. I was disappointed to learn you left Johns Hopkins and took a post as a pathologist in a small town in Arizona, but was happy to see you continued to publish."

"Luke Hospital," Spencer says. "As in Luke Air Force Base." He had studied the pilot's charts.

"Yes, Mr. Hansen—"

"Please call me Spencer." *Not used to being in such high company.*

"Spencer. If you are traveling with Dr. Deschene, you are much more than *Spencer*. But I will agree with your wishes."

The sheriff has become antsy with the back-and-forth among his visitors and interrupts the introductions. "Dr. Semi, please tell them what's going on."

Dr. Semi's briefing, complete with visuals projected on the HDTV in the sheriff's conference room, describes bodies similar to what Dr. Deschene and Spencer have seen.

"I understand you contacted Ms. Bass at the Grand Junction body farm?" Dr. Deschene says.

The sheriff takes that question. "Yes, and she flew down and examined two of the victims before they were cremated or buried."

"Why the difference?" Dr. Deschene pounces.

"We identified one from her clothing and the missing person report. DNA analysis confirmed her identity, and her family claimed her body for burial. The other had no identification and did not match any missing person report. The county cremated him."

"The third one?" Dr. Deschene prompts.

"I keep hoping we can identify him," the sheriff says. "Dr. Semi says he's only fifteen years old. Still no ID and he doesn't match any missing person report."

"Do you agree animal and insect activity caused the evisceration?" Dr. Deschene asks.

"If you thought so, you would not be here," Dr. Semi says. "But I understand your question.

"Predation caused some damage, but not all. The young woman was clothed. The clothing that covered her torso was shredded, but was intact on her back. No organ harvester would leave a victim's clothing, not even socks and shoes. The young man is naked. His body was discovered before extensive animal activity occurred. I am certain the evisceration involved significant surgical intervention."

The sheriff escorts the party to the morgue. An attendant rolls out the body of the fifteen-year-old. "Here and here," Dr. Semi says. "Bones cut too cleanly to be an animal." She points to other, less obvious markers before everyone returns to the conference room. "Here are my notes and those of Ms. Bass. I've redacted the names. Use them as you will – and please keep in touch."

~~~~~

Dr. Deschene's estimate of six hours on the ground is spot on. He and Spencer arrive at the private airstrip just as the pilot completes his pre-flight inspection. "Glad they have avgas," he says. "We could make it back to Folio on what was in the tanks, but it's nice to have a reserve. It won't appear on your bill, doctor."

The night flight enraptures Spencer, especially when the pilot turns off the instrument panel lights except for a single red light illuminating the whiskey compass. In just a few minutes, Spencer's eyes adapt to the darkness, and he sees the stars. Living in the high desert, Spencer has seen more stars, including the Milky Way, than people living in cities and towns. Still, seeing them from eight thousand five hundred feet above sea level on a cloudless night is awesome.

When they reach the general aviation terminal at Folio, both Dr. Deschene and Spencer thank the pilot. Dr. Deschene issues orders to Spencer. "Sleep in, tomorrow. Then, go to the coffee shop you like so much, and write a paper about what we learned. You may refer to the body farm – by its proper name – but keep other locations secret. I will explain this in my note to your professor."

In response to Spencer's frown and furrowed brow, Dr. Deschene continues. "Even though you are completing coursework on the internet, you owe papers to your professors. I will expect you in my office tomorrow afternoon. Say, 4:00 PM?"

"I think I can wake up by then," Spencer says.

Spencer cannot sleep in as Dr. Deschene ordered. He is too excited. By 9:00 AM, he is in the coffee shop with his laptop computer. By 2:00 PM he has completed a paper describing the bodies found on the Navajo territory, those found by the Tularosa sheriff on and near the Mescalero Apache reservation, and two at the body farm. He debates including photographs. *I'll have to get Dr. D's permission.* He does not draw conclusions in the paper, although he is convinced there is a link, somewhere, between them. There is not enough evidence to prove a link, but Spencer is sure.

Carlotta Krafft

The NSA analyst listens closely to the next intercept. She reports to her supervisor who leads her to the office of the Director of Domestic Operations.

"Carlotta Krafft is traveling in the United States on a Romanian passport and a tourist visa. Today, she reserved a G6 to fly six people from Folio, Arizona to Luke Air Force Base on Friday. She asked if the charter company could get a PPR number. That's 'prior permission required,' to land at a military installation, for Mr. Kuznetzov, who has an appointment with Colonel North."

The analyst takes a deep breath before continuing. "I reached out to our people at Luke and learned there is no Colonel North. That is a code word for a CIA operation located there. The Luke command post confirms they issued the PPR number.

"Mr. Kuznetzov is traveling on an Estonian passport. His H-1B visa was issued on orders from the State Department. He is not known to be working in the US. He is an employee of an Estonian company that makes systems for both electronic intelligence and jamming. We have no record of him except his entry into this country at New York.

"We see money transferred from accounts in Malta to Kraft's accounts in Bermuda. The Malta accounts belong to Kuznetzov."

~~~~~

There are two classes of prisoners in U.P.S. #9. Cell Block 11 holds men in solitary confinement. Three other wings hold men in two- and four-person cells. The latter cells surround a common area in which the men congregate, watch television, and exercise using free weights. The prison yard is open to these men for several hours each day.

Some things are common among the prisoners. They all wear indestructible plastic anklets, which hold an RFID chip. Scanners at cell doors, in the dining hall, common areas, and mob showers at the end of each wing read the chips. Guards have scanners on their belts. The RFID chips need no power; their power comes from the ubiquitous scanners. The scanners report over a WiFi network to a central computer, which monitors and records every movement of every prisoner.

Only a few employees know the truth about the two hundred special prisoners in Cell Block 11 of Unified Prison System #9. Some of these prisoners are convicts, placed by the courts. A few are waiting for an arraignment that will never happen. Some are transferred from other prisons in the state prison system. Pony Boy and his Reapers bring others. Their DNA has been sequenced. They have been screened for drugs and diseases including HIV and the Hanta, Ebola, and Zika viruses. The lesson that Ebola can live for months, hidden in a victim's body, has not been lost. These prisoners are isolated to make sure they don't become infected.

Since his partnership with Gospoden Kuznetzov, Warden Sam Red Horse receives encrypted email through a private system on the dark net. Numbers represent genetic markers that show the degree of potential transplant rejection. Sam doesn't understand the email technology, and does not understand what "11001001" means, even when it decodes to PI3Kγ. All he knows is how to decrypt the message and make his computer compare the results with inmates' medical files, which, like the software, hide somewhere on the dark net.

An early morning message decrypts to a request for one kidney from someone with AB-positive blood and certain histo-blood group antigen markers. The offered price is $200,000 with a bonus for speed.

The computer takes only seconds to search the inmate medical files before finding a candidate. He's a good one, well worth the fee promised by Sam's mysterious comrades. The donor is a twenty-year-old Caucasian, rare in the prison but perfect for this transplant. The warden tells the software to search for customers for the candidate's other organs, something he could not have done before his alliance with Kuznetzov.

Sam knows Kuznetzov represents the Russian Mafia but the money outweighs any qualms he might have. Sam picks up the phone, calls the special wing, and orders the prisoner from Cell Block 11 to his office.

"You may remember when you came here we did extensive medical testing, including DNA analysis. We did that so we can identify you easier if you commit another crime. Other tests let us know if you would be eligible for medical research. You have not been part of the research, so you weren't told any more. Today, you can participate in a research project. If you agree, you will receive an injection of a drug being tested by the Food and Drug Administration. It is completely safe, but the FDA wants more tests to determine its effectiveness.

"If you agree to participate, your sentence will be commuted to *time served.* Cooperation will make you free. Please sign the release form on the clipboard."

The clipboard holds a stack of at least twenty pages, all in small print. The inmate glances at the papers, sees the warden's impatience, and signs.

Days later, the inmate wakes in a bed in a hospital room. He is weak. An intravenous catheter connect to a bottle that drips something into his arms. "What...?"

Nurse Grassier, seeing the inmate is awake, approaches. "You are awake. I'm surprised."

"What happened?" the inmate asks.

Grassier looks around the room. "I'm not really the one to tell you this, but you had a bad reaction to the test drugs. Did terrible damage to your kidneys. We had to remove one, but don't worry, the other is working just fine, now." He injects something into a port on the intravenous line, and the inmate sinks into darkness. Two hours later, an anesthesia nurse comes in and injects a different drug. The inmate from Cell Block 11 is returned to the operating room where the darkness becomes permanent. After a week in a coma, the inmate is declared brain dead and the rest of his organs are harvested.

The kidney is suitable, and the computer finds buyers for the second kidney, the liver, and the heart. Sam Red Horse's pay envelope and those of two guards and a surgical team at the Glen Canyon Medical Spa are filled with cash. Six weeks later, a younger son of a Russian oligarch returns home knowing he will not die, at least not as soon as he thought.

≈≈≈≈≈

The NSA analyst, her immediate supervisor, and the Director of Domestic Operations meet in a shielded room, safe from being overheard.

The analyst provides a summary. "My contact at Luke reports the G6 landed, and a motorcade took the passengers to the CIA building. The passengers were five men and one woman. Four of the men appeared to be bodyguards. The fifth man appeared to be the principal.

"The principal is Ivan Kuznetzov who entered the US with an Estonian passport. He represents an Estonian electronics firm. The meeting with the CIA may be associated with that business.

"The woman is Carlotta Krafft. Intercepts of her cell phone began this investigation. We have seen Kuznetzov transfer money to her accounts. We conclude she is his mistress. My counterpart at Luke described her as 'quite a looker.'"

The analyst sees the DDO frown. "His report includes a photograph taken with a telephoto lens.

"There was no special operational security associated with the visit. The motorcade cars were driven by un-cleared airmen assigned to the base motor pool. The CIA hosted a lunch at the officers' club. It was held in a private room, but that was likely due to the size of the party. The room was not swept before the meeting."

The DDO sits for a moment before she speaks. "Good work; thank you. Continue monitoring and report any new information."

After the analyst and her supervisor leave, the DDO reaches out to one of her people in the FBI. *Perhaps he can find out if the FBI has an open investigation.* She picks up a secure phone and punches six buttons.

~~~~~

Friday is payday throughout the Unified Prison System. The prison company doesn't believe in direct deposit. On payday, every employee – warden, clerks, guards, medics, cooks and bottle-washers – receives an envelope with a check. Some envelopes are fatter than others, stuffed with cash. Everyone knows about this; only the select know why. Some of the cash comes from a thriving business delivering drugs and cell phones to inmates. The rest of the cash comes from a more secret and more lucrative business. Those who aren't select hope to become select. That hope – and fear of the warden and his personal guards – keep them silent.

Chris Schultz holds his bracelet to the RFID scanner. Unlike the prisoners' anklets, Schultz can remove his bracelet when he leaves after his shift. The scanner beeps and displays Schultz's picture. The clerk confirms the man's identity, and hands him an envelope. Later, Schultz counts the bills. "Looks about two Ben Franklins short," he says to his friend Mona Goth.

"Lungs weren't any good," Mona whispers. "Needed some rare genetic marker besides the blood type. Heard a scavenger crew lucked out with an Indian kid who wandered a little too close to the bus station. We'll not get the bonus."

"Scheisse!" Chris says.

≈≈≈≈≈

The message sent to the next of kin of the inmate whose lungs were not suitable was brief. *Inmate 93526 died of bacterial meningitis on Friday last. In accordance with established policy for those dying of a contagious disease, his remains were cremated. As listed next-of-kin, you may accept his ashes upon payment of two hundred dollars for handling and processing. If you do not claim his ashes within thirty days of his death, they will be scattered in the prison yard. One death certificate is enclosed. Additional certified death certificates are available upon request for twenty-five dollars, each. Sincerely, Sam Red Horse, Warden.*

≈≈≈≈≈

The laughter of gulls is drowned out by the engines of trucks moving shipping containers at the Port of Long Beach. The port handles over 500,000 containers every month. Unloading, sorting, and moving the containers is orchestrated by a computer program, and watched by supervisors and customs agents with tablet computers. Many containers hold junk from China, bound for the nation's Sprawl-Mart stores. Some have less innocent contents.

118

On a summer morning in 2018, a supervisor's cell phone bleeps. "Boss? We got a problem."

The supervisor drives his golf cart to the site of the reported problem. Two of his men are there. One points to a container. A viscous, stinking liquid is seeping from under the doors.

"Step back," the supervisor orders, and thumbs a single button on his cell phone.

The supervisor's supervisor takes one look and a single whiff, orders the area evacuated, and calls for a Hazard Materials team. The HAZMAT leader breaks the customs seal on the door and snaps the lock with a bolt cutter. He swings the lever that holds the door shut and pulls it open. When they see what is inside, two members of the team vomit inside their suits and have to be rescued, themselves. The liquid seeping from under the door is waste from the thirty women and children locked inside the container.

The HAZMAT chief calls for ambulances. By the time the ambulances reach a hospital, six of the containers' prisoners are dead. The others are so dehydrated and starving it is days before they can be questioned. Most know nothing except their name and the name of their village, and that they were promised freedom in America. Those who know more are afraid to speak. They know the power and reach of those who put them in the container. They are very unresponsive to questions.

"Where did the container come from?" This is the first question ICE – Immigration and Customs Enforcement – asks.

"Nicaragua, according to the computers," the dock supervisor answers. "The port and the company whose name is on the manifest deny knowing anything about it."

"There's no way to get anything more from them," the ICE supervisor asserts.

A member of the dock team is first to leak the news to the press. As soon as the *Los Angeles Times* gets the information, it is impossible to stop the story. Television stations demand access. Even the Lompoc paper sends a reporter. The editor of the *Washington Banner* wishes Susan Calvin still worked for him. This is something she could run with.

White House reaction is swift, predictable, and terse.

<<@RealUSPOTUS more #illegals we must stop them! build #Mywall>>

The improbability of a wall stopping a shipping container carried with as many as 10,000 others on a ship from Central America does not occur to the White House.

Further investigation finds the container was mistakenly offloaded in Lázaro Cárdenas, Mexico. It sat on the dock for six days before being put on another ship. The ICE supervisor connects the dots and fills in the blanks. "If the container arrived when expected, it would have been picked up in Long Beach, loaded on a truck, and taken to a large city where the women would be given the choice of deportation or prostitution. The children would not be given the first choice."

The ICE supervisor knows one of the Mexican drug cartels, the self-styled Knights Templar, controls the port of Lázaro Cárdenas. He knows there is no chance of getting information from them. The scenario he envisions is plausible and makes it easy to close the case. His conclusion is plausible, but wrong.

≈≈≈≈≈

Ivan Kuznetzov does not trust the Overlook Resort's switchboard, no matter how obsequious the operators are, and makes calls on his cell phone.

His first call on this morning reaches Gerald Michelson, the Americanized name of Yury Mikhailov, the head of the California Bratva. "Yury, why do I have to get bad news from the media?" This is all Kuznetzov needs to say.

Kuznetzov's use of his Russian name puts Gerald on alert. Kuznetzov is more than displeased; he is angry.

"*Gospoden*, the container of goods was held in Mexico for six days. Our contact in the Knights Templar says the shipping line claims an error in the original manifest. When the container arrived at Long Beach, our agent there notified us. By then, it was too late. The authorities in Long Beach had opened it. The contents are out of our reach."

Kuznetzov allows himself a few moments to fume before addressing the situation. "Notify our supplier in Nicaragua we expect a new shipment at no charge and a refund of fifty percent of the price we paid for the first shipment. We have people waiting for those organs."

He dismisses his minions and summons Carlotta to his suite. A tap on the door is followed by a click as the lock opens. Carlotta steps in; the single bodyguard steps out. He will wait in the hallway. The lock clicks.

"An important shipment of goods was delayed, damaged, and then seized by the authorities. I have ordered another shipment. I am having second thoughts about one aspect of my operation. What do the cards say?"

Kuznetzov shuffles the cards and returns them to Carlotta. Since Kuznetzov did not ask a specific question, Carlotta uses the full deck and the Celtic Cross pattern.

She turns over the first card, in the "Present" position. *Three of Wands*, inverted. "You are facing a situation created by someone who has less power than you."

The second card, the "Challenges" card, is *The Page of Swords*. A somewhat androgynous figure stands on a promontory at the edge of the ocean. The figure holds aloft a sword and is looking over its right shoulder. Carlotta pauses. "*Gospoden*, this card puzzles me. It tells me something is troubling you more than the loss of one shipment." She waits.

"I am surrounded by imbeciles," Kuznetzov says. "You are the only one who I trust, and the only one who has any sense. The shipment was lost because of incompetence. The most modern ships in existence move thousands of containers around the world flawlessly every day. My container is offloaded at the wrong port and delayed six days. The people who were being brought into this country were six days and more in stifling heat. Some died."

"*Gospoden*, you were bringing in prostitutes? You said you had created a better business."

"See, you remember things. That encourages me. No, not prostitutes. Our contact in Nicaragua has a sophisticated medical clinic. He screens peasants according to our criteria and sends them to us. In return for donating a single kidney or a lobe of their liver, they receive papers, green cards, and start-up money." Kuznetzov does not tell Carlotta some of his cargo would donate more organs and would not survive. Nor does he mention the growing demand for child-sized hearts.

Kuznetzov gestures to the cards and Carlotta continues the reading. The next seven cards are innocuous. The tenth card, the "Future" card, is *The Hanged Man*, warning of unknown influences in Kuznetzov's future.

Carlotta stares at the card for longer than usual before saying, "You will encounter someone who is not your friend. You must be watchful and take swift and decisive action."

Although neither happy nor satisfied with the reading, Kuznetzov crosses Carlotta's palm with silver before telling her to arrange an immediate flight to Los Angeles and quarters for them and his guards. "You will travel with me. I can no longer wait a day or two for you to arrive."

The NSA analyst finds it easy to match her shift with the hours kept by Carlotta. "Become familiar with her," her supervisor says. "Look for patterns, including her sleep patterns. It is important you know her. The more you know, the easier you will spot anomalies. But do not get too close to her. Remember, she is an enemy."

Carlotta's calls a travel agency to arrange a suite and four more rooms. The credit card she uses links to an account in Malta, one known to the NSA. Another flag goes in Carlotta's file.

Carlotta does not try to coordinate charter flights from the Folio airport to Phoenix and then LAX, but asks the travel agency to make the arrangements. After a slight pause, during which Carlotta hears computer keys being pressed, the pleasant voice of the agent returns. "Ms. Krafft, there isn't a G6 in the nation I can get to Folio tomorrow. I can get you from Folio to Denver on a very nice Bombardier, where a G6 will meet you. Denver weather is forecast to be clear and warm. You can transfer from one plane to the other on the tarmac. I can make sure they park next to one another. If you prefer, I can get a Bombardier or G6 from Folio to LAX on the next day."

Carlotta thanks the woman, muses for a second, and says, "We really need to travel tomorrow. Please lock in the two planes."

The travel agent confirms the planes and the departure times, then asks, "Will you need a car when you arrive at LAX?"

"A helicopter, please," Carlotta says, and provides the final destination.

Carlotta does not know about Kuznetzov's earlier call to Gerald Michelson, head of the California Bratva. She calls him to arrange a meeting.

The call to Michelson is the one that betrays Carlotta. Michelson's phone is also on an NSA intercept list. A computer makes the connection in a microsecond. The analyst's connection to Carlotta's phone is cut in another microsecond. She punches in a call to her supervisor.

"I have a link between the person of interest and a five-star number. I don't have access to that kind of number."

The analyst's supervisor reaches the woman's cubicle in minutes. The supervisor knows his subordinates often work in ignorance. *What's the old saying? Treat them like mushrooms. Keep them in the dark and feed them manure?* He tries to make his people understand the importance of what they are doing and to bring them into the action, but he is not always successful. After Edward Snowden betrayed NSA, and the NSA was hacked and many of its own hacking tools stolen and sold, security was tightened. *The Director must have overdosed on Imodium, he was so tight*, the man thought. The image in his mind gives him one of the few moments of laughter he ever feels on the job.

An hour later the analyst and her supervisor meet in the DDO's office.

"You know the person you are monitoring has been linked to Ivan Kuznetzov. The five-star number she called was that of the head of the California branch of the Bratva – the so-called Russian Mafia. You need to know we believe Kuznetzov is the head of the Bratva in the United States. The woman associated with him – her travel plans have mirrored his. Now, she seems to be making those plans for him. He contacted the CIA operation at Luke Air Force Base. He is a Bratva power player who controls drug and human trafficking networks that extend into Nicaragua. The coincidence is troublesome. Tell me what you have."

After listening to the analyst, the supervisor realizes this intercept goes into territory beyond NSA's authority. "Call the FBI." She provides a contact's name and phone number. "Use the white phone system; it is self-authenticating."

"Tell your contact at the FBI Ivan Kuznetzov will meet with the head of the California Bratva. They will understand. Give him the details. Be sure to record the call and send me a transcript of the conversation.

"You have found an important link. Your work will be recognized."

~~~~~

That night, diaphanous figures fill Carlotta's dreams. At first, they are women and children, on their knees, arms extended, and hands open as if begging for something. Then, they dive into the depths of a dark sea. They tug Carlotta's clothes. She realizes she, too, is submerged in the sea. The figures swirl around her, dragging her down as they cry for … for what? For rescue? For justice? She wakes with her heart pounding in her chest. Her mind fills with questions. Who are these people? Why are they reaching out to her? How is Kuznetzov involved, for he certainly is?

126

An Anonymous Victim

Johnny Two-Horses carries the cooler of ice, water, and light beer from his truck to the edge of the bluffs where Sam Little Crow is waiting. Sam is fiddling with a radio, a scanner that switches between the center, approach control, the tower, and ground control, stopping when it detects speech.

"Yá'át'ééh, Sam. What 'cha got, new toy?"

"Yá'át'ééh. Scanner. Got it set to the airport frequencies. Listen."

"G6 Romeo Golf, Folio approach. You are cleared straight in runway 33. Contact tower 121.5 at outer marker."

"Folio approach, Romeo Golf, roger. Cleared straight in 33, tower 121.5 at outer marker. Good day, sir."

"Sam, that's the best damn toy you ever bought. Where is he?" Johnny sets down the cooler and lifts his binoculars. "I see him! One of them fancy Gulfstreams. Some rich dude come to play golf?"

"Probably. Wait. What's on the tarmac? Ambulance. Maybe someone really bad off going to the hospital."

Sam and Johnny watch as four people in blue scrubs run down the steps of the G6. They're carrying a small picnic cooler. "Looks like they brung their own beer," Johnny says as the ambulance drives off, red lights flashing and siren blaring.

Sam and Johnny watch ninety minutes later when the ambulance returns with the people and their cooler. The G6 has been serviced and is waiting with engines running. The two men listen to the scanner as the plane is given immediate clearance for takeoff.

"Sam, you still got a buddy in the flight service station?"

"Yeah."

"Find out where that plane is going, can't you?"

Sam's buddy appreciates the donuts Sam brings when he drops by to catch up on things, and has no reason not to tell Sam about the G6. "Medical priority flight, headed for Rochester."

"Minnesota, like the clinic place?"

"No, New York, like the Kodak place. That's the second medical priority flight this week."

During the next several months, Sam and Johnny watch fast planes – Gulfstreams, Citations, even a Beechcraft Starship – become frequent visitors. The passengers are always the same. A team of four or five people, one or two with red and white picnic coolers. They go to and from the airport in ambulances.

Had Sam and Johnny been a little more curious, they would have figured out the ice chests carried not beer or soda, but organs for transplant. Kuznetzov's plan and system are working overtime.

≈≈≈≈≈

Susan Calvin, Dr. Deschene, and the E'e'aahjigo Kiva meet in Dr. Deschene's laboratory among the autopsy tables. Dr. Deschene opens the meeting. "We have received the DNA testing on the young woman we found two months ago, and the scat found near her. The scat was from a coyote and contained human DNA matching both the still-unidentified young woman and her fetus. DNA markers show she is of Athabascan, and likely Navajo ancestry. Spencer and Chuchip assisted with her autopsy. Chuchip, would you describe what we found?"

Chuchip looks at a tablet computer, clears his throat, and begins. "The cadaver is a female age approximately 18, who was exposed to the elements and both animal and insect activity in the high desert for approximately four months. That estimate was made by Spencer based on what he learned at the body farm in Grand Junction. Dr. Deschene confirms the estimate."

Spencer blushes. The others pretend not to notice.

"The cadaver was missing eyes, lips, tongue, all organs of the chest and abdomen, and the softer, external parts of her reproductive system. Ribs were torn away and most were missing. The partial remains of a fetus, of approximately seven months gestation, was located at the bottom of the abdomen.

"She wore tattered clothing which appeared to be a pair of cotton shorts and a cotton maternity blouse." He looks up. "We got that from the label, by the way.

"Toxicology revealed traces of Rohypnol in the victim's flesh. Indications are the Rohypnol was administered shortly before death."

"The cause of death cannot be determined given the condition of the body."

"The Navajo Nation Police are unable to match her with any missing persons report in the Navajo Nation or in any of the Four Corners states."

Chuchip swipes the screen of the tablet. "That's all from the autopsy. Based on the human DNA in the scat, it is the team's opinion at least some of the post-mortem damage was due to animal activity. We do not rule out organ harvesting; however, the presence of clothing suggests otherwise. Why would anyone dress a corpse before dumping it?"

"Rohypnol. That's roofies, right? Why would anyone give a date-rape drug to someone seven months pregnant? That's sick!" Ahote crosses his arms over his chest and glares at the group.

Spencer takes that question. "We learned about roofies. They are just a fast-acting sleeping pill. If someone wanted to knock her out to take her organs, maybe they'd use that." He thinks for a moment and adds, "And maybe the guy was sick."

"Maybe the guy was the father of the baby, and wanted her and it out of the way." Everyone looks at Cha'tima after he speaks. A couple of them nod.

"Any other ideas?" Spencer asks.

Susan steps into the conversation. "Pregnant and missing for four months, and not reported. Do you still have her body?"

"Yes," Chuchip says.

"Is her face… preserved?"

"Eyes, tongue, cheeks, lips missing."

"Skull intact?"

"Yes."

"I assume you took dental impressions?" Susan is on a roll.

"Yes."

"May I take a series of photographs of her face, and can you get me X-rays of her skull – an MRI would be better – and may I send them to James Holomon University? They have the best computer software for re-creating faces. Maybe it's time to get some publicity. Her image and an article. I'm sure United Press Universal will accept it."

"Holomon University's anthropology department, of course," Dr. Deschene says. "They started with Neanderthal skulls a few years ago. Now, they do a lot of work for the United Nations on bodies found in mass graves in Syria. I suspect they would recognize my name and—"

"Probably, Sweetie, but my ex-boyfriend is likely the better approach," Susan says.

Dr. Deschene looks over the top of his glasses at Susan – except he's not wearing glasses. It just seems that way. "Ex?"

"Absolutely, but we've collaborated since then. A body found in the tiger cage at the National Zoo."

"Hoppin' Higgs!" Ata'halne' says. "I remember that." The others could almost see his mind working. "You're the Susan

Calvin who cracked the case. Convinced the police it was murder. And now you're here, working with us! Way, way cool."

Now, it is Susan's turn to blush.

"What about the uncanny valley?" Niyol asks.

"The what?"

"It's a thing in CGI, the computer-generated graphics in movies like *Polar Explorer*. The characters were close to human, but there was something odd about one boy's ears. Just close enough to human but odd enough to make some people uncomfortable. The big videogame people ran into the same problem. And, those reconstructed Neanderthal heads they show on the so-called educational channels are just not quite right."

"I think they will surprise you with their progress," Susan says. "Will you trust me on that?"

A brief susurrus of whispers subsides. "Yes, ma'am," Cha'tima speaks for the group. Niyol nods.

"Some excellent thinking," Dr. Deschene says. "Anyone have answers to our list of questions about Jessie?"

Niyol had asked about the large number of autopsies in Rough Rock County and did the research, so he answers that question. "Of the total of 213 autopsies in 2017, twenty were forensic autopsies, conducted because of a suspicious death. The others were routine – where people died alone and not under a doctor's care. The problem I see is 193 routine autopsies in one year is way, way above normal especially when compared to population. I dug a little deeper, and found nearly 100 already this year. I was able to get into the coroner's files – most of the routine autopsies, last year and so far in 2018, are deaths of prisoners at U.P.S. #9."

"Huh?" A couple of the boys blurt.

"Unified Prison System Number 9 … the one across the river."

"That's especially interesting," Dr. Deschene says. "All deaths while incarcerated or in law enforcement custody are supposed to be autopsied by the state medical examiner. What we have here, boys and girls, is one big red flag."

"Um, Susan is the only girl, here, Dr. Deschene, and she's a woman."

"Just an expression. My apology, Susan."

"It's okay to call me a girl." She looks around. "I'm saying that to Dr. D and not to everyone, you understand."

The older boys snicker. The younger ones seem confused.

"I'm not going to ask how you accessed those records," Dr. Deschene says, "but, were you able to find cause of death for the prisoners?"

"No, sir. I haven't gotten that far, yet. Is it important?"

"There are reported to be about 3,500 prisoners in #9," Dr. Deschene says. "More than a hundred deaths in one year among 3,500 people, even if they are prisoners, is another red flag. I don't need to remind you to keep all this among yourselves, do I?"

The young men voice their agreement.

"Anything else?" Dr. Deschene asks.

Ata'halne' stands. "Chief Joe asked a judge to subpoena Jessie's phone records from the carrier. The judge will issue an order. We can only hope the cell service hasn't deleted the information."

Ahote adds, "We've all been asking around who might have gotten a call from Jessie before he went missing. No luck, though. We'll keep trying."

Susan raises her hand. Dr. Deschene smiles and recognizes her.

"I put on my reporter's hat and visited the Rough Rock County Coroner. Told him I was writing a series of articles on the service coroners provide, and perhaps get them some recognition for doing such a thankless job. I also wore a low-cut blouse and a push-up bra."

Several of the boys – and Dr. Deschene – smile at that.

"I suggested, for a human interest angle, he describe some of the personal effects found with victims. I was thinking he would tell me about photographs, lockets with pictures, trinkets, and house keys, stuff like that. However, this guy collects souvenirs. I can't imagine it's legal. He opened a drawer filled with stuff. Including an orange rubber flash drive bracelet."

Susan pauses just long enough. "Did I mention I was a bit of a kleptomaniac?"

She pulls the bracelet from her pocket. "No chain-of-custody, so this would not be of much use in a criminal prosecution, but perhaps one of you young gentlemen would like to examine it?"

A low rumble fills the room as the young gentlemen pound the stainless steel autopsy tables with their knuckles in approval.

"Good work, everyone," Dr. Deschene says.

Niyol closes the meeting with a Navajo blessing.

Susan corners Ata'halne' before he leaves. "The Police Chief is your uncle, right? Why don't you call him *uncle* when you speak of him? Is there some trouble between you?"

"Yes, Miss Susan. He is my uncle. No, there is no trouble. However, being the nephew of the Chief of the Navajo Nation Police is about as far away from my friends as I can get. Three of them don't know who their father is. Many don't have uncles, and the ones who do, receive no guidance from them. None of them have grandfathers to tell them the stories. I have all those things. They live in old, ten-wide trailers, and use the bathrooms for storage 'cause they don't have running water or sewage, but get water from a horse tank under a windmill and use an outhouse a few yards away from the trailer. I live in my uncle's house with electricity, hot water, and flush toilets. I do everything I can to blend in with them. It wouldn't work except that they are all great guys and good friends."

≈≈≈≈≈

A week later, the E'e'aahjigo Kiva, Susan, and Dr. Deschene gather again in the pathology lab.

"Chief Joe got Jessie's cell phone records," TomTom – Ata'halne' – reports. "Including the location of the phone until the battery ran out – or the phone was destroyed.

"The last calls were made to Jessie's girlfriend, but were not answered. They were made from Gallup. Somewhere in a three-mile radius of a cell tower in the center of town. The last known location of the phone was also within three miles of the tower."

"His body was found … " Niyol looks up from his tablet computer. "More than 200 miles away from Gallup, in a different state. Another red flag."

"Can we get a map? Is there anything in the three-mile circle around the cell tower that stands out?"

"Gimmie," Niyol says to Ata'halne'. He takes the report, finds the coordinates of the cell tower, plugs them into Google Maps, draws the three-mile circle, and projects the result on the HDTV.

Everyone stares at the map. "Awful lot of stuff, there." Ahote says. "What time were the calls?"

"About one each hour from 8:17 to 11:30 PM," Niyol says.

"What's open during those hours? What about this diner?"

Dr. Deschene offers Niyol access to a second desktop computer. The young man finds the diner. "No. Closes at 9:00."

"He could have been there until nine and made the last calls after he left."

The boys find business after business. All are negative until someone finds the bus station. "It's open twenty-four seven."

"Do we have a picture of Jessie?"

"Yes … the JV team had pictures made a week before Jessie went missing. I got one and blew it up," Niyol says. "Had to clean it up a bit, but it's pretty close."

"Someone, at least two of us and maybe more, need to take his picture to the diner and the bus station."

134

"Ahote and I, but not in uniform. I'll clear it with the chief," Niyol says. "We have no jurisdiction in Gallup, and uniforms would make people keep silent."

"Do you think he was running away?"

"We need to talk to more of the JV team and his girlfriend," Cha'tima says. "Who's up for that?"

More boys volunteer than are needed. Cha'tima selects two, Cheveyo – an older Hopi – and Hok'ee. Hok'ee beams with pride at being selected for an important task.

"Good work, everyone," Dr. Deschene says. "I will prepare a summary for Chief Joe."

RMS Queen Mary

The NSA analyst provides her FBI contact the details of Kuznetzov and Carlotta's travel arrangements. The Denver FBI spots Carlotta and Kuznetzov when they transfer from the Bombardier to the G6. Two and a half hours later, the G6 lands on LAX Runway 24 Right, and taxis to the general aviation terminal, where a private helicopter takes them to their hotel in Long Beach.

"What is this?" Kuznetzov demands.

"The Royal Mail Ship Queen Mary," Carlotta says. "You have the best of the First Class cabins. Although they're not up to your standards, you are sleeping in history." Somewhat mollified, Kuznetzov follows her to his quarters, a large and well-equipped suite.

Kuznetzov expects a tense but cordial meeting with the head of the LA Bratva. His guards disabuse him. "There's a sniper on the roof overlooking the pool. You're not in his sights. A diversion, likely." The lead bodyguard explains.

"What is the plan?" he asks.

"You came in by helicopter; you will leave by boat. The Queen Mary's lifeboats are all operational. We have made simple adjustments to the one closest to your quarters."

Kuznetzov thinks for a moment. "You are sure our Komerade of the L.A. Bratva plans something?"

"Yes, *Gospoden*."

"Then this is what we shall do."

After 6:00 PM, there is only one way onto and off the Queen – the gangplank or "brow" as sailors call it for reasons lost to history.

Kuznetzov's people are ready. Some tourists, looking for a drink on a bar overlooking the port, or supper at the Clam House, are walking up the gangplank. Among them, and not at all convivial or inebriated, are seven men in dark suits.

"*Blyad*'," one of Kuznetzov's guards says. "Could they be any more obvious?"

"Wake up!" Dmitry Ivanovich, the leader of Kuznetzov's detail says. "The most obvious, the least obvious. Keep your eyes on the tourists."

Ivanovich is correct in his assessment. The seven young men in cartoon T-shirts declaring them to be members of "Goofy's Bachelor Party" are neither as inebriated nor as childish as they seem. Three of them claim a large table at the Clam House. Four walk toward the men's room before ducking down a service corridor.

Long before they reach the First Class section, twelve bullets fired by Kuznetzov's guards from silenced 9-mm Glock pistols, interrupt their planned visit.

Ivanovich reports the battle just as Kuznetzov terminates a cell phone call. His agent has killed the leader of the California Bratva.

Kuznetzov, himself, leads the assault on the three who remain in the Clam House. By the time the son of the leader of the California Bratva recognizes Kuznetzov, Kuznetzov's men have disarmed the young man's two guards. Kuznetzov sits at the table.

"Your father took a great risk. It did not provide the reward he expected, and he has paid for that."

The young man blanches. He knows Kuznetzov means his father is dead and he is about to follow him. Kuznetzov's next words give him some hope.

"You showed courage in coming here, but courage is not enough. You are now the head of the California Bratva and report directly to me and not through the Pacific Coast Bratva. We will discuss your responsibilities tomorrow."

138

Kuznetzov returns to his stateroom and commands Carlotta. "Get us out of here. A hotel in LA tonight and tomorrow night; then back to Folio. It will not be necessary to use the lifeboat."

While Kuznetzov washes his hands, Carlotta calls her travel agent to arrange a hotel in Beverly Hills, a car to pick them up immediately, and a G6 to take them to Folio in two days.

≈≈≈≈≈

The NSA notifies the FBI of Carlotta's travel plans. The FBI learns about the bodies found on the Queen Mary, a dead man with a sniper rifle on the roof of a nearby parking garage, and one found in a penthouse in Los Angeles, but cannot, however, tie the bodies to Kuznetzov.

If truth be told, they don't try especially hard. "The head of the Russian Mafia in California was found in his bathtub. His throat was cut. The four bodies found on the Queen Mary and the sniper are members of that gang. The California Russian Mafia is in turmoil. Someone got rid of their biggest player and five soldiers. Maybe, someone will take out more of them. It will save us a lot of work."

≈≈≈≈≈

October weather in Folio, Arizona, is what the Greeks named *Halcyon Days*. It is the time when Aeolus – god of winds – calms the waters of the sea so his daughter, transformed into a halcyon bird in one of the endless Greek tragedies, can lay her eggs on the beach without them being washed away. The time is also known as *Indian Summer*.

Johnny Two-Horses and Sam Little Crow have toted their lawn chairs, cooler, scanner radio, binoculars … "And the kitchen sink? Did you remember the kitchen sink?" Sam grumbles. He looks in the cooler as if expecting to find the sink there. "Beer? Real beer and not the lite crap you usually bring. What's the occasion?"

"No occasion," Johnny says. "ABC-123 was out of lite beer. We'll need to take it easy. Hey, look, it's the 757 again."

Sam puts down his beer and picks up binoculars while Johnny fiddles with the scanner.

"Nope, different registration," Sam says as he pokes the characters into a Google search window. "Saudi Arabia, again, though. They must got a lot of sick royalty."

"They got a lot of royalty," Johnny says. "But not as much as they used to. Remember last year when a bunch of princes got arrested?"

By now, Sam and Johnny are accustomed to seeing convoys of black SUVs escorting a windowless, white Mercedes van that serves as an ambulance. They can follow the convoy on 10th Street until it turns north. "Headed for the spa, all right."

≈≈≈≈

The convoy pulls under the portico at the back of the spa. Men wearing dark suits, dark glasses, and ear buds attached to curly wires leap from the SUVs and form a semi-circular cordon, facing outward. Two others watch the doors of the spa open, and examine the ID badges of the two men who exit. "Dr. Standart. My Prince asks me to greet you. Who is with you, please?"

"This is Nurse Grassier, my right hand man. He will assist me during the Prince's stay and will be responsible for his care team."

A wheelchair is brought to the Mercedes van. "For His Highness's comfort, I most respectfully ask he allow us to transport him in the wheelchair," Dr. Standart says. The Prince needs little encouragement. His condition has weakened him. He appreciates the game Dr. Standart plays to pretend the wheelchair is for his comfort.

The Prince is comfortable in his room – in a reclining lounge chair, and in his own robes rather than the Western suit he wore on the plane. The suit is an important part of his disguise, although no one thought to disguise the registration number of the plane. Dr. Standart explains to the Prince what his treatment will entail.

"The most critical element of your treatment is the heart transplant, itself, and the subsequent recovery. We anticipate it will require eight weeks before you can be a passenger on your plane. When you are well enough, we will operate to remove the bunion on your left foot, since the bunion is the ostensible reason you are here. That, and enjoying the luxuries of our spa … which cannot compete with the luxuries of your own home, but, perhaps, may be different enough to be, how shall I say, *exotic?*

"Following eight weeks of recovery, you will return home. I understand your plane will return to Riyadh tomorrow and will be summoned here when you need it. Do you have any questions, Your Highness?"

The Prince does not respond, but gestures to a member of his entourage. The man wears neither the white robes and ghutra of the Saudi royalty nor the dark, Western suits of the Prince's guards. Rather, he wears what appear to be gray scrubs – although the material is silk – and velvet slippers of the same color.

"*As-salāmu 'alaykum*," he says, and bows toward Dr. Standart.

"*Wa'alaykumu as-salām,*" Dr. Standart replies and bows, surprising the man.

"I am Doctor Singh," the man says. "And I thank you for your blessing. I will consult with His Highness's doctors and care team regarding every aspect of the surgery, and I will be present in the operating theater during removal of the donor heart and its implantation in His Highness. You have already agreed to these terms. However, I am a consultant only, and will not take part in any physical aspect of the procedure. I believe you and I can continue the discussion elsewhere without taking up His Highness's time."

"I was pleasantly surprised," Dr. Singh says, "when you responded to me in Arabic." Dr. Singh and Dr. Standart sit at a conference table and have been served strong coffee.

"My preparation was reasonable, although I had expected to exchange the greeting with His Highness. I was pleasantly surprised to hear it from you. I am glad my studies had a convivial result."

Dr. Singh smiles. "The matter of the heart. I understand you have a donor? A living donor?"

Dr. Standart is unprepared for this. The understanding was the Prince would remain at the spa, being pampered and entertained until a donor was located. The sharp eyes of Dr. Singh keep Standart from equivocating.

"We have a donor. He is a prisoner nearby. He does not, of course, know he will be a donor. His Highness does not need to know these details."

"Of course not, Dr. Standart. We have an understanding. However, I am concerned the donor is a prisoner."

Dr. Standart spreads a sheaf of papers on the table. "This donor has been in isolation for eleven months. He understands and agrees to participate in medical research. He believes his cooperation will make him free. We test him monthly for sexually transmitted diseases, and especially for the HIV virus. We also test for the Hantavirus, the Zika virus, and the Ebola virus. Here, you see the results.

"Dr. Singh, His Highness is an important guest. His health and the outcome of this procedure are as important to us as to him and you. I want you to visit the donor and supervise any tests you feel appropriate."

The donor is transported to the spa. He is a Jicarilla Apache, arrested for armed robbery and held without arraignment. He is happy to see a new doctor's face and submits to blood drawings and sampling of urine and feces. If Dr. Singh realizes the young man has been lobotomized, he says nothing.

Dr. Singh is grateful the procedure will be conducted in this American surgery. There is nothing in India, his home, to compare with the facilities here. There is nothing in Saudi Arabia, either. *Say what you will about their decadent society, the Americans do have some amazing medical equipment.*

~~~~~

The operating suite has two identical tables, two sets of high-intensity lights, two racks of patient monitors, two heart-lung machines, and two anesthesia machines. Trays of instruments are sealed in plastic. Two nearly identical teams of surgeons and nurses enter the room. One team stands by each table.

The Prince and the Apache are rolled in on gurneys. They are already sedated, and don't notice or react when they are lifted onto the surgical tables.

Anesthesiologists affix masks to each patient while others connect the patients to monitors. At a signal from Dr. Standart, each team begins its work.

Dr. Standart and his counterpart crack the chests of their patients. Dr. Standart clamps off arteries and veins and then attaches them to a heart-lung machine, which keeps oxygenated blood flowing in his patient. The counterpart team does so, as well. Not to keep their patient alive, but to ensure his other organs – all of which have been bought by bids on a dark net auction – will remain suitable for their clients.

In a single, orchestrated move, the heart of the Apache crosses to the table of the Prince. Dr. Standart places the heart in the Prince's chest and reattaches veins and arteries. On the other table, lungs, kidneys, the liver, and spleen are removed, packed in ice, and taken from the operating suite to people whose planes have emergency clearances from Air Traffic Control.

Kokopelli

The kiva members sit on the floor of Dr. Deschene's office. The doctor and Susan are in chairs in the bay window, but have turned them around to become part of the circle favored by the kiva.

Niyol reports first on the coroner's causes of death among inmates of U.P.S #9. "Last summer, there was an outbreak of bacterial meningitis. That caused 23 of last year's deaths. Thirty-seven of the others were listed as 'failure to thrive.' I don't know what that means."

"In this case, it means 'complications of AIDS,'" Dr. Deschene says. "Not unexpected, but still a high number, especially since the courts ordered prisoners with HIV receive the drug cocktail that has been so successful in delaying the onset of AIDS."

"Another avenue of investigation," Ahote says. "Is the prison selling the drugs on the black market?"

"The remaining 100 prisoner deaths were a hodgepodge of causes including suicides and fifty-seven heart attacks – all of them coronary thrombosis—"

"Niyol, please forgive me for interrupting, but did you copy the causes of death exactly as written?"

"Yes, sir." Niyol hands the list to Dr. D. who studies it.

"These are not the words a doctor would use," he says, "although the Rough Rock County Coroner, who is an MD, signed the reports. That's another red flag. And, there may be another one. Niyol, can you learn if anyone reported the outbreak of bacterial meningitis to the Rough Rock County Health Department or the state Health Department?"

Niyol agrees, and then reports what he found on Jessie's flash drive bracelet. "Someone erased the flash drive, but it wasn't a safe-erase. All the erase did was delete the names of the files so they wouldn't be visible. The files, themselves, are still there."

Ata'halne' asks, "Why would someone erase Jessie's bracelet and put it back on him?"

"Or, did Jessie erase it, 'cause he knew how to recover files after a safe erase. Maybe he did it so someone finding it wouldn't be as likely to see his files?"

"Have you looked at the files?"

"A few. Starting with the most recent and working backwards. It's a 128-gig drive, and there are hundreds of files. So far everything is homework and something that looks like a story he's writing, maybe for an English lit class. I don't think there will be any clues, but I'll keep looking."

"What about the other questions?"

Spencer-Atsa puts the list on the HDTV.

"Was it Jessie? Confirmed, especially since Susan found the bracelet and Niyol has read some of the files. I still wish we could test DNA, though."

Gaagii breaks the long silence that follows. "You know I am studying with a Shaman to learn the chants and ceremonies of our people. I asked to learn first The Blessing Way. Beginning Friday night, the Shaman will take me through the entire two-day ceremony. Can you all be there? That includes Dr. D and Ms. Susan, if they wish."

"I think we would all like that," Ahote says. "The Shaman, he won't mind if some Hopi are present?"

"Not any more than if two Bilagáana are there," Gaagii says. He laughs and Susan and Spencer know he's not laughing at them. "We welcome anyone, as long as they respect our traditions and the ceremony."

146

The kiva agrees, and the meeting continues reviewing the list of questions.

"Who is working on the hikers?"

Dr. Deschene takes that one. "I've filed a FOI – a Freedom of Information request – for police reports and any notes the coroner has related to Jessie's death. If they don't have the hikers' names I will put an ad in the newspapers, although I doubt it would do much good."

Cheveyo raises his hand. "A lot of Rough Rock County is a designated wilderness area. If the hikers registered with the Park Service – and they should have if they were entering a wilderness area – the Park Service might have a record."

"Do you suppose they would release information if we did an FOI?"

"It's worth a try," Dr. Deschene says.

"Can you give me a few days, first, Cheveyo asks. "My boyfriend works for the Park Service ... ... I didn't mean to say boyfriend." He puts his hands over his face, bends down, and curls into a ball.

"Spirit Warrior," Cha'tima says. "Brother." He stands, steps to Cheveyo and puts his hand on the young man's shoulder. "Do not hide your face from us. You are one of us. What pains you also pains us."

"Besides," Ahote says. "We all know you are blessed with two spirits. We've known it since, like, seventh grade."

Cheveyo looks up. "Really? And you said nothing? Not even when we were still in scouts?"

"No," Ahote says. "Like Cha'tima said. You are our brother. You have always been our brother. You will always be our brother."

Cha'tima seals the boys' agreement with a blessing. Each of the young men clasps Cheveyo's hand as they leave.

≈≈≈≈≈

One of Kuznetzov's guards summons Carlotta to the boss's suite. She knocks, enters, and then closes and locks the door. Kuznetzov has newspapers spread over the couch. They are open to display the same image. The image appears to be a photograph of a young woman. *Hispanic or American Indian*, Carlotta thinks. *And he is angry about something.* Carlotta walks cautiously toward Kuznetzov.

"*Gospoden?* What is it?"

He pulls his eyes away from the images and thrusts a newspaper into her hands. "Read this."

≈≈≈≈≈

"Folio, Arizona (UPU). The body of this young woman was found, abandoned in the desert. Her body and the body of the unborn baby she was carrying were savaged by animals, including at least one coyote. Had she lived another month or two, she would have given birth. The baby would have lived, breathed, and become a person. As it is, however, she and the baby died and their bodies were desecrated. This was not a sky burial as practiced by some cultures, but the exact opposite. It was an abomination, not only to the ways of the Diné, but also to the ways of the Bilagáana.

"There was barely enough left of her for caring people to recreate the image of her face. Do you find the images disturbing? They should be. They were constructed by computers. However, they are the best and closest pictures we will have of this young woman unless some friend or relative comes forward with a photograph.

"Hers is not the only body found abandoned and desecrated in the desert. At least four others are being investigated."

The article continues with stories, some clearly labeled as speculation, including speculation about illegal organ harvesting from other bodies found in the desert.

"The dry air and hot sun of the high desert leave few clues. If you know this young woman, or if you know of anyone who is missing under strange or questionable circumstances, please contact the Navajo Nation police."

A toll-free number and an email address follow.

≈≈≈≈≈

"Who is behind this?" Kuznetzov demands, although he knows Carlotta will not have the answer. His call to Isaac Peterson, head of the Arizona Bratva, is more direct and specific. "Find out who she is and where she is getting her information."

Carlotta returns to her room and stares at her crystal ball. The ball is silent, but her mind races with questions. Not just who the woman is and where she gets her information, but why the story angered Kuznetzov. A chance remark she made during a reading comes back to haunt her. The *Death card could be as simple as starting a chain of funeral homes. But it's not funeral homes. He's behind this, and it really is organ harvesting.*

Carlotta does something she seldom does. She shuffles the cards and deals the Celtic Cross for herself. The cards are full of warnings of danger, but are too vague to be of any immediate use.

≈≈≈≈≈

An intern at the Organ Procurement and Transplantation Network stares at a terminal. He is tired of sitting around waiting

149

for something to happen. The agency's entire attitude is "hurry up and wait." The intern idly pages through the records of people waiting for organs, hoping to find something interesting.

He blinks. The record he is looking at disappears from the screen. The next record appears. *Glitch*, he thinks, and hits the *page up* key. What appears is not the record he had been reading. He frowns. The name was easy to remember. He types it into the search box. No hits. Not found.

The intern walks to his supervisor's desk. "Ma'am? Why would a record disappear from the database? Did someone's name get withdrawn? Did someone die or become ineligible? I just saw a record vanish."

"Look over my shoulder," she says. "See? That icon opens your filter settings. This record is marked *filled*. If you turn on the *filled* filter, you won't see them. Here's one marked *removed*. See the code? This list shows the codes for the reason. Your filters are turned on. It was just a coincidence."

"Thank you, ma'am." The intern returns to his terminal, turns off the filters, and searches for the record he had been examining. Still not there. *I must have misremembered the name.* He resumes his browsing.

≈≈≈≈≈

Kuznetzov depends more and more on Carlotta to make travel arrangements and schedule visitors. After reading Susan's article, he orders her to find a more permanent place in Folio. The town and its airport are the center of his organ-harvesting, drug smuggling, and human-trafficking empires. But first, the cards. He summons her.

"Carlotta, should we remain in Folio? Am I in danger? What do the cards say?"

"Your question is broad," Carlotta says. She lays the cards in a spread unfamiliar to Kuznetzov.

150

"What…?"

"This is a new way to spread the cards," Carlotta says. "It is associated with business and commerce rather than love and relationships. I see it as more suited to your question."

Kuznetzov nods. He knows Carlotta's prescience is not limited to the cards.

Carlotta turns the first card. *Ten of Cups.* "This reflects your purpose," she says. "You have chosen a new focus. It brings a new ally."

"The next card tells your motivation." *Four of Pentacles.* "This alliance must be about more than money."

She continues to turn cards until reaching the sixth and last. *The Hanged Man*, inverted.

"That one keeps turning up," Kuznetzov grumbles. "I can't help feeling there's something dangerous ahead."

"This card lies in the future position. Inverted, it tells you are facing not the unknown, but the known.

"You asked if you should remain in Folio. Taken as a whole, the cards say so. The cards also say you are on the correct path, and you must plan for what the Americans call *the long haul*."

≈≈≈≈≈

Kuznetzov thinks about the reading and then issues orders. "Find a house for me, you, and the hangers-on. I'll need an office. Security and communication are essential. Ivanovich will arrange phones and computers. Otherwise, you decide," he commands.

Carlotta places calls, which an NSA computer forwards to the analyst. She finds a realtor who sounds competent, and outlines her requirements. She does not say "security," but says, "isolated and quiet," and insists the home must have reliable high-speed internet. "My son is quite the video gamer," she says. "I indulge him too much, but I have promised he may continue his hobby."

The report to the FBI is brief. "Subject of investigation 2017-19330130 Carlotta Krafft contacted a real estate agent in Folio, Arizona and made inquiries about a five-bedroom house. It is likely the house is for subject Ivan Kuznetzov."

≈≈≈≈≈

White House reaction to Susan's story about the unknown woman and her baby is swift.

<<@RealUSPOTUS discredited reporter with more #fakenews disgusting why allowed to publish?>>

≈≈≈≈≈

Near Window Rock, the spiritual center of the Navajo Nation, Chief Joe sits in the emergency command post. Six members of the E'e'aahjigo Kiva sit at phones and computer terminals. They all have read Susan's article. A copy of the Folio newspaper is on top of a stack that includes newspapers from Red Rock, Gallup, Denver, Salt Lake City, Phoenix, and elsewhere. United Press Universal bought the article and sent it to every newspaper in the United States, Canada, and the British Commonwealth. Joe presses his fingers to the top of his nose. *It's going to be a long day and night,* he thinks as the phones start ringing.

Cha'tima skims the automated transcripts of phone calls. Although the software isn't perfect, it gives him a good idea of what is being said. After two hours, he speaks to Chief Joe, and then calls out. "Listen up, everyone. Let the phones ring for a minute.

"Rule 1: If any caller says anything about alien abduction, Big Foot, crop circles, UFOs, the New World Order, conspiracy, or anything like that, say *Thank you, this isn't what we're looking for*, and hang up. Then block that number.

"Okay, back to work."

Ahiga puts aside his headset and walks to Cha'tima's position. "Cha'tima, I got a call about a government cover up. Is that the same as a conspiracy?"

Chief Joe hears, and steps toward the two. "What about a cover up?"

"Someone who would not identify themselves said they knew the Arizona State Medical Examiner had covered up deaths at Arizona prisons. He said the prisons were being run by a company hired by the state. He also said people raised questions about the contract. Politicians brushed off the questions."

Chief Joe purses his lips in thought. "Cha'tima, please tell your people to be alert for anything associated with the Arizona prisons, the company that runs them, or the Arizona state medical examiner's office."

Cha'tima nods. He does not interrupt the activity, but walks from position to position, telling each person one at a time. His persistence pays off when another call comes in. Spencer is on the phone with a caller. He raises his hand to signal Cha'tima.

After the call is over, Spencer queues up the recording. "My brother was arrested in Jake's Lake. We don't know why. Him and his friends were hanging out at a convenience store, maybe buying beer, but they were all 21 and it's not on the Res. A cop pulled up and hassled them. My brother complained and they hauled him off. We never heard from him, again. The county sheriff's department said they never arrested him. They kept hassling the boys who said they'd been there. A year later, we got a letter from the warden at the prison saying he'd died from a heart attack, and we could claim his ashes for two hundred dollars. It's not the same as that woman found in the desert, but nobody will listen to me, so I called you."

They hear Spencer thank the caller, get contact information, and hang up.

"Hoppin' Higgs," Cha'tima says after Spencer plays the recording. "Let's get the Chief in on this one."

Chief Joe listens to the recorded call, and thanks Spencer and Cha'tima. "Another link in the chain," he says. "Make a transcript, and both of you sign and date it, please. And add another question to your list. How was he held for a year without his family knowing where he was? When were the arraignment and trial? What were the charges? Who was the judge?"

"Uh, that's five questions, Chief," Ahiga says.

Chief Joe smiles. "Go figure."

≈≈≈≈≈

Two days after Susan's article appears in a Farmington newspaper, an elderly woman reaches the Navajo Police Headquarters in Window Rock. She shows the desk sergeant a photograph and an article torn from the newspaper. The photograph is clearly the young woman whose picture is in the article. The desk sergeant rustles up a patrol car and a female officer to take her to the command center.

"Found her, Chief," the officer says. "Her grandmother is just outside."

"Yá'át'ééh, amá," Chief Joe says

"Yá'át'ééh," she replies and continues in Navajo. Joe listens carefully. The old woman says the girl in the newspaper is her granddaughter. The girl was pregnant and had been seen at the free clinic. She was living in a trailer with a man. The grandmother's voice becomes venomous when she names the man.

The chief gently interrupts the old woman, and issues orders. A few minutes later, an officer is on the phone asking for a warrant for the man's arrest on suspicion of murder. It takes only a few more minutes before a fax machine spits out a copy of the warrant.

It takes considerably longer to find the man, who has fled. The Phoenix police find the truck abandoned near a Salvation Army shelter, and find the man sharing a bottle of muscatel with two others in an alley outside the Sallie. Federal Marshalls drive him to Window Rock where a judge finds sufficient cause to order a DNA test. The results are 98% match with DNA from the fetus. Susan's next article features the photo the grandmother provided and the headline, "Case Closed."

When the kiva meets next, the boys' happiness is muted. They have closed one case, but there are still others to be solved.

≈≈≈≈≈

Susan is puzzled by the invitation to the next meeting of the kiva. It will be held not in Dr. D's pathology lab, but in the backyard of a trailer home southeast of Folio. Susan stands in front of a mirror in Dr. Deschene's home putting on the little makeup she wears. Dr. Deschene steps behind her, clasps his arms around her waist, and presses his body into hers.

"You are beautiful, you know?" he says. "All the boys know that. The younger ones think it's *cute,* I suppose. Older ones are oddly not jealous. It's as if they understand the bond you and I have created."

"What does this mean?" Susan asks. She picks up the invitation.

"They mean to bring us into their *kiva society*. They will ask us to accept as true some things that are not part of your upbringing. Can you do that?"

Susan pulls from his embrace, and turns. "What sort of things?" she demands.

Dr. Deschene thinks for several moments. Susan gives him time to do so. She sees how important this is.

"That the Judeo-Christian-Islamic god you grew up with is not the only aspect of the Creator. That while humans are fallible, we are not created in sin, as the Christian Bible says. Therefore, we do not need to be saved from sin by a blood sacrifice. Things exist in this world ... things that are real, but not in your understanding."

"I was with you until that last," Susan says. "But, I've got a pretty broad understanding." She smiles, and steps into Dr. D's embrace.

"You'll need it," he says. "But I will be with you."

The fire that a year ago greeted Spencer has been rekindled. Cha'tima stands by the fire pit. He wears only a breechclout and moccasins. His hair is unbound. Gaagii greets Dr. Deschene and Ms. Calvin when they arrive. He is dressed similarly. "Please come with me," he says. "Others will join us and be your guides."

Dr. Deschene and Susan follow Cha'tima toward the flames and see the boys and young men they know – but not in their present aspect. The young men do not wear the torn blue jeans and faded T-shirts that Dr. Deschene and Susan expect. All, including Spencer – the pale and white-haired son of Norwegian mining engineers – wear traditional buskins or moccasins, breechclouts, and necklaces. Their faces and bodies are marked with stripes and pictographs. *That's Navajo*, Susan thinks. *That's Hopi,* Dr. Deschene realizes.

Their escort leads them to seats on a log, one of several surrounding the fire.

"The Blessing Way ceremony is both sacred and private," Gaagii says. "The Shaman has agreed to conduct the ceremony for members of my kiva society. He knows we are a mix of Navajo, Hopi and Bilagáana. With his understanding, we meet tonight to add two people to our kiva, Dr. Nastas Deschene and Ms. Susan Calvin."

"Chohooi," Niyol responds. "It is necessary."

"One is Bilagáana," a voice in the darkness calls.

156

"So am I." It is Atsa's voice. "You trusted me. We need to trust them."

"It is so," Gaagii says.

The initiation is brief. Cha'tima asks Dr. Deschene and Susan to swear loyalty to the Kiva Society. There is a brief bit of confusion when Dr. Deschene says he has taken the doctor's oath, the Hippocratic Oath. "I cannot swear an oath that violates an earlier one."

After Dr. Deschene recites the Hippocratic Oath, the members of the Kiva whisper among themselves. "It is agreed," Gaagii says. "It is right the older oath has precedence over the newer one. We accept your condition."

Susan had never made an oath except the one time she served as a juror in a petit larceny case. She has no reason not to swear oath to the kiva.

Minutes later, both Dr. Deschene and Susan Calvin are members of the E'e'aahjigo Kiva.

Niyol gives Susan a necklace; Ahote gives Dr. Deschene a silver belt buckle. "This is a gift from my uncle. I pass it to you in both brotherhood and my hope for my people."

Dr. Deschene recognizes the hallmark and name on the back. "Ahote, this is priceless, I cannot—"

"Priceless. That is Bilagáana talk," Ahote says.

"No! I mean, yes. I mean, no," Dr. Deschene sputters. "It is priceless because of its history and because it is a gift from your uncle. I am not worthy—"

"Those are the same words I said to my uncle when he gave it to me. He assured me I was worthy. He also foretold that someday I would pass this on to someone who was worthy, and he would become a friend and ally. That has happened, tonight."

Dr. Deschene nods his head in acknowledgement of the younger man's words and the wisdom of the boy's uncle.

Later that evening, Susan stares in the mirror at the necklace she was given at the ceremony. Four strands with tiny olive seeds, pipe bush, turquoise, and shell alternate in a pattern. She counts beads, and realizes it's a 4/4 times 4/4. *It's the four things, again,* she thinks. Four sacred mountains, four winds, four colors, four seasons … *The things Doli and I talked about. It is a gift from my kiva society. My kiva, with two Bilagáana – one a young man and one a woman. Will wonders never cease?*

Dr. Deschene steps into the vanity where Susan is looking at the necklace. "It's beautiful," he says. "Something one of the boys' mother or sister made."

"I thought they were all discarded by their families."

"Officially, I think so," Dr. Deschene replies. "Still, some have contact with relatives. The belt buckle they gave me is Hopi Work. Ahote says it was a gift from his uncle. I think he is not quite forthcoming about how important his uncle is.

"After World War II, a handful of Hopi veterans used the GI Bill to learn silver-smithing and then worked to recreate the ancient, traditional, and classical Hopi designs and techniques. They found patterns and symbols used by their ancestors in the old pawn pledged against loans and never redeemed, in jewelry passed down from generation to generation, some from before the time the Spanish Catholics arrived to corrupt the Hopi traditions. They found images in pictographs scratched in rock. They melded these with their own creativity and imagination. This buckle was made by the son of one of the greatest of the modern Hopi silversmiths."

158

"The figure on the buckle is Kokopelli," Susan says. "I recognize him. What are the other symbols?"

Dr. Deschene laughs. "You recognize Kokopelli without his most remarkable feature."

"I know what you mean, you dirty-minded Indian." Susan laughs. "Besides being a trader who traveled from what is now Utah to Mesoamerica, I know Kokopelli was a fertility god. Older images show him to be amply endowed for that function, but modern re-creations, made for tourists, omit that critical feature."

≈≈≈≈≈

It is late Friday afternoon, the day after Dr. Deschene and Susan's initiation into the E'e'aahjigo Kiva. Members of the kiva arrive at Chief Joe's home. He offers the use of his hogan since a central theme of the ceremony is the hogan as a symbol of order and harmony. A large horse-watering trough, carefully cleaned for ritual baths, stands beside the hogan. The Shaman arrives at dawn and creates patterns in the sand using cornmeal and dried and crushed flower petals.

The ceremony begins Friday night and continues, with breaks for ritual baths, on Saturday. Chants fill Saturday night. The Shaman knows this is not only a ceremony to bring harmony to the kiva, but is also a teaching moment. He describes and explains each step to the participants.

On Sunday morning, the Shaman erases the patterns in the sand. Chief Joe and his family serve a traditional meal. By noon, his yard is empty where once a handful of pickup trucks and one Land Rover, Dr. Deschene's vehicle, had been.

Spencer Hansen Undercover

Father Sontag meets after the last Sunday mass with the lay leaders of the Ignatius Catholic Church. They are the trustees of the church. More important to Father Sontag, they control the money – including the pittance he is paid. He is on his best behavior and prepared with his best arguments.

This week, he rails against the unknown thieves who have twice robbed the church. The first time, they stole a gold-plated cross, a silver chalice, and a silver ciborium. He had locked up the replacements; however, an ancient monstrance containing a host was left in the church. Two weeks later, it was stolen.

"The host has been displayed in this church since its reconstruction," Father Sontag says. "There must be some way to do so without having to worry about thieves. The monstrance was of no great value except for its historical importance."

"The monstrance has been recovered, Father. Someone tried to pawn it in Tucumcari. The pawnshop operator understood its significance and accepted it as collateral for a $40 loan. He contacted us. We have reimbursed him. It will arrive here in two days. We know the identity of the thief. We will deal with him."

Father Sontag has learned to trust the men of the Lay Council. Further, he has a great deal more on his mind than the fate of a petty thief. His emolument is to be reviewed in two months, and the Lay Council has final say.

~~~~~

Johnny One-Feather roller-skates from the kitchen to cars at a drive-in in Tuba City. *How does he expect to reach the order button?* Johnny wonders. An SUV, the largest model made, has pulled into one of the bays. The menu board and speaker are two feet below the driver's window.

Not to worry. The driver's arm belongs to a gorilla, and his voice is loud enough the kitchen doesn't need the speaker system to get his order. Johnny is *at bat*, as the carhops say, and it is his turn to take the gorilla's order from the kitchen to the car.

His co-workers know Johnny well. No one is surprised when the SUV returns at shift change, a door opens, and Johnny disappears. No one wonders when Johnny doesn't show up for work the next day, or the next. It is nearly a week before anyone files a missing person report.

Johnny is one of the fortunate ones. He doesn't wake when a needle is pushed into his arm. He is still asleep when his kidneys, liver, lungs, and heart are removed. He slips from sleep to death, unaware of what was done to him.

≈≈≈≈≈

"Chief Joe got a missing person report, yesterday."

The E'e'aahjigo Kiva is meeting in the pathology lab. Tommy, also known as both TomTom and Ata'halne', is speaking. The room smells of formaldehyde and other less pleasant and less easily identified odors. "Johnny One-Feather. We followed up on the report. Johnny worked at the *Roller Rink Drive-In* in Tuba City."

"The one with the carhops on roller skates, right? I thought they only hired cute girls," Gaagii says.

"Not always. They hire good-looking carhops and Johnny was always – well, he was a rent boy, and often met his johns at the drive-in. His co-workers knew, but they all liked Johnny, and covered for him. After nearly a week, one of them reported that one day after work he got into a huge, black SUV, and hasn't been seen, since."

162

"Huge black SUV," Ahote snorts. "Could be anybody. ICE, Homeland, ATF. They're all a-holes with AK-47s, armor, and attitude. Sorry, Miss Susan."

"No apology needed, Ahote. Sometimes, a strong word is the best way to describe someone, and *a-holes* does the job, here." The young men are not all successful at suppressing their snickers. "You don't want to overdo it, however," Susan concludes. "It looses effectiveness if you do."

"Did anyone see the plates on the SUV?" Dr. Deschene asks.

"No sir, at least not according to the report."

"Then Ahote is correct, it could be anyone."

"Sir," Ahote says. "Niyol and I have been watching the prison. With binoculars, from the hills. Black SUVs arrive nearly every week. Sometimes two or more in one week. They stop at the guard posts just before reaching the concertina-wire fence. They don't spend long at the guard post before the gates open and they disappear behind the walls."

"We also see black SUVs leave the prison and head to Folio," Niyol says. "We've followed some of them to the hospital and others to the Glen Canyon Spa."

"Prisoners needing medical attention," Dr. Deschene says. "Although I'm surprised any are being sent to the spa. Must be *pro bono* work to create tax deductions – or milk Medicaid."

He asks if Ahote or Niyol have recorded license plates.

"The ones going to the prison are too far away for us to read the license plates, but we can tell they're Arizona plates … they're colorful. The ones going into Folio, we checked and they're all registered to the Arizona Department of Corrections."

No other member of the E'e'aahjigo Kiva has anything to add, and the meeting breaks up. Dr. Deschene hands each one of the young men a homework sheet, with questions about anatomy and physiology. This is part of the deception, the notion these young men -00are exploring medical careers. Not that the hospital administration is overly watchful. Still, Dr. Deschene hopes some of the boys will follow up.

~~~~~

"How would you like to do some undercover work?" Dr. Deschene's question surprises Spencer. "The spa?" Spencer asks, and frowns as he thinks of his rapport with Dr. Standart.

"Actually, no. I still have some friends at the State Medical Examiner's Office in Phoenix. If I were to call one of them I could get you there for about a week. An expansion of your in-service.

"What would I be looking for?" Spencer goes directly to the heart of the matter.

"Two things. Most important, any samples saved from Jessie Long Tree's tox tests. Second, any indication of collusion between the state ME and Homeland ... or anyone else."

"Yes, sir," Spencer says. His eyes light up at the thought of this challenge and relief that he would not have to betray Dr. Standart.

On Saturday, Susan takes Spencer shopping for clothes. "You need something besides scrubs," she says, "although you will need those, too. You'll be *hanging out*, as you say, with the techs your age. Nothing too fancy, but not torn blue jeans and that T-shirt. Where did you get it, anyway?"

Susan points to Spencer's faded green T-shirt with a stylistic fish, but with legs and the word, "Darwin" inside the outline."

"Sallie secondhand store?" Spencer says.

Susan *humphs* and pushes him toward her car.

Dr. Deschene tells Spencer what he knows about the office of the ME, the people who work there, and those who he still knows. "Mention me only to them. If the ME gets wind you're my protégé, he'll throw you out on the street."

164

On Sunday afternoon, Spencer takes a commuter plane from Folio to Phoenix, and a cab to a motel near the state office building. Monday morning, at 7:45 AM, he presents himself to a sour-faced rent-a-cop at the entrance to the building.

"Yeah? What do you want?" the guard asks. It is obvious from his five-o'clock-shadow and disheveled appearance he is night shift, and ready to get off work.

"Spencer Hansen, sir. I have an appointment with Dr. Markus in the Medical Examiner's office."

"Don't open till eight. You can sit there." The guard points to a row of plastic chairs.

Before Spencer can move away from the guard post, a young man with a nametag calls to him. "You're Spencer? I'm Kerry, autopsy tech and gofer. The ME calls me Gomer, though."

Kerry turns to the guard. "Give him a visitor's badge, please. He's with me."

"Yeah, yeah, whatever. Sign here."

"You're doing an in-service with Dr. Deschene," Kerry says as the two boys walk down a hallway of white tile and even whiter florescent lights. "That's awesome."

Spencer isn't sure how to respond.

"It's okay," Kerry tells him. "Dr. Marcus is Dr. Deschene's friend, and my supervisor. He told me to look out for you. Your secret is safe.

"He also told me you would be looking for samples left over after a tox test. I know where to look, but we can't just walk in there."

Spencer, relieved he has a possible friend, is introduced to the ME, who quickly dismisses him. Kerry takes him to meet Dr. Marcus, who outlines a schedule of autopsies and tox tests. "You'll get to see and operate some pretty impressive equipment."

On Friday, after two days of learning and using the most modern equipment available, Kerry and Spencer run tox tests on several samples sent by a coroner in Yuma. The tests are positive for opioids; the level is high enough to suggest an overdose. "We'll send samples to a lab in Denver to confirm," Kerry says. "Won't hear from them for at least a month, though, maybe more.

"Come on," Kerry adds. "We need to put the extra samples in the storeroom." His voice lowers. "And I checked the computer for Jessie Long Tree. He's there as a John Doe. Well, at least some of him is. Or was."

The room is refrigerated and the boys' breath puffs in white clouds. "Four degrees Centigrade below zero?" Spencer asks.

Kerry nods. "We don't want to stay here, long." He puts on a pair of gloves. "And don't touch anything."

Cabinets fill the store room, but they don't look like office file cabinets. The drawers are only a couple of inches high, and broken into numbered partitions. Kerry opens the pouch he carries, removes the samples, consults the labels, and puts them in the appropriate drawer. Then, he looks at a number he has written on a card and leads Spencer deeper into the room. The drawer he opens yields three vials with that number. Kerry removes them, puts them in the pouch, and hands the pouch to Spencer. "I've just broken the official chain-of-custody, which means these can never be used for criminal prosecution. My mentor believes Dr. Deschene knows what he is doing, and that's good enough for me. Just don't get caught."

Spencer looks at the labels on the vials. They all bear the initials of the ME, himself.

"They were ordered destroyed by the ME," Kerry says. "But he keeps cutting our budget. We're about ten years behind in destroying evidence. Just don't seem to get around to doing it."

166

After a long lunch of certifiably unhealthy food and several pitchers of beer shared with Kerry and a few other techs, Spencer is on a plane to Folio.

Dr. Deschene and Niyol are waiting at the Folio airport. After greeting Spencer, Dr. Deschene gives the vials to Niyol, who goes to the gate serving the next flight to Denver. "He'll deliver the vials for testing. And don't worry about chain-of-custody. That's not what we're looking for."

≈≈≈≈≈

An aura of mystery and something more, something undefinable, blankets the next meeting of the E'e'aahjigo Kiva. The boys are happy to see Susan wearing her necklace and Dr. Deschene sporting his Hopi silver belt buckle attached to an FQO belt. While "Full Quill Ostrich" is not part of their tradition, they understand its meaning to their brothers of far-away nations.

Cha'tima calls the meeting to order. "The E'e'aahjigo Kiva is assembled." Because they are in Dr. Deschene's pathology laboratory, sage smoke is not a part of the opening ceremony, although the boys recite brief chants from both the Navajo and Hopi traditions.

Niyol's report is first. "The outbreak of bacterial meningitis was not reported to the Rough Rock County Health Department. At least," he adds, "there is no record of it in their files. It was reported to the Arizona Health Department. There is a record of an email sent to them. Not who sent it, and there is no further record, anywhere. We note, that the State Medical Examiner is a senior official in the state Health Department. Our hypothesis is that the report was suppressed."

Dr. Deschene smiles at Niyol's words. He has tried to impress on these boys the difference between suspicion and hypothesis, between hypothesis and theory. Perhaps some of that has sunk in.

"Another red flag," he says. "Why did the State Medical Examiner not take action, or at least investigate?"

Cheveyo makes his report. "We identified the hikers. They are students at the community college, so I asked Spencer to go with me to question them. We told them straight-away we thought the body they'd found was a friend, but we needed to know for sure so we could conduct a chant to set his spirit at rest."

"They thought they understood our culture and knew what we meant. They thought we wanted to keep his spirit from becoming *yee naaldlooshii* – a skin-walker," Atsa says. "We didn't contradict them."

Cheveyo continues. "We spent a couple of hours talking to them. They saw what they thought were bones – maybe rib bones – about a hundred yards away from the rest of the body. They confirmed they saw no clothing and admitted they had a morbid fascination and took pictures with their cell phones. They showed us the pictures and sent us copies. I'm afraid there was nothing in them that wasn't in the coroner's report. It looks like Jessie really was savaged by animals."

Spencer reports on his visit to the state ME's office. "Two things stand out. First, the ME ordered the samples from Jessie destroyed. It is only because he is so cheap that they weren't. Second, I learned that samples sent to Denver for detailed tox tests never come back for at least a month. You know I picked up the samples, and Dr. D sent them to a lab in Denver. Oh, and the ME's initials were on the sample containers."

"That's actually three things."

"We still haven't ruled out organ harvesting," someone interjects into the silence.

"No, but it suggests we focus our energy elsewhere," Tommy says.

"Here is a place for us to focus," Cha'tima says. "Atsa and I monitored a call from someone who claimed his brother was

168

arrested in Jake's Lake – the county seat of Rough Rock County – and not heard from until a year later when they got a letter saying he had died in U.P.S. #9. I was able to get his name, but the records of the Rough Rock Sheriff and courts are not computerized. They are, however, public records. Perhaps two of you would like to spend some time searching musty, dusty, and likely almost illegible records."

The kiva agrees this will be included in their investigation. Assignments are made and accepted.

Dr. Todd Standart

Father Sontag stands in front of the sink, cleaning his privates while his acolyte on this Sunday lays out the robes they will wear.

A bit more than an hour later, he ends the service with the Dismissal, "Go and announce the Gospel of the Lord." The congregation responds, "Thanks be to God."

Seven members of the congregation are especially impatient for those last words. They are the lay leaders of the church and are anxious to meet with Father Sontag. He has asked for funds to support the Navajo orphanage but the Lay Leaders are not in favor of that. They are surprised, however, when Father Sontag asks not for money, but help to remove another bunch of rowdy young men.

"They are interfering with the charitable works you have approved," the father says.

"In what way?"

"They leech the resources of the Church. They present an unwholesome example for the youngsters," Father Sontag says.

His charge against these young men leads to only a little discussion among the Lay Councilmen.

"We will handle this, Father," the Council Chair says. "You need not concern yourself."

"Doesn't he even want to know what will happen to them?" one of the Council asks as the men walk to their cars and pickup trucks.

"No." The Council Chair says. "He has washed his hands of them saying he can not save them."

≋≋≋≋

Dr. Deschene is a most fortunate person. Five and sometimes six or seven days a week, he goes to a job he loves. He looks forward to Monday not as a return to drudgery but as a chance to explore new avenues of knowledge and to solve new mysteries. In the past months, he has become surrounded by mystery, and he relishes it.

On this Monday, he walks into his office to find the door guarded by Niyol, in uniform and armed. "Dr. D, I'm so glad you're here. Chief Joe is in your office. It was burglarized over the weekend. Your secretary called us as soon as he got here."

"Niyol! I've not seen you armed, before. You got the job?"

"Yes, sir. Chief Joe decided he needed an officer with computer skills and pushed me ahead of a lot of other applicants. I'm a rookie officer, now, not just an auxiliary. As soon as you check in with the chief, he will ask me to at look your computer for signs of tampering."

"You think that's why someone broke in?"

"Not really. Probably someone looking for drugs, but I'll take any chance to shine for the chief."

Dr. Deschene winks. "Let's see what I can do, then."

"Good morning, Joe. Looks like I missed an exciting weekend." Dr. Deschene shakes hands with Chief Joe and looks around his office. "Really trashed the place."

"Yes, and we're pretty sure they didn't find what they were looking for."

Dr. Deschene raises an eyebrow. "Oh?"

"That's one thing the television cop and CSI shows get right. If they found what they wanted, they would have stopped searching at some point. Whoever did this didn't stop until they'd ransacked or destroyed nearly everything."

"I saw Niyol outside. Can we get him in here to look over the computer?"

172

Chief Joe laughs. "He got to you, didn't he? Yes, of course, we'll bring him in, but you must not let on we know he is most anxious to impress you."

"And you," Dr. Deschene says.

After Niyol comes in, Dr. Deschene and Chief Joe accept the young man's recommendation they move Dr. D's computer to another room and hook it to the hospital's intranet just as it had been in the office. Niyol sits at the keyboard and looks at the list of user IDs and passwords Dr. D has written for him.

"Let's start with the routine – hospital records."

"Isn't it more likely something in one of my autopsy reports, or FOI requests, or … well, something, would yield more?"

"Think *The Purloined Letter*, by Edgar Allen Poe, Doctor," Niyol says, leaving Dr. Deschene and Chief Joe open-mouthed.

After an hour, during which Dr. Deschene goes to the cafeteria for high-calorie, high-caffeine drinks for Niyol, the young man asks, "Dr. D? Should your account have access to these records?"

Niyol finds, among the minutia and details of everyday cases, a set of autopsies from nearly fifteen years ago. All are on letterhead of the state ME's office; all are signed or countersigned by Dr. Nastas Deschene.

"Probably not," Dr. Deschene says. "Those autopsies were conducted when I was an assistant ME at the state medical examiner's office in Phoenix. I had a little help getting copies. I wanted to see if there might be some relevance to current events. I certainly think if my name is on them, I am entitled to see them."

"We're not judging you, Dr. D," Niyol says.

"I know," Dr. Deschene says. "But if you found this so quickly, others might, too."

"Why are these autopsies special?" Chief Joe asks.

"They are autopsies of the bodies of young, healthy Navajo, Hopi, and Apache found in the desert, desiccated and eviscerated,"

Dr. Deschene bows his head. "May all the gods of my people help us. It's happening, again."

Both Chief Joe and Niyol are afraid to ask what Dr. Deschene means, but they are both certain they understand his fears.

Dr. Deschene, Chief Joe, and Officer Niyol find both privacy and strong coffee in the back room of a coffee shop in Folio. The barista knows the rules – the room is reserved for book signings and the regular meetings of three groups of secular humanists, two writers' circles – one poetry and one prose – morning classes of ESL, and after-school classes in Navajo for kids who want to preserve their heritage. However, the calendar is empty. "Until 4:00 o'clock, Chief. Then the language classes start. Will that give you enough time?"

Chief Joe nods, accepts his coffee, and tips the barista five dollars.

When they are settled, Joe asks the burning question. "How many, and over what period of time? I was in law enforcement then. Why didn't I know?"

Dr. Deschene answers, quietly and somewhat reluctantly. "We found eighteen. There may have been more. There's no way to know. All over a period of less than two years. DNA showed them all to be of Athabasca ancestry – Navajo, Hopi, and Apache. No one outside the task force knew, and the task force was sworn to secrecy. I escaped the oath. It was a bureaucratic oversight. Still, I felt bound by the oath until now.

"The leaders of the task force were sure after the second body was found it was the work of a ritualistic, maybe Satanic, serial killer. I thought they'd been watching too much television. I assisted the ME in twelve of the autopsies, and conducted the other six, myself. If it were a serial killer, he was a surgeon. And he had help. Toxicology tests found traces of Propofol—"

174

"That's what killed that rock star," Niyol says. Chief Joe chastises the boy with a stare and a raised eyebrow. Niyol ducks his head and remains silent while Dr. Deschene continues.

"There were also traces of lidocaine, which is often used to lessen the pain of the initial propofol injection."

Niyol couldn't keep silent. "First, do no harm. Second, make it easy when you do kill them," he says.

Dr. Deschene forestalls Chief Joe's admonishment. "Yes," he says. "Exactly. The surgeon – surgical team, it would have to be – was, at least, merciful murderers.

"I proposed organ harvesting as a motive, but the ME and the head of the team were fixated on a serial killer – and the publicity they would get when they caught him. Organ harvesting was just too much for them to deal with, I guess. I was only an assistant ME, and no one was willing to listen to me.

"When the murders stopped – at least, when bodies stopped being discovered – the case was closed with a putative declaration the isolated, single, serial killer had died. Or moved. All the files were sealed."

Dr. Deschene sets down his empty coffee cup. "I got the files with the help of a friend. The only thing he could find were the autopsies. It appears no other records exist."

"And you think this same group, this same surgical team, is working again?"

"Not necessarily the same group, but the same *MO* or *modus operandi* as you say," Dr. Deschene answers Chief Joe.

Niyol asks, "Did anyone ever question why they were all *Indian?*"

"Because," Dr. Deschene replies, "we Indians are at best second class citizens. We are undesirables, especially to those who want to run oil pipelines through our sacred lands, to mine uranium and coal on the Navajo lands without paying us royalties, and to strip the trees from our sacred mountains to build ski resorts."

≈≈≈≈≈

Early on a Friday morning, Dr. Deschene accepts an envelope from a courier, and examines it. It is an expensive piece of stationary, cream, with his name written in black ink. The handwriting is impeccable. He opens the envelope and removes a folded notecard with the Cyrillic letters "ИК" embossed. The note, in the same impeccable handwriting, is an invitation to play golf with a *Gospoden Ivan Kuznetzov* on the next day at 8:00 AM at the Glen Canyon Country Club. *An 8:00 o'clock tee time on Saturday is golden. This Kuznetzov must have some connections – and a lot of money.*

Dr. Deschene does not advertise that he is a member of the club. He enjoys golf, and finds the club to have the only decent course in the area. Besides, he uses his access to sign up other members to support charities that aid Navajo children. *More money than I could have generated on my own*, he thinks. *A good ROI – return on investment.* He chuckles. *Wonder if this Kuznetzov will be good for a donation.*

The next morning, Deschene arrives at the club a few minutes before 8:00 AM. The pro introduces him to Kuznetzov, but not the two other members of the foursome. Their golf cart has no clubs. *Bodyguards*, Deschene thinks. *He's either very important, or thinks he is.*

The game is perfunctory. Dr. Deschene has had little time to play recently, and his game is off. He's lucky to achieve par for the course. Mr. Kuznetzov, his host, is five strokes under par at the end of the game.

"Well played," Kuznetzov says. "Will you be my guest at lunch?

176

He wants something more than a game of golf, and he still hasn't said how he knows me. I think I need more information, Deschene thinks. "Thank you, lunch would be very welcome after the energy I spent chasing balls into the rough."

Kuznetzov laughs. Deschene echoes the laugh. *Who is fooling whom?* Deschene wonders as he accompanies Kuznetzov to the dining room.

The camaraderie of the golf course evaporates at the table.

"Dr. Deschene, I understand you have been troubled by some unusual autopsies," Kuznetzov says after tasting his gumbo.

"My reaction, even the fact I conduct a particular autopsy, is not a matter of public record," Deschene says. All his senses go on alert. *Someone at the state ME's office leaked? No, only my friend and I knew. Niyol was concerned about the autopsies on my office computer? Is that how this man know about them?*

"No, no! Of course not. But there are reporters, paparazzi, even here in Folio. One autopsy, the young pregnant woman, made national headlines."

"That is true," Dr. Deschene says. "But I give the tabloids no more credibility than they deserve, which is often none. I trust there is more to your invitation than following up on gossip and rumors."

Kuznetzov understands he will get no further with Dr. Deschene and tries to salvage what he can from the meeting. "Certainly not. I am, however, fascinated by the American press … the freedom given to the tabloids to print stories that are at best gross exaggerations of the truth."

No matter how hard he tries and no matter how he approaches the subject, Kuznetzov is unable to delve into Dr. Deschene's mind.

Have I met an honest man? Is he a dangerous adversary? Kuznetzov wonders, and decides to ask Carlotta for a special reading.

That afternoon, Kuznetzov summons Carlotta. "The *Dancing Bear* hacker team found several autopsies on the computers of the hospital where Dr. Nastas Deschene is pathologist. They were autopsies of – as the ally put it – young people who had sacrificed themselves so others might live. Dr. Deschene refused to discuss the matter, even to admit to any interest. Is he too honest to deal with?"

Deal with? You mean, subvert. Chance remarks overheard come together in Carlotta's mind, although she attributes the thought to her prescience. She hands Kuznetzov the full deck to shuffle, and then deals the Celtic Cross.

One after the other, the cards reveal Kuznetzov is facing a powerful adversary, and warn against pursuing him.

Kuznetzov greets the reading with mixed emotions. While he regrets the loss of a possible ally, he appreciates the warning not to reveal too much to Deschene.

~~~~~

Kuznetzov has calmed considerably since the debacle with the container of Nicaraguans. The second container and the refund have arrived. The refund is delivered to Kuznetzov's suite at the Overlook Resort in person and in cash by a nephew of the Nicaraguan boss. Kuznetzov appreciates the gesture and relishes the young man's obvious fear. He also remembers Carlotta's prediction he would find a new ally and must focus that alliance on more than money. "Tell your uncle I accept his gift, and invite him to visit me, sometime. He should bring you on that visit."

The young man stutters his thanks. Kuznetzov smells the stink of the boy's fear.

Kuznetzov stands. The young man shrinks back, then finds his courage and stands tall.

Kuznetzov extends his hand. "Take my hand." The boy does. His palm is moist, but his grip is firm.

178

"Hector, I feel your fear. I watch you fight it and win. I respect you for that. As long as you and your family meet your obligations, you and they are safe."

Kuznetzov picks up the briefcase of money and hands it to the young man.

"Give this and my assurance of friendship to your uncle, and remind him we have opportunity to achieve a great deal more than this."

Hector understands. Kuznetzov has placed him and his uncle under an obligation. He nods and thanks *Gospoden Kraznachey*. And another puzzle piece falls into place.

As soon as the young man departs, Kuznetzov summons Carlotta.

The Nicaraguans, she realizes after the reading. *This was about the shipping container that was in the news a few months ago. He denied it, but he is bringing in prostitutes, including children. The dream – the women and children begging me, dragging me to my death – they were from that awful container. He is responsible. Children! I didn't know. My gods protect me, but I didn't know! Am I powerless, or is there something I can do?*

Her thoughts are interrupted when Kuznetzov does not cross her palm with silver, the usual signal that he has finished with her. Carlotta dares to ask, "Is there more, *Gospoden?*"

"Yes. I will play golf with Dr. Standart tomorrow. We will be alone and isolated, for much of the game. I wish to know how to proceed."

Carlotta hands him the full deck and watches as he shuffles.

She then deals the cards in the Celtic Cross.

The cards' meaning is not unusual, until Carlotta reaches the eighth card, in the "What You Need to Know" position. It is *The Hanged Man*.

"That card seems to be turning up too often," Kuznetsov grouses.

"You see it as a harbinger of evil," Carlotta says. "You are wrong, *Gospoden*. I hesitate to say this for I fear your anger."

Kuznetsov leans forward in his chair. "Do not fear me, Carlotta. Do not fear my anger. Continue."

"The most important meaning of this card in this position is to urge caution. Some of those you encounter soon will be allies, reluctant, but loyal. Others may become traitors. You must use all your resources to separate the two."

"My greatest enemy at the moment is Dr. Standart. He resists my proposals – and my control of his operation. He resists what he sees as an incursion into his secure little world. But, he has no idea of the danger he would face if the American-Italian Mafia or the FBI get wind of what he is doing."

"That, then, is your approach," Carlotta says.

"The cards say this?"

"No, *Gospoden*, I see this."

The golf game between Kuznetsov and Standart is predictable. Kuznetsov watches as Standart ensures Kuznetsov will win the game. Kuznetsov's attempts to get Standart to suggest an approach to Dr. Deschene yield nothing. Still, Kuznetsov's win over Standart continues to cement the dominant-submissive nature of their relationship, and a reluctant Todd Standart picks up their lunch check.

≈≈≈≈≈

Thurmond snorts when he sees the four tourists waiting for their helicopter tour. They are all wearing designer *safari* clothing, including hats that would have embarrassed Teddy Roosevelt, and have cameras with telephoto lenses or binoculars slung around their necks. One is talking on her cell phone; another is texting.

Won't get a signal in the canyon, Thurmond thinks. *Wonder what they'll do then? They pay the bills, though, and running a Bell 206B helicopter makes a lot of bills.*

Thurmond lucked into the purchase of the helicopter. The original owner had defaulted on his loan. The bank was eager to dump it, and Thurmond has a friend at the bank. Instead of the one-million-plus purchase price, Thurmond got the craft for less than three hundred thousand dollars. His monthly payments are pretty steep, but there are a lot of tourists too lazy to hike down the canyon, too afraid to raft down the rapids, and too rich to do anything they don't want to do.

Thurmond makes most of his income at night, flying nap-of-the-earth to avoid radar. Flying to a set of GPS coordinates, always different. Finding men who speak Spanish among themselves and who load Thurmond's helicopter with sealed boxes which he delivers to a twenty-wide trailer at another set of GPS coordinates where he is met by men with heavily accented English. *Something Eastern European,* Thurmond thinks. He's carried tourists from all over the world, speaks Spanish and Navajo, and thinks he has an ear for accents.

Life is good until Thurmond's night-flight customer brings a visitor to the airport. Thurmond recognizes power when he sees it. The man wears a business suit that cost more than Thurmond nets in six months. Dark, but still gray and not black. *Probably a wool-silk blend,* Thurmond thinks, and remembers from his childhood the Biblical admonishment not to wear garments of two different materials. He smiles inwardly. There's no doubt this man's sins are far greater than that.

Four others follow the man. Thurmond is certain they are armed bodyguards, and is surprised when the man dismisses them and Thurmond's contact. The man and Thurmond are alone in the pilots' ready room of the Folio Municipal Airport.

"Thurmond, you may call me *Gospoden Kraznachey*. The Russian translates to *Mister Paymaster*, and I am the paymaster for your frequent night flights. You know, of course, their purpose."

Thurmond can read faces as well as a trained Athabascan can read tracks in the desert, and answers quickly. "Yes, *Gospoden*, moving drugs from delivery points to the place they are adulterated and repackaged for distribution."

The Russian nods. "I have more work for you, specifically transporting prisoners from various prisons to the unit across the river from Folio. You will continue to provide hair-raising flights through the canyon for tourists. It will provide a legitimate cover. I see questions and doubt in your eyes. Understand, you have no choice. Evidence of your *night flights* to the trailer has been collected and could be provided to the Drug Enforcement Agency at any moment. It would not be difficult for me to acquire another trailer – or another helicopter. You are being offered an important place in a very lucrative business, and you already know I am a generous paymaster."

Thurmond needs no time at all to consider the offer – and the clear threat. "I understand, *Gospoden*. I am surprised the kingpin of the operation meets with me, today."

The Russian leans back in his chair and laughs. "Komerade Thurmond, I am not a fool. Neither are you. You just proved that. You will be very close to the center of our operation, and you will easily comprehend what the operation is. I would rather you enter with your eyes, how you say, *wide open*."

Thurmond nods and the Russian describes the operation. "Certain prisoners from throughout the prison system are kept isolated until they can be screened for diseases, including the Human Immunodeficiency Virus and the Hanta and Zika viruses.

"Those who are clear of disease are moved to Prison Number Nine, nearby. They are kept in isolation until offered an opportunity to participate in medical research or, in some cases, an opportunity to donate a kidney for transplant. Occasionally, I will need a swift transfer from another Arizona prison to Unit Nine."

Thurmond understands some of these prisoners will donate more than a single kidney, and will die. He is smart enough to say nothing of this, however.

"I understand, *Gospoden*. And I thank you for your confidence in me."

Kuznetzov smiles. *No fool like an old fool,* he thinks.

~~~~~

Karl Hilflinger, owner and operator of the Peaceful Rest Mortuary and Crematorium, stares at the numbers on his spreadsheet. Each cremation requires about 100 mega-joules of energy, or about 100 cubic feet of natural gas. That's average, and those figures are from years ago. His legitimate clients are often what Henry Belka describes as porkers – people much too heavy for their height, and therefore more expensive to burn. The infestation of fast-food outlets in the Four Corners area opened the door to obesity, high blood pressure, cancers, and other environmental ailments. Hilflinger's other clients, much more numerous, have no internal organs or blood, and therefore require less natural gas. *I wonder if anyone can figure this out from the gas bill*, he thinks. He pushes this thought aside to look at the total number of cremations. *These numbers cannot be hidden from inspectors*, he determines. *There are too many for a town this size, despite our contract with the prison.*

Another thought arises to trouble him. The refractory bricks that line the oven – the crematory retort – should endure through more than 2,000 cremations. Questions would be raised if he had to replace them sooner than scheduled. His paymaster demands the near-total destruction of remains by cremation. That niggles at the edges of his thoughts. He sits, paralyzed with indecision, until the fire alarm sounds.

183

Hilflinger glances at the fire control panel on his way down the hall. *The crematory. What has Henry done, now?*

When the fire department arrives, Henry takes them to the room housing the cremation oven. There is no fire, Henry explains to the firefighters, the police officers who responded, and to Hilflinger. "The retort. Lined with refractory bricks. They crack. Usually, the inside layer will expand with heat and seal the cracks. That's normal.

"Somethin' happened. Probably a couple of bricks on the inside fell from the side wall. The next layer must have been cracked, too. We're running more than 1,800 degrees in there. The fire broke through the last insulation and the outer wall and set off the fire alarms. I shut off the gas, and the fire went out. It's still too hot to open but you can see through the periport." The firefighters and police officers are not interested in that, however.

When the first responders have left, and the oven is cool enough, the door is opened. Henry's prediction is correct. A pile of refractory brick lies atop the half-disintegrated corpse.

"The bricks are supposed to last through maybe 2,000 cremations. What happened?" Hilflinger demands.

You bought the cheap bricks. You had them installed by the lowest bidder – some guy who runs a garage and builds fireplaces in fancy homes as a sideline, Henry thinks. "Don't know, boss. Flaw in the bricks, maybe."

"What are we going to do, Henry? I can't just go to Amazon dot com and order a new retort."

"Not just the retort, boss," Henry says. "The whole thing. The fire blew through the control circuits."

Hilflinger pales. "You're talking more than two hundred thousand dollars, and at least a month, maybe two. We can send this one…" he gestures to the retort, "… or what's left of it, to a company in Flagstaff to finish up. We can send our regular clients there, too. But we can't send the special clients. And we can't turn them away, either."

Hilflinger thinks hard. "Henry, the number of cremations we conduct cannot be justified by the number of clients we receive from our public operation. Not even by the legitimate bodies we get from the prison. Frankly, Henry, I fear we are being used as a cut-out between the spa and the law."

Henry's face is immobile. He sussed this a long time ago, and wondered when his boss would figure it out – or admit it to Henry.

Hilflinger waits until he realizes Henry will not speak. "Henry, I want to bring you in as a full partner in the … off-books activities of this mortuary. It will be an expansion of the extra duties I have paid you for. From today, if you agree, you will receive half of the net income from these activities. You must, however, agree to complete secrecy. And, your duties will consist of the complete disposition of, shall I say, *special* bodies by some means other than cremation."

Henry understands. He may be poorly educated, but he's not stupid. He knows Hilflinger can keep secret the payments he receives, and even if Henry had access to the mortuary's financial records he would never understand them.

Henry sets the terms. "I can't be driving home with body bags in my car. I can't be ridin' out with a body bag slung over a horse. But, there is a way."

Hilflinger is impatient. "Well? What is it?"

"Thurmond's helicopter."

"Thurmond? Who is he? And why should we trust him?"

"Thurmond runs one of them *See the Canyon from the Air* helicopter tours. He flies all over, though, showing 'em the desert, the mountains, and such."

"Can we trust him? Why?"

"Thurmond and I go way back. And, he knows I know he sometimes carries things that ain't on the manifest."

185

"Smuggler?"

"You could say that. You could say drugs or illegal immigrants. I'm not sayin' though. And he bought a really expensive helicopter. He'll be needing money."

"Henry, I think we need to recruit your friend, Thurmond. How much do you think he would want per flight?"

Henry and Hilflinger negotiate a deal. Henry will recruit Thurmond and pay him from Henry's share of the cash. After preparing for shipment what's left in the now-cool cremation oven, Henry drives to the airport.

"Yá'át'ééh, Thurmond."

"Yá'át'ééh, yourself, you dumb Injun. Where you been keeping yourself?"

Henry describes his job at the mortuary. "Mostly just watching the machinery, 'cept when something goes wrong."

"Got enough dead uns to keep you busy?"

"Too busy." Henry tells of bodies picked up at the spa. "I'm the one gets to take them out of the body bag and put them in a cardboard coffin to go into the oven. And I can see they all been operated on. I may be a dumb Injun but I can tell they've had things cut out of 'em – sometimes, they don't even sew them back up. At least, they bleed 'em out before I get 'em."

Thurmond is quick to understand. "The spa is doing organ transplants."

"Yeah, and they're using prisoners' organs."

"How do you know?"

"Prison tattoos, mostly." Henry doesn't have to say how he recognizes prison tattoos; Thurmond knows Henry's history as well as Henry knows Thurmond's.

Henry and Thurmond agree. Henry will pick up bodies at the spa and deliver them in body bags to Thurmond who will dump them from the bags somewhere over desolate territory.

186

"I know just the place," Thurmond says. "There's a ravine I sometimes fly over. It's narrow and deep. It runs east-west and it's dark even when the sun is straight up. Coyote and Raven can reach the bodies, but no human will ever climb down." Thurmond does not think it necessary to tell Henry about a twenty-wide trailer some two miles east of the ravine, a trailer that is one of Thurmond's regular stops.

The next morning, Henry explains the plan to his boss. Hilflinger agrees, and is able to conceal his smile. *Good. Henry is asking much less than I had expected. He is aptly named,* Squirrel, *but he has no idea of the nuts I'm storing for the winter.*

Hok'ee

Eight weeks after the samples from the drawers of the state ME's office reach Denver, Dr. Deschene receives the analysis. The analysis not only provides Jessie's DNA, but also shows the samples from Jessie's body have traces of two different anesthetics. "That supports the hypothesis of organ harvesting. Now," Dr. Deschene says. "Now, we need DNA samples from Jessie's family."

It is not easy to get those samples. Had Dr. Deschene not been Navajo, and had Chief Joseph not sent Niyol with him, Jessie's aged parents would not have cooperated. Spencer does the analysis in Dr. Deschene's laboratory using the "128-banger electrophoresis DNA sequencer" Spencer had convinced the doctor to buy. The results sadden the kiva. They confirm the body is Jessie.

"Even though the first samples were tested by the ME, himself, we have no link, no proof of organ harvesting. Still, it was a worthwhile exercise," Dr. Deschene says.

"Yes, sir," Spencer says. "And I've found some more really neat equipment you need for your lab. Don't worry, it's not expensive."

≈≈≈≈≈

Johnny Two Horses and Sam Little Crow's perch on the bluffs overlooking the Folio airport allows them to follow ambulances moving toward the Glen Canyon Spa, but it does not let them see the black SUVs that move from the south and west toward the prison. Johnny and Sam's focus is aircraft. After all, that had been their careers. Had they seen any of Thurmond's landings at the prison, they would have been interested, but they could not see U.P.S #9, across the river.

Johnny is monitoring the scanner. "Hey, lookee lookee, the little Cessna … a student pilot about to solo."

"Didn't your nephew get a private pilot's license?" Sam asks.

"Nah, he was working on it, but he got kicked out of the church scout troop – and my sister disfranchised him, or whatever it is they do."

"Disfellowshipped," Sam says. "You mean, she kicked him out of the family?"

"Yeah, the men who run the church, they made her do it. Dragged him in front of the Bishop and Stake President and made her say the words. She still keeps in touch with him, though."

"Johnny Two Horses, you are his maternal uncle. You owe him something more than a card on his birthday."

Sam's words bring back lessons Johnny learned as a teen, before he joined the Air Force.

"Sam, you're right, but I wouldn't know what to do, or how."

"Can I help?" Sam asks.

Johnny has sunk back into his lawn chair. "I don't know, Sam. I just don't know."

"Call your sister," Sam says.

The call to Johnny's sister is awkward, but she relents and gives Johnny the phone number of one of her son's friends. A few calls later, Johnny is able to speak to Hok'ee. The call is not what Johnny expected. The boy insists one of his friends be with him when he meets Johnny at the diner in Tuba City.

~~~~~

At midafternoon a week later, Johnny enters the diner. There are only two other customers – a teen and an older boy, a white-haired Bilagáana.

"Yá'át'ééh, nephew. I see my sister's eyes in you," Johnny says as he sits.

"Yá'át'ééh, brother of my mother," the younger boy says. The man's gut tightens, but he understands why the boy does not call him *uncle*.

"I know you as Tahoma," Johnny says. "Have you gone on spirit quest? Do you have another name?"

"I have and I do," Hok'ee says. "But that name is only for my kiva."

Johnny's stomach drops to his feet. His face becomes pale. Then, he pulls a knife from the top of a boot and draws it across his palm. Blood pools in his hand as he says, "Tahoma, by my blood I acknowledge I have failed you. By my blood, I promise to overcome that. Will you let me be your uncle?"

Tahoma, also known as Hok'ee, *Abandoned*, watches his uncle's blood drip onto the table. He grasps the man's hand and presses their palms together. "Yes, Uncle – *Adá'í Bidziil* – yes."

The waitress at the diner is an older woman who seems to understand. What happened at her table is more important than her tip. Without being asked, she cleans up the blood. Then, she brings a bandage, tape, and three Navajo Tacos.

"These are the only part of the tradition that can be offered here, but…" She pauses. "My grandfather was a Shaman, and he taught me many things, including some not usually open to women."

She smiles. "I am glad to see that here, today."

≈≈≈≈≈

Carlotta surveys her suite at the Overlook Resort. She is pleased Kuznetzov seems to need her and includes her in his plans. However, he has not called her to his room for more than a week. *What is he hiding? Does he suspect I know …* Her mind refuses to acknowledge the things that frighten her.

When she learns Kuznetzov will be on the golf course most of Wednesday, she decides to make time for herself. She visits the tourist destinations in Folio, shops at Navajo jewelry dealers, and visits a few pawnshops offering old pawn.

Carlotta has given up finding something genuine that does not have a history of poverty when she enters a coffee shop. Her senses are alert. She realizes this is the first place she has visited today that has neither the logo of a national chain nor a miasma of greed. Carlotta orders a latte and a pastry, and looks around for a place to sit.

It is late morning, and people hoping to get energy from caffeine and sugar to carry themselves through the day fill the place. Only one table is not full of fast-talking young people. Carlotta looks at that table, sees a woman her own age, and signals the barista. "I'll be over there," she says, and adds a ten-dollar tip. The barista nods. "I'll bring it."

"Hello," Carlotta says. "May I join you?" She gestures to the other tables, filled with people and spirited conversation. "I don't think I would fit in."

"Yes," Susan says. "Please do. I'm Susan Calvin."

Carlotta's schooled reaction is muted, but she knows immediately who Susan is. *The woman who wrote the story.*

"Thank you. I am Carlotta Krafft. Am I correct in thinking you are the Susan Calvin who writes for the *Washington Banner?"*

Susan looks at Carlotta and decides. *She isn't a groupie looking for someone famous with whom to rub elbows.* "Yes, I'm that Susan, although I no longer work for the *Banner*."

Susan is pleased Carlotta doesn't question her firing from the *Banner*. She is more interested in Susan's opinions about the history and the culture of the Four Corners. "I am Romany – what many call Gypsy," Carlotta says. "My people are nomadic, like many of the peoples of this area were before being herded into reservations. We were similarly persecuted."

192

When they have exhausted their drinks and conversation, Susan gives Carlotta a business card. She crosses out the email address tied to the newspaper and writes a new address on the back. "The phone number is still good. Perhaps we can get together another day."

~~~~~

Chief Joe and Niyol study a map that covers one wall of the chief's office. The map displays the Navajo Nation and much of the surrounding states and holds stickpins representing crimes. Red are violent deaths; green are assaults; blue are crimes against property. Computers can display the same information more rapidly and precisely, but Chief Joe used his map for years before computers, and likes the breadth of its display. Recently, he has added both yellow pins to represent bodies found eviscerated and white pins to show reports of missing young people.

"What do you see?" the chief asks Niyol.

"The white pin at Jake's Lake. The boy arrested there?"

"Yes," Joe replies.

Niyol knows why that boy is included. Ahiga and Ahote spent a week in Jake's Lake. They claimed to be pre-law students at the community college and had a letter from the provost confirming that. What they found was disturbing. Benny Little Cloud was arrested and appeared in the county court. He was found guilty of both disorderly conduct and assaulting a police officer. The public defender who handled thirty cases on that day had no record of him. The court records are sparse and there is no record of him at the sheriff's department.

"White pins in Gallup. They cluster around the Sallie and the bus station. Not all those kids caught a bus. Someone's taking them."

"You see that. Good." The chief stares at the map. "What about that cluster around Tuba City?"

"The diner is a hangout. So is the drive-in where Johnny One-Feather worked. Homeless kids, panhandling. Someone's taking them."

"Same someone?"

"I don't think so. Too far apart. Gallup is the Tonaleah gang's territory; Tuba City, the Moenkopi gang's territory. They don't mix."

"How do you know about the gangs?"

"Everyone knows it – everyone who is the right age and poor."

"Do the gangs have anything to do with the missing people?"

"When I was six or seven, I heard stories. Older kids, not in the gangs, stories of body snatchers and skin walkers. I thought it was just to scare the youngsters."

Niyol and Chief Joe remember what Dr. Deschene had said: *It's happening, again.*

"We need to find out more about the bodies Dr. Deschene autopsied fifteen years ago. Do you suppose you can find any more records of the task force?" Chief Joe knows he is asking Niyol to skirt the law, perhaps to break it. "It would take too long to go through official channels, even with a court order which might be hard to get. An official request would also give someone time to destroy records."

"I understand, sir. And Dr. D said since he had performed the autopsies he has a right to see them. I believe he has a right to see the rest of the records since he was a member of the task force."

~~~~~

Hok'ee calls and asks Spencer to meet him and his uncle near the Folio airport at one of the many fast-food joints that infest the Res. Spencer is puzzled, but agrees.

194

"Yá'át'ééh," Spencer greets Hok'ee and Johnny.

"Yá'át'ééh," Hok'ee says. He launches into the reason for this meeting. "Spencer, my uncle knows something we need to know."

Spencer understands *we* means the members of the E'e'aahjigo Kiva.

"Uncle Johnny and his friend, Sam, have nothing better to do than watch air traffic at the Folio airport," Hok'ee begins, and then giggles. "I do not say this to criticize them. They both served honorably and retired from the Air Force. Uncle Johnny is a Chief Master Sergeant. His friend, Sam, is a Senior Master Sergeant. They found something that may be of interest."

Hok'ee describes the frequent flights of teams of people with ice chests and fast planes. "Uncle Johnny and Sam keep a log of all the planes they see at the airport, including these."

"I've seen stuff like this on TV," Johnny says. "They're organ harvesters. Those ice chests hold organs. And it's suspicious."

"How do you mean?" Spencer asks Johnny.

"There are too many of them. Way too many."

≈≈≈≈≈

Before Hok'ee or Spencer can get this information to Chief Joe, the Drug Enforcement Administration and Homeland Security invite the chief to a meeting. Homeland pushes its authority on everyone and chairs the meeting. "We have information that drugs brought in from Mexico are being transshipped from Phoenix to the Four Corners area where they are broken up and sent to low-level distributors. We think we know where they are being broken up." He points on the map to a spot in Navajo territory east of Kaibito.

Then, he projects an aerial photograph. "This was taken just two nights ago by a NASA U-2 using a multispectral camera." The photo shows a trailer, larger than most on the reservation, with a helicopter parked beside it. A handful of SUVs and pickup trucks are parked haphazardly around the trailer.

"We believe this is the place where distribution throughout the Four Corners area begins. We will raid it as soon as we determine the helicopter is back."

Helicopter. He wants the helicopter. Probably worth more by itself than all the pickups parked around the trailer, Chief Joe thinks. *The raid is more about property seizure than crime.*

≈≈≈≈≈

Auxiliary Navajo Police Officer Kyle Running Deer's supper is interrupted when another aux officer pounds on his door.

"Time to rock 'n' roll," the man says. "Suit up and bring your dog. DEA's got a raid, and we can get in on the action."

"She's a cadaver dog, not a drug sniffer."

"Doesn't matter. If we recover money or vehicles, we get a cut based on the number of people we have on the task force. Come on, let's go."

From Kyle's perspective, the raid is a non-starter. As an unarmed auxiliary officer, he is not part of the action, but finds a place in the command center monitoring radios. Kyle's dog is antsy. At dawn, Homeland declares the all clear. Kyle checks with Chief Joe and takes the dog for a run in the desert. They've not gone more than a hundred yards before the dog takes off, barking and howling.

She's found something, Kyle thinks. He runs behind the dog. His breathing is not yet labored when he reports through the radio. "Aux Officer Running Deer. My dog's found something," he says.

"More drugs?"

"No, she's a cadaver dog. Maybe a dead coyote or something. She's stopped running. Not a coyote. That's her body-bark."

"Location?" Chief Joe's voice comes over the radio.

196

"Two miles due west of the command post," Kyle says after checking his watch. *Twenty minutes. A little much for two miles, but…*

Kyle's dog stops at the edge of a ravine. Kyle lies on his stomach, his head over the edge. The smell is obvious even to his nose. "Death," Kyle turns his head and says to his dog. "No smell quite like it." A quiet bark confirms Kyle's assessment.

He shines his tactical flashlight into the darkness of the ravine. Then, he triggers his radio.

"There's a body down here. Maybe more."

Manaba Begaye

Within an hour, the police command post has moved closer to the ravine. Chief Joe demands Homeland stand down and takes control of the scene. "You have concurrent jurisdiction in some instances," he says. "But you are not in charge."

The head of the Homeland team grumbles. He's always been able to force locals to follow his orders and is unaccustomed to any resistance. He thinks about calling Washington for a warrant or reinforcements, but realizes he has little to justify either, and his superiors would see his request as weakness on his part.

It is dawn before the first team is ready to rappel into the ravine. Kyle insists on being a member. "My dog found this."

"But what did she find?"

Had the team been a few days later, the heat and low humidity of the high desert might have mummified the newest body, and there would be no smell for the dog to detect. However, the body is fresh. It is a young woman. She is lying face down on top of at least three other bodies. There are others, scattered along the bottom of the ravine. By noon, the team finds forty more bodies in the ravine. They put the young woman in a body bag, which is lifted to the top of the ravine. By this time, the senior Homeland officer, who still hopes to horn in, has called the Arizona State Medical Examiner. The State ME shows up in a helicopter just after noon.

"Wave that helo off!" Chief Joe yells. Two officers who understand what he means cross their arms over their heads, back and forth. Ignoring the signals, the pilot lands beside the ravine, and blows dust and sand into the air to settle on the plateau and in the ravine.

"Tell the pilot to shut down and stay shut down, and don't take *no* for an answer," Joe orders an officer. "Cuff him if you have to. And you," he speaks to another, "bring the passengers here before they do any more damage."

The State ME thinks he is being honored by the escort until he faces Chief Joe. Joe pulls no punches. "Your pilot landed only yards from a crime scene and blew dust into the ravine from which we are retrieving bodies. You may have destroyed or damaged evidence. Why are you here, anyway?"

"To take charge of this investigation."

"Not in your wildest imagination," Chief Joe says. "You are on the territory of the Navajo Nation – and not even in Arizona. Neither you nor your friend in Homeland is in charge. In fact, you are trespassing. I will have someone drive you to Kaibito. You won't get a cell signal there, but there's a payphone at the gas station. You can have someone pick you up."

"My helicopter ... " the ME says before wilting under the chief's gaze.

"Your helicopter has done enough damage. I will allow it to leave after we have finished with the crime scene."

The State ME sputters. Then he catches sight of Dr. Deschene. His eyes and mouth open wide. "Deschene! What are you doing here?"

Dr. Deschene's manner is decidedly cold. "Assisting in the investigation," he says.

"You're not an ME anymore," the State ME says.

Deschene laughs. "I am, however, assistant coroner for the Navajo Nation. And I am one of only one hundred-twenty certified forensic anthropologists in America."

"I know all about you," the State ME is livid and almost frothing. "You work at some community hospital. You have no credentials—"

200

"The *regional* hospital is within the Navajo Nation, *Doctor*," Deschene says. "Now, I understand this police officer will take you to the gas station at Kaibito from which you can call for a ride. Enjoy the trip."

One of the Navajo officers gestures Chief Joe to him. The officer points to two parallel scratches in the rock. "These were made by just a little forward motion when the helicopter landed just now," the officer says. "When the rotor wash blew away dust and sand, it uncovered a score of similar marks."

"What does this tell you," Joe asks.

"The bodies in the ravine were – may have been – brought here by helicopter."

"Good work. You will supervise the CSI team. I want every inch of the helicopter at the trailer checked not just for drugs, but for traces of blood and for any evidence it carried the bodies. And measure its skids. Full crime-scene protocol."

"Yes, Chief."

≈≈≈≈≈

"Chief, there's something odd about this," Dr. Deschene says to his friend two evenings later. "Why did Homeland call the State ME when you had declared this to be your crime scene and your case?"

"He hoped the State ME could get in the act where Homeland couldn't," Chief Joe says.

"No, the Homeland guy is a jerk, but he's not an idiot."

"Cover up, then," Joe says. "You think there's a link between Homeland and the State ME." It is not a question.

"Kót'é – it is so."

≈≈≈≈≈

After only a brief look at the bodies retrieved from the ravine, Chief Joe asks Dr. Deschene to perform all the forensic autopsies. "You saw," Joe says. "All eviscerated, and not by animals. Coyote couldn't get into the ravine. Raven, perhaps. Spider, perhaps. But not Coyote."

The young woman whose body was atop the carnage in the ravine is identified as a teacher at the Navajo college in Tsaile – and the daughter of a member of the Nation's Council. How she arrived in a ravine 150 road-miles away from the college is only part of the mystery. How she died is the second part.

Dr. Deschene greets the Chief when he arrives at the pathology lab. "I hear you got a call from the State ME and chewed him out, again. What's the story, there? It's more than blowing dust over an already dusty crime scene."

Chief Joe knows Nastas Deschene still has friends at the state ME's office. His voice holds no humor when he answers. "I do not trust him to be thorough or honest. He's a political appointee who gave up his license to practice medicine to escape charges of performing unnecessary surgery and overbilling both US Medicaid and the Navajo Nation's Health Program."

Dr. Deschene gestures to the autopsy table and then nods to Spencer and Chuchip, who remove the sheet covering the young woman's body. Joe leaves the laboratory for the observation room.

"There's already gossip about this," Susan Calvin says to Joe when she walks into the observation room. "Is there anything I can do to help?"

Chief Joe agrees a simple, unadorned article in the Farmington newspaper might calm the gossip that has begun, despite his attempts to keep this secret. He and Susan sit in the observation room and discuss the article while Dr. Deschene, Spencer, and Chuchip begin the autopsy.

Dr. Deschene addresses the microphone hanging over the autopsy table.

"This is the body of a young woman who has been identified as Manaba Begaye, age 24. The body was eviscerated, missing all thoracic and abdominal organs. The body was found face down. Eyes, lips, tongue, and external genitalia are not damaged, ruling out the likelihood the evisceration was due to animal activity. There is clear evidence of surgical intervention including marks on the ribs consistent with Finochietto chest retractors and bone cutters.

"The proximate cause of death cannot be determined; however, no one could live without the missing organs. Further, the body was completely exsanguinated."

Dr. Deschene takes samples of hair, skin, and flesh for toxicology.

When the autopsy is complete, Dr. Deschene asks Joe, "Has the family been notified?"

"Yes. They ask the body be taken to the nearest crematorium. That is Peaceful Rest. I'll call them to arrange pickup."

Henry Belka is surprised to see a body he thought he'd disposed of. He has heard about the discovery of the body of a popular teacher who was daughter of a Tribal Council member, but the circumstances are still closely held.

~~~~~

Manaba Begaye's family wants to put her ashes in a columbarium at the Window Rock cemetery. The TV station in Farmington sends a remote van and sets up outside the monument. Chief Joe keeps them from bothering people at the funeral, but the press tracks people to their homes.

By this time, news the Navajo Police recovered forty bodies, has been leaked.

The kiva assembles in Dr. Deschene's office. "Why is there so much hoopla about her, and not about the other bodies?" Susan asks.

"It's people's attitude – *Only the poor are murdered.* It's an old Navajo saying. Actually, it's a new Navajo saying," one of the young men answers.

"No it's not … not a Navajo saying, that is. But it's the way a lot of people think," another says.

"Everyone knows she was murdered. The family released the autopsy report. It was clear her organs had been harvested. Susan got an exclusive interview and it's gone viral," Atsa says.

"Here's a real Navajo saying. *If you want more pinyon pine nuts, shake the tree,"* Chief Joe says. "I think we've shaken the tree."

It takes only a few more autopsies before what falls from the pinyon tree is revealed. Dr. Deschene works quickly but is thorough. With help from Spencer, Chuchip, and the four pathology techs, Dr. Deschene can conduct two autopsies simultaneously. It's more than wanting information; the hospital has only ten drawers to hold the remaining bodies.

Eight days after he began, Dr. Deschene, the rest of the E'e'aahjigo Kiva, the techs, and several officers meet in Chief Joe's conference room.

"In brief," Dr. Deschene begins, "All bore evidence of surgical intervention and were missing all or most thoracic and abdominal organs. Some had veins stripped from their legs. All were exsanguinated.

"Thirty four of the male bodies had prison tattoos. I find that to be remarkable; a red flag.

"This bears the mark of an extremely thorough and well organized organ harvesting operation."

"Why would such an organization be so sloppy disposing the bodies?" Susan asks.

Ata'halne' breaks the long silence. "Subcontractor," he says. He looks around the room. "It makes sense. If it's a big operation, it's broken down into specialties. Reapers, handlers, surgeons, distribution, disposal crew."

"A good point," Susan says. "Keep it in mind. Can you tell us anything from the crime scene investigation?" She asks.

"What I will say is off the record. None of you must speak of it. Agreed?" Joe looks for nods from everyone. "Ms. Calvin, please get with me, after, and I'll tell you what the public has a need to know – and what we might learn from the public."

Joe then uses the HDTV to illustrate his points.

"The helicopter at the trailer is the one Thurmond uses for tours of the canyon. And a lot of drug running. The CSI team found enough cocaine in cracks and crevices to charge him with possession with intent to distribute.

"They also found traces of blood. It is probably not enough to do any sort of analysis. It does allow me to hold the helicopter which the Homeland chief is anxious to sell as forfeited property. He's going to be disappointed, since the bank, which holds the mortgage, gets first dibs."

"Not necessarily," Niyol says. "In *Bennis v Michigan*, the Supreme Court ruled a car, joint property of a husband and wife, could be seized because the husband had a liaison with a prostitute in the back seat. And that was just under a city's nuisance laws. The bank is probably SOL."

Joe raises an eyebrow and looks at Niyol, but continues his lecture.

"They also found a strip of black plastic, caught in a rivet in the doorframe. The plastic is unique, and is identical to that used in body bags. If we can find a bag with a matching tear, we have another link in the chain. This information is very secret.

"Thurmond refuses to admit knowing anything about the bodies. He is being charged with illegal movement of bodies and desecrating a corpse. Actually, multiple counts of desecrating a corpse, but we're going to need more than skid marks and a strip of plastic to prosecute him for that."

Chief Joe looks around the room where the E'e'aahjigo Kiva mixes easily with his lead officers. "Any questions?"

"Why is Thurmond not being held on suspicion of murder?"

"May I answer that, Chief?" Dr. Deschene asks. When Joe nods, Dr. Deschene explains. "All the bodies died after extensive surgical intervention. Thurmond could not do that. Thurmond was one of the subcontractors Ata'halne' suggested."

"Who would be? Capable of such surgery, I mean," Gaagii asks.

"There are only two places nearby, this hospital and the Glen Canyon Spa. I am confident this did not occur at the hospital."

"The prison tattoos. Does that mean the prison and the spa are allied? But what about Manaba Begaye?" someone asks.

"It seems there is more than one route bodies take to the organ harvesters."

"The prison and someone else."

"Reapers, like Ata'halne' said."

"Thurmond must have had help. A sub-subcontractor." Hok'ee, says and then giggles. He does this more often than before, and the kiva are happy to see it.

"You are correct," Chief Joe says.

206

Carlotta Krafft

Kuznetzov calls Carlotta to his room. At first, she is glad for the summons. When she reaches Kuznetzov's room, she removes the Tarot Cards from her purse. Kuznetzov grabs them from her hand and puts them on the table. "These are crap," he says.

"The cards do not compel," Carlotta says. "They only foretell. I cannot—"

Kuznetzov's arm reaches across the table and slaps Carlotta. She raises her hand to her cheek, but not before the imprint of Kuznetzov's hand appears, livid against her dusky skin. A rivulet of blood flows from a gash from his signet ring.

"No," he growls. "The cards do not compel; you compel. You have been leading me, driving me."

He slaps her again and then picks up the stack of un-dealt Tarot Cards, turns them over, and spreads them across the table. The Magician is missing from the deck.

"You removed The Magician. You know The Magician foretells better than any other what my future will be. You stacked the deck and dealt from under and not from the top. You marked the cards. You have been cheating, telling me what you want me to hear, not what the cards say."

Carlotta shakes with fear. Kuznetzov is right. She used all her skills to bring him to America; she used all her skills to steer him to dominate the American Bratva.

"Why?" Kuznetzov asks.

"*Gospoden*, I … I see much farther in both space and time than the cards see. I know, better than the cards can tell, what the future brings. Remember, you brought me to yourself after I saw your future in my crystal ball. I was right, then. It was you who insisted I use the cards. I continued to use my talent, the Romany power to see into the future. That is the only reason I 'stacked the deck' as you say."

Kuznetzov frowns. "I don't believe you. Do you still have the crystal ball?"

"Yes, *Gospoden*."

"Bring it here. We will see if you tell the truth."

"Yes, *Gospoden*."

Ignoring the cards, but taking her purse, Carlotta leaves the room and walks down the hallway toward the elevator. She is glad the realtor has not yet found a house Kuznetzov approved. It would have made her escape impossible.

She does not go to her room, but takes the elevator to the lobby. The doorman hails a cab, and Carlotta disappears into traffic. Her destination is not the Folio airport, but one some thirty miles west. Cash and a smile guarantee an immediate departure. "To escape a vindictive husband," Carlotta touches her cheek when anyone questions her. The barely healed gash from Kuznetzov's ring and the bruise on her cheek are evidence enough to convince anyone.

The plane takes her to Denver. It is easy to find the Hispanic ghetto, with its bodegas, small clusters of unemployed men looking for day-labor jobs, and worn women carrying mesh bags of day-old bread and week-old produce. Carlotta learned Spanish in Europe, but she adapts. She passes among these people and finds someone to produce new documents.

"A complete identity," she says. "Birth certificate, social security card, drivers license, passport."

"I can give you a drivers license, today. The rest? Three, maybe four days. Payment in advance. Cash. Four thousand dollars."

"One thousand when you deliver the temporary drivers license. Three thousand more on delivery of the rest," Carlotta says.

The man wants to haggle, but Carlotta is resolute. He logs onto the dark net and shows her options – people whose identities were stolen and placed for sale.

The forger looks closely at her. "You could be as young as 22; as old as 32."

"A good range. Go with that." In fewer than 30 minutes she has found who she wants to be. *Jessica Martinez. A good, solid Hispanic name.*

She leaves with a Georgia driver's license bearing a name and address pulled from the internet and a gold star to assert positive proof of US citizenship. It won't help her if she gets stopped for a traffic violation, but she has no plans to drive. The card will, however, allow her to get a drink in a bar and rent a room in a hotel.

Two days later, she possesses a Colorado driver's license, a US passport, a certified copy of a birth certificate, and a social security card – all of which will pass a federal police check.

"Don't get a job using that card," the forger warns. "The person whose identity you are assuming is real. She is a housewife in Pueblo. She has never traveled outside the country and has no criminal record – not even a traffic ticket."

The next day, Carlotta takes a commercial flight to Gallup and a commuter flight back to Folio. She uses the internet to book a B&B on the other side of town from the resort.

She changes her appearance and identity. Adorned with silver and turquoise jewelry and with her hair in a ponytail, she fits in on the streets of Folio as either a tourist or a local.

There is some risk Kuznetzov or one of his guards will encounter her, but she has a powerful reason to be in Folio, a reason named Susan Calvin.

The couple who operate the B&B in their home understand lost luggage. The woman joins Carlotta on a brief shopping trip to purchase a few things.

Carlotta has selected this B&B for two reasons. First, it offers a long-term stay, not just an overnight. Second, their website says they have secure WiFi.

Before leaving the B&B for her supper Carlotta uses the secure WiFi connection to access Kuznetzov's accounts. Her thoughts are no longer muddled, either by loyalty to him or by the visions in her mind. It takes only minutes to transfer money from his accounts into hers. She then splits the money among new accounts of which Kuznetzov does not know.

Her last step is to change the passwords on Kuznetzov's accounts so he can no longer access them. Finally, she sends a long text file to Susan Calvin.

Francis Falco

"She's been off the grid for five days," the NSA analyst reports. "She turned off her phone and made no calls. We tracked the phone's GPS to Denver and back to Folio, Arizona. Today, she used the phone on a secure WiFi system. This case is not high enough priority to get the hackers to crack the WiFi. However, we have back doors into two of the bank accounts she accessed. She transferred twenty-two million dollars from Malta to Bermuda and then emptied the Bermuda account. We traced the money to accounts in the Channel Islands. More money from accounts we haven't flagged appeared in the Channel Island accounts. We're working to identify those accounts."

The DDO ponders this news, and orders the WiFi at the B&B cracked.

≈≈≈≈≈

Niyol and Gaagii sit across the desk from Chief Joe.

"Thurmond refuses to talk. He's been arraigned, and an attorney we know he cannot afford is demanding we release him on bond," the chief says.

"Can you arrange for me to visit him?" Gaagii asks. "Can you video the meeting without him knowing?"

"I see no reason I can't," Chief Joe says. "We tell prisoners we record every encounter, except with their lawyer. We don't have to tell him, again."

Four hours later, Gaagii stands in an interrogation cell at the headquarters of the Navajo Nation Police. He wears only moccasins, a breechclout, and a necklace of turquoise, abalone, jet,

211

and shell. Bands of color mark his face and arms. His hair is unbound and falls over his shoulders.

Two guards bring Thurmond to the cell. They push him into a chair and fasten his handcuffs to a staple on the table.

"Who are you supposed to be?" Thurmond sneers.

Gaagii answers, keeping his voice soft so Thurmond must strain to hear. "You have been *Thurmond* for so long you have forgotten your heritage. At one time, you were Anáá, *One with eyes wide open*. Then, you rejected that name, and became Thurmond Smith, and adopted the ways of the Bilagáana."

"How do you know that? And who are you?" Thurmond asks.

"I am Gaagii, Raven, and I see the darkness of your spirit and its depravity. Know you, the *chindi* of many of your brothers, abandoned in the desert and denied the chants, summon the *yee naaldlooshii* – the skin-walkers – to ask for vengeance. They want you. The skin-walkers will find you. This prison holds you in but cannot keep them out. They will find you."

Thurmond tries to stand, but the staple on the table keeps him from rising to his feet. He sits back heavily. "You know things you can't know. You are a Shaman. Are you real?"

Gaagii walks around the table. Thurmond – Anáá – flinches when Gaagii touches his shoulder.

"The spirits of those you desecrated cry to you. You must allow us to put them to rest. Only by freeing them and cleansing yourself can you find peace," Gaagii says and leaves the room.

When the guards return, Thurmond says. "I want to talk to the chief. I transported those bodies."

≈≈≈≈≈

Susan is surprised to find the message on her new email account. Only Dr. Deschene, the Kiva, and some of her closest friends know the address. Then, she remembers giving it to Carlotta. She reads the attached file. *Hopping Higgs, as Atsa would say*, she thinks, and rushes to Dr. Deschene's office. He skims the printout and calls Chief Joe.

≈≈≈≈≈

The private clinic in New Jersey is designed and equipped to handle wealthy patients with trivial problems. The chance to provide post-operative support to the son of a very wealthy client is too lucrative to refuse. Especially since this client is *connected* – he is the head of an Italian Mafia family. The boy received a kidney transplant. The Glen Canyon Medical Spa sends two nurses to help with the first week following the surgery. Easy money – until the principal nurse from the care team pushes his way into the director's office.

"I don't know an easy way to tell you this," Nurse Grassier says "But your patient is infected with HIV. We are certain the infection existed before the surgery."

Bull, is the clinic's director's first response, but he does not say this. "We screened him for STDs including HIV before we sent him to your spa."

Grassier responds, knowing what he says cannot be challenged medically. "It can take months for HIV to appear in testing. It was at your assurance and insistence we accepted this patient before testing could be complete. His CD4-T cells dropped to below 200, and he is running a fever – suggesting infection. We are no longer responsible for him, and will leave immediately."

As soon as he receives this news, the patient's father calls one of his lieutenants. "Scout the place in Arizona, then call for as many soldiers as you need. I want the people who procured the donor and everyone involved in the surgery dead. Collateral damage is acceptable."

≈≈≈≈≈

An eerily similar scene happens at the Glen Canyon Medical Spa. A patient has died of bacterial meningitis after receiving one of Johnny One Feather's kidneys. The patient's father has arrived in the United States with a team of Swiss doctors.

The immunoglobulin masked the initial symptoms, Dr. Standart thinks. Before he can explain this to the British team, their lead doctor speaks.

"Your donor was infected with bacterial meningitis. Your screening was inadequate."

Dr. Standart tries to appear confident when he responds. "It is most likely this patient's immune system was so weakened by the anti-rejection drugs he contracted meningitis despite the sterile—"

"Dr. Standart, your explanation does not satisfy the Emir of Qatar." Dr. Standart watches as the man follows the body of the patient from the spa to the hearse.

~~~~~

The call from Nurse Grassier is more frightening than the unstated threat from Qatar. "How could this happen?" Standart demands.

"Your friend, Warden Red Horse," Grassier says. "He got greedy and didn't screen the donor. We are about to board. We'll be in Folio late tonight."

It's falling apart, Dr. Standart realizes. It takes only a few moments for him to decide. He removes a Brazilian passport, an open ticket on American Airlines, new credit cards, and a briefcase full of cash from a safe in his office and walks from the building to his car. It's a five-hour drive to Denver – the nearest place he can use his airline ticket. The flight to Rio will last fourteen hours. Once there, he can access additional money from accounts all over the world. He sighs. His work is not done, but he can continue it in Brazil. Someday, he will reach the final solution of organ rejection.

~~~~~

214

The E'e'aahjigo Kiva and selected police officers assemble in Chief Joe's conference room. "We have three out-of-town visitors," Chief Joe says. "This is Sheriff Edmonds of Tularosa County, who encountered situations similar to ours. He has met with Dr. Deschene and Spencer Hansen."

He introduces a woman wearing a nametag with FBI in large, blue letters. "This is Special Agent Gabby Winder. She has information that will help us understand what we have learned."

The chief introduces another man. "This is Assistant United States Attorney Francis Falco, from the Flagstaff Office. His office prosecutes federal crimes and felonies on Indian territories. He agrees to listen to what we know and what we suspect. He will decide how to proceed. Our task today is not to convince him to ask for a Federal Grand Jury, but to give him the information he needs to convince himself."

Mr. Falco stands. "When he invited me, Chief Joe told me very little. He said you believe you have evidence of a major criminal operation on and around the Navajo and Hopi Nations, including felonies that cross state lines. Either of these can trigger action by the United States Attorney's office. We are especially interested in anything that would fall under RICO – the Racketeer Influenced and Corrupt Organizations Act. I am happy to listen to what you have to say. I understand this session is being recorded in both audio and video. I see not only Chief Joe's officers and Ms. Winder from the FBI, but also a dozen civilians. Perhaps you could begin by describing your role."

"Spencer," Chief Joe says, "that's you."

Spencer stands and takes a deep breath. The members of his kiva have agreed to what he will say next, but he is still nervous. "I am Spencer Hansen, a pre-med student at the Folio Community College and an intern at the Navajo Western Regional Hospital.

All the *civilians*, plus two police officers, are members of the E'e'aahjigo Kiva – that's *Westward Kiva*. In the kiva, I am Atsa."

The Navajo policemen and women exchange glances. They realize the E'e'aahjigo Kiva includes not only this Bilagáana but also a woman and both Navajo and Hopi members.

Heads wag, but Spencer ignores them. "Two years ago, I worked as an orderly at the Glen Canyon Medical Spa." He describes the Emir's liver transplant and Nurse Emile Grassier's description of a locator anklet on an organ donor. "The spa was not licensed to do organ transplants until months after that.

"Next to speak will be my mentor, Dr. Deschene."

Dr. Deschene addresses Mr. Falco. It is clear they know one another. "Frank, it's good to see you, again. I'm sorry it took something like this to bring us together.

"For the record, I am Dr. Nastas Deschene, MD, and am honored to be a member of the E'e'aahjigo Kiva."

Dr. Deschene operates a hand-held control and an autopsy photo appears on the screen.

"This is the body of a still-unidentified person. It is one of forty recovered from a ravine on Navajo territory. The location of the bodies protected them from predation. All bore clear evidence of surgical intervention – specifically, surgical removal of their organs.

"I have certified copies of the autopsies for you. I will not ask everyone to sit through forty autopsy reports, except to say these people lost organs under circumstances that point to massive, illegal organ harvesting."

"The young men of the kiva began their investigation two years ago when the body of one of their friends, a schoolboy, was found in the desert, eviscerated and mummified. The Rough Rock County Coroner with support from the Arizona Medical Examiner's office conducted his autopsy. I have evidence that the

216

autopsy was mishandled – I will not say *covered up* until I learn more.

"Here is a copy of his autopsy, and that of a young man who appears to have sold a kidney and then died when the remaining kidney failed."

Dr. Deschene briefly and clinically describes the marks showing surgery on the bodies found in the ravine. He displays on the HDTV, images of prison tattoos. He asserts the surgery could only have been done at a medical facility as sophisticated as the Glen Canyon Medical Spa or the regional hospital and avers that he is certain it was not done at the hospital. "The forty bodies were found about thirty-five air miles southeast of Folio. It is unreasonable to think they were brought from a greater distance."

"Occam's Razor," Chuchip says. Chief Joe, Dr. Deschene, and Mr. Falco nod.

Chief Joe calls on one of his officers to explain the tattoos and associate them with known prison gangs. Then, he calls Ahote to the microphone.

"I am Ahote, *Restless One*, a member of the E'e'aahjigo Kiva and an auxiliary officer in the Navajo Nation Police."

Ahote shows images of documents from the public record showing the spa's contract to perform legal organ removal from deceased prisoners. "The State of Arizona Department of Corrections, or 'AZ-DOC,' awarded this contract without public comment or oversight. There may be evidence of political or financial pressure, but we have not found it."

He also presents a copy of a contract between the AZ-DOC and the Peaceful Rest Mortuary and Crematorium. "This is public record, but buried deeply in the archives. They contracted the mortuary to cremate the bodies of deceased prisoners. We hypothesize that instead of cremating bodies, the mortuary dumped them in the desert. We searched for data to support or refute that hypothesis. The Folio Fire Department reports a fire recently destroyed the mortuary's cremation oven. This supports our hypothesis.

"We observed one of their employees meeting with the helicopter pilot, Thurmond. The employee, Henry Belka, and Thurmond have extensive and interrelated encounters with the legal system. Their meetings are always inside the hanger where Thurmond keeps his helicopter.

"Thurmond was arrested in a recent drug raid. Two days ago, he confessed to receiving bodies from Henry Belka and dumping them in the ravine. As soon as Belka signed the confession, Chief Joe called us to this meeting."

The chief asks Susan to present her information.

"I am Susan Calvin and honored to be a member of the E'e'aahjigo Kiva."

Heads wag, again; again, they are ignored.

"I am a journalist and understand everything said here, today, is off the record until released by Chief Joe.

"I received an email from a young woman, Carlotta Krafft, who I met once in a coffee shop in Folio. In the email, she claims to be a psychic working for the head of the Russian Mafia. His name is Ivan Kuznetzov. She said he is the head of a nationwide organ harvesting, human trafficking, and drug distribution network. The message included significant details, including names and contact numbers of twenty of Kuznetzov's associates."

"I met Mr. Kuznetzov," Dr. Deschene says. "We played golf and had lunch. He pumped me for information about certain autopsies – autopsies he should not have known about. He is, in a word, smarmy. And wealthy. He bought membership in the Glen Canyon Country Club for at least six million dollars."

Special Agent Winder stands. "I think this is my cue to jump in. Chief Joe assured me you all are trustworthy and discreet. What I am going to say must be kept secret until the National Security Agency and the FBI release it.

Eyes open wide and people perk up when Ms. Winder mentions the NSA.

Winder continues speaking. "You have uncovered links, facts, and details neither the National Security Agency nor the FBI know. You have done some truly amazing work. Here's what I can tell you about what we know.

"Carlotta Krafft is a close associate of Ivan Kuznetzov who is the head of the Bratva, the Russian Mafia in the USA. The FBI suspects he ordered the murder of one of his lieutenants in Los Angeles and of five members of that organization. We have uncovered a link between him and a Nicaraguan cartel known to smuggle people into this country. Together, they are responsible for the deaths of a number of these people. I can document this.

"We have found links between Kuznetzov, Dr. Todd Standart at the Glen Canyon Spa, the Arizona State Medical Examiner's office, and—"

She looks up. "The last thing I will tell you is extremely sensitive. We believe there is a link between the Medical Examiner and the Head of Homeland Security in this area although we do not yet have proof. That is why Homeland is not here."

Hok'ee' is next. He describes the organ flights from the airport and planes arriving from throughout the US and from foreign countries. Mr. Falco perks up, again.

Chief Joe stands and addresses Mr. Falco. "Frank, this is an official request. The next testimony was gathered by hacking computers in state offices. I ask for blanket immunity for the presenters."

"Chief, you have it. Lend me a secretary later, and find a notary, and you'll have it in writing before the day is out."

Joe nods. He expects nothing less of his friend. "Niyol, you're at bat," Joe says.

"I am Niyol, called *Wind*, a member of the E'e'aahjigo Kiva and a rookie officer in the Navajo Nation Police. My specialty is computer crime. I don't often commit it, myself."

A chuckle runs through the room. When it dies, Niyol continues. "When the E'e'aahjigo Kiva first suspected the extent of this operation, and before I was a sworn police officer, I looked into the records of the Rough Rock County Coroner. While Rough Rock County is not well represented on the internet, he sent his reports to the State ME's office where they were scanned and indexed. I discovered the Rough Rock Coroner was conducting autopsies of state prisoners even though those autopsies should have been performed by the state ME. The number was high – over two hundred during 2017, and a higher rate so far in 2018. A large number died of bacterial meningitis. The Red Rock Coroner reported this to the State Health Department, but they never acted on it. We hypothesize someone suppressed the report.

"The autopsies include an unusually large number of prisoners who may have died of AIDS. We hypothesize they were being denied the drugs ordered by the courts, and someone might have sold those drugs on the black market."

The next boy stands. "I am Cha'tima, *The Caller*, of the E'e'aahjigo Kiva. Chief Joe put me in charge of a telephone bank when we were seeking the identity of a young woman whose body and her unborn child were found in the desert. She had been eviscerated. Evidence pointed to animal activity. Toxicology tests showed she had been drugged with Rohypnol shortly before her death. The likely perpetrator has been arrested and arraigned. His trial for murder is scheduled for next month.

"One caller was very insistent that the State ME had covered up deaths at Arizona prisons. Another caller reported the arrest of a man in Jake's Lake. That's the County Seat of Rough Rock County, across the river. The man disappeared in the prison system – until the family received a letter from the warden of Prison #9 saying he had died and been cremated. We found irregularities in the records of the sheriff, the public defender, and the court.

"We have certified transcripts of both calls and of copies of documents."

Chief Joe takes the remote for the HDTV. "If I can get this thing to work," he mumbles. A map of the Four Corners area appears. "The white numbers at Tuba City and the Gallup bus station represent missing youngsters, ages twelve to twenty-five, in the past two years. The reports come mostly from casual conversations with other youngsters, but we have the last known location of one missing person's cell phone in Gallup. His body was found in Arizona. Not much good as evidence, except it points to interstate kidnapping. We may be able to show more if we can get DNA from families of missing youngsters to match DNA from the bodies we've recovered." Chief Joe sits. "Dr. Deschene will wrap this up."

Dr. Deschene holds a sheaf of papers. "Sixteen years ago I was a member of a task force that investigated what the medical examiner in charge decided was the work of a serial killer. Eighteen bodies of young, healthy Navajo, Hopi, and Apache were found in the desert, desiccated and eviscerated. I assisted the ME in twelve autopsies and conducted another six by myself. The killer was a surgeon. Toxicology found traces of lidocaine and

221

propofol. The ME rejected my hypothesis of organ harvesting and ordered the records sealed. I hope your offer of immunity holds for me since I couldn't otherwise explain how I got these copies.

"The ME on the task force was the man who is now the State ME."

He hands autopsy copies to Mr. Falco.

At that moment, Niyol's phone buzzes. He looks at the screen and pumps his fist in the air. "Yes!"

"Officer Niyol?" Chief Joe says. "I hope that's more important than my niece accepting your invitation to a date, Saturday."

Niyol stands. "No, sir. I mean, yes, sir. It's a message I've been waiting for. Dr. Deschene described the task force sixteen years ago that was investigating bodies found in the desert. The message confirms the head of the task force was a young FBI agent who is now in charge of this area's Homeland office.

"Our hypothesis is that they were engaged in shenanigans then and are still involved."

Niyol sits.

"That is the final piece in the puzzle," Chief Joe says. "But you still have to meet my niece's parents."

After the chuckles stop, Mr. Falco takes the floor. "Chief Joe told only part of the reason I am here. I need enough information to convene a Federal Grand Jury and enough information that search warrants and evidence collected for the Grand Jury can stand up to a trial judge's scrutiny. If warrants are ruled invalid, then the evidence gathered is also invalid.

"I have never seen as much evidence collected so well by such an – I'll say an *eclectic* and dedicated group of people. I would like copies of your documents and a copy of the recording of this

222

meeting. I will fly to Flagstaff, and present this to a judge of the district court. I will ask that a Grand Jury be convened. Before I leave, I will write the letters granting transactional or blanket immunity to those who need it. You know some of you will be called to testify before the Grand Jury and likely at trials."

On the Record

Before the team from the New Jersey Mafia can assemble, an FBI task force armed with search and arrest warrants reaches the Glen Canyon Medical Spa. They enter from both the front and the rear porticos, and push their way to the administration wing and patient rooms. They do not find Dr. Standart, Nurse Grassier, or any patient records.

They find a computer with a dark net browser and unidentifiable communication apps. Special Agent in Charge Winder turns the computer over to an NSA team that arrives in Folio. They do not penetrate the apps before they disappear, wiped from the computer.

The FBI arrests twelve spa employees on charges of illegal organ harvesting and murder. Whether they can be prosecuted is problematic without records. Chief Joe recruits Sam Little Crow and Johnny Two Horses to assemble records of suspected organ flights. It is a long shot, but perhaps something will pop out of that information.

~~~~~

The raid of the Peaceful Rest Mortuary and Crematorium finds blank death certificates signed by the Rough Rock County Coroner. A federal judge issues an arrest warrant for the coroner. The FBI takes Mr. Hilflinger and Henry Belka for questioning. Neither the US Attorney nor later a jury is impressed by Henry's protestations that he was "just following orders."

~~~~~

An earlier scene at the Overlook Resort is no less exciting than any in Folio.

"*Gospoden*, we found the B&B where she was staying, but she's gone. Not in her room. She won't go far. Everything is still there."

"Find her! But first, get me out of here," Kuznetzov orders.

"Where to, boss."

"Kazakhstan." *The US has no extradition treaty and my Estonian passport will get me in without a visa. When I get to Kazakhstan, I can become someone else, and escape whatever she has planned for me.*

≈≈≈≈≈

As soon as the raids begin, Susan buttonholes Frank Falco. "You've seen the message Carlotta sent," Susan says. "She's given away big chunks of Kuznetzov's network."

"Not all?" Falco asks.

"Not all. I suspect it's much bigger than she knows. You know her email is worthless as evidence unless she corroborates it, in person and on the witness stand."

Falco nods. "Carlotta deserves protection. It would be hard to prove she knew more than she put in the message. I will guarantee immunity and, if needed, entry into the witness protection program. You'll have something in writing within a day."

Susan thanks him and composes an email to Carlotta.

≈≈≈≈≈

At 9:00 PM on the day of the raid on the spa, Susan Calvin receives a call from the editor of the *Washington Banner*. "Susan," he says. "Thank you for taking my call. You know we would like an exclusive and I know that's unlikely. However, may I at least get a few words from you?"

226

Susan is prepared for this. The FBI, the US Attorney, Chief Joe, and the young men of her kiva helped assemble her notes. Had the editor not called her, she would have called him. The *Banner* is still the most-read newspaper in the US and the world.

She reviews what is *on the record*. She looks at the notes on the table. Her voice is strong and confident when she replies, "Here is your exclusive – the whole thing. I trust you are recording because I'm not sure I can bear to tell it more than once."

Every major news outlet in the world – except Al Jazeera and Al Arabia – picks up Susan's story. Apparently, some of the information hits too close to home for Qatar and Saudi Arabia. The Associated Press, BBC, *The Guardian*, the Canadian property Reuters, Sputnik and RT, and dozens of others headline the story.

≈≈≈≈≈

Susan's article swamps the foxprop news outlets and impacts all branches of the government. The president's tweets do not let up.

<<@RealUSPOTUS #fakenews to destroy America greatness #MAGA Make America covfefe Again>>

Analysts at a TV news network tied to the administration watch their viewer numbers plummet.

"Not to worry," Gloria says to her producers. "What do we have to distract them tonight?"

"The president has challenged the North Koreans, again, to 'Let's Make a Deal—'"

"Great," Gloria says. "Fear always sells, and the North Koreans are the only scary enemy we have, any more. 'Let's Make a Deal!' We'll run with it. That will be the theme of tonight's show." She glances at her watch. "I've got somewhere I need to be. You work on it and put the notes on the teleprompter. We have 30 minutes until show time."

Twenty-seven minutes later, Gloria stands in front of a sink washing her privates while an intern lies on the leather couch. Gloria makes it to the studio with 10 seconds to spare.

≈≈≈≈≈

Sam Red Horse learns of the raid on the spa. He learns of the raid on the mortuary. He learns the state's contract-prison system is being investigated. Two of his top guards, Mona Goth and Chris Schultz, have disappeared. He fears they may be in a witness protection program. He knows he cannot withstand an investigation.

Sam swivels his chair until he is facing his "I Love Me" wall. The drug he puts into the double old-fashioned glass dissolves in the 30-year-old Scotch whiskey. Sam sips, and then drinks. He barely has time to set the glass on his desk before he is lost in eternal darkness.

Special Agent in Charge Winder does not make the same mistake she made at the Glen Canyon Spa. She brings Niyol to Sam Red Horse's office. "The NSA crashed the spa's computer before they cracked it. This one is probably the same. You reckon you can figure it out?"

'Yes, ma'am. The gang was Russian. The *Dancing Bear* hacker team created their software. They think they're gods of the internet but they have feet of clay – and they always use the same set of tricks."

≈≈≈≈≈

The leader of the Western Bratva calls his subordinates to a meeting in Reno, Nevada.

"The American FBI exposed the operation set up by Komerade Gospoden Kraznachey. Our suppliers and customers are in turmoil.

As Lenin told us, confusion and change offer opportunities. We will assume control of both the national and the international operations.

"We control the servers with the data on hundreds of prisoners and potential customers. Kuznetzov depended on greed – Hilflinger, the owner of a mortuary and his employee; Warden Red Horse and his guards; Standart at the spa. We will not make that mistake, but will govern with force.

"We still control most of the for-profit prisons in the western US and seven so-called not-for-profit hospitals. We only need to move the principal source of organs to the prison in Denver. Given our access to the dark net, it will not be difficult to rebuild."

The reaction to the message is mixed. Nevertheless, enough of the state lieutenants of the Bratva are convinced. What they do not know is that Niyol has cracked the late Warden Sam Red Horse's computer. He and the FBI are monitoring every one of the Bratva's transactions.

~~~~~

Spencer sits in front of Dr. Deschene's desk. It has been just over two years since Spencer began his in-service, but only a day since Susan's article exposed the huge organ harvesting operation.

"I know you've not applied at a college," Dr. Deschene says. "And I know the reason. You throw yourself into whatever is important *at the moment*. For two years, the mystery of organ harvesting has been that moment. Therefore …

"Therefore, I have applied on your behalf at _____." Dr. Deschene names a prestigious university whose medical school is the gold standard.

"They accepted you. Here is the information you need and a ticket to the airport nearest the university. Hok'ee, who has won his private pilot's license, insists on taking you to the commercial airport in Phoenix."

"Dr. D, I cannot afford this," Spencer says. "I'm sorry, but—"

"The Navajo Nation will pay your tuition, books, and fees," Dr. Deschene says. "The bank account into which the hospital has been sending your pay will receive a monthly allowance for living expenses and a little more. Normally, we would ask you to sign a contract to spend the first five years of your practice on the Res. I do not believe we need to do that."

"No, Dr. Deschene. I am Bilagáana by birth, but Diné by choice and by adoption into the kiva. This is my place."

≈≈≈≈≈

Before Spencer leaves for university, the E'e'aahjigo Kiva asks Gaagii and Cha'tima for an Enemy Way Ceremony to dispel the ghosts of the non-Navajo who visited evil on to them and to bring the kiva society back to harmony.

Instead of his hogan, Chief Joe arranges for one of the great kivas to be opened to them.

"The kiva has been reconstructed, but we were careful to use the proper materials and methods," the Navajo Park Ranger explains. "We will close the kiva to tourists for the next three days, for a religious ceremony. This will disappoint some tourists. Others will take it as a validation of our beliefs – or of their beliefs about our beliefs."

The two ceremonies require no longer than had the earlier Blessing Way ceremony. Both nights and the intervening day are filled with chants, smoke, and fasting. On the third day Chief Joe's family provides a traditional breakfast.

≈≈≈≈≈

Nurse Emile Grassier's escape plans are interrupted by three men in dark suits who meet him at the Denver International Airport. Their credentials mark them as Immigrations and Customs Enforcement. There is no doubt in Grassier's mind. He has been discovered. His protestations, his French passport, his H1-B visa, nothing is of any use. He finds himself secured by plastic tie-ties, hand and foot, in an SUV with blacked-out windows.

Grassier expects he will be taken to a police or sheriff's station, where he will be allowed to contact a lawyer. He is surprised to be taken to what appears to be a super-max prison and placed in a solitary cell.

"Welcome to the Colorado prison system," his guard says. "The good news is you won't be in a cell with Bubba. The best news is your participation in a medical research program will speed your release. Cooperation will make you free."

The End

232

Author's Afterword

Illegal organ harvesting is real but may be not as pervasive or well organized as it appears here. On the other hand, it is growing. Urban legends and conspiracy theories abound on the internet; however, there are also scholarly articles from legitimate sources. I invite you to

http://www.ajkd.org/article/S0272-6386(09)01177-9/fulltext.

It's a long article and a long scroll, but well worth reading. There are other articles listed in the "Internet References" near the end of the book.

The great disparity between people needing organs and people willing to donate their organs is real, and results in thousands of unnecessary deaths, each year. If you are not registered as an organ donor, please become one, and make sure your next of kin know your desires.

This novel grew from a 2017 NaNoWriMo challenge, and a great deal of fascinating research – although it was never intended to be a research paper. Some of the research is documented at the end of the book. I've not listed all the links offered by Wikipedia articles, nor all of the YouTube videos, but both are easy to find.

Except where specified or patently obvious, the locations and institutions in the story exist in a fictional reality, not the one in which you are reading this, and are intended not to represent or reflect anything in our reality. All characters are completely fictional.

I have used "aboriginal," meaning "before the beginning," as a collective adjective for the various peoples and nations (e.g.,

Navajo, Hopituh Shi-nu-mu, Apache) who appear in the story. "Indian" is a relic of a mistake made in 1492 when Columbus brought disease and removed slaves from some Caribbean islands.

The chants and ceremonies are both sacred and private. I have redacted the descriptions. The kiva initiation and the scene between Hok'ee and his uncle at the Tuba City Diner are pure imagination.

Acknowledgements

My very enthusiastic thank you to Beta Readers Mary L. "Lani" Clancy, Charlotte E. Robinson, and Michael Weinstock.

Many non-English words and phrases were obtained from the Google translate web site. Distances and air travel times, as well as inspiration for the fictitious locations came from Google Maps.

Characters

_____, Ab al Hakim, Emir: Client of both Dr. Standart and Gospoden Kuznetzov.

Anáá: "One with eyes wide open." See "Smith, Thurmond."

Bass, Roseanne: Forensic anthropologist at the Grand Junction "body farm."

Begaye, Manaba: Navajo young woman whose body is discovered, eviscerated. Manaba = "Bright Flower."

Belka, Henry: Employee at Peaceful Rest Mortuary. (Belka = "Squirrel")

Calvin, Susan: Investigative reporter for a major eastern newspaper.

Chee, Tommy: Nephew of Navajo Nation Police Chief, Joseph White Eagle. Nickname, "TomTom." Also known as Ata'halne' of the E'e'aahjigo Kiva.

DDO: Director of Domestic Operations, National Security Agency.

Deschene, Dr. Nastas MD, Fellow College of American Medical Examiners, Diplomate American College of Forensic Pathologists. Navajo. Pathologist at Navajo Western Regional Hospital.

E'e'aahjigo Kiva Members: E'e'aahjigo ("Westward")

Bilagáana: Spencer Hansen, later Atsa ("Eagle"); Ms. Susan Calvin.

Navajo: Ahiga ("He Fights"), Ata'halne' ("He Who Interrupts") AKA Tommy Chee; Gaagii ("Raven"); Hok'ee ("Abandoned") originally Tahoma ("Rock"); Niyol ("Wind); Dr. Nastas Deschene.

Hopituh Shi-nu-mu: Ahote ("Restless One"), Cha'tima ("The Caller"), Cheviots ("Spirit Warrior"), Chuchip ("Deer Spirit")

Gaagii and Cha'tima are studying their cultures' traditions in order to become Shamans.

Ahote and Niyol become auxiliary police officers; later, Niyol gets a regular officer's position.

Niyol is an accomplished computer hacker.

Spencer plans to become a doctor; Chuchip shows interest and helps with some autopsies.

Later additions: Chief Joseph White Eagle (Shiehe'e, "Father"); Dr. Nastas Deschene, Susan Calvin.

Falco, Francis: Assistant United States Attorney, Flagstaff, AZ.

Franklin, Dr.: Provost (senior academic administrator) at the Folio Community College. Golfing partner and friend of Dr. Deschene.

238

_____, Gahtsoh: ("Rabbit") Navajo young man, member of a one-time gang. Gahtsoh is crippled by polio and wears braces on both legs.

Goth, Mona: Guard at U.P.S. #9.

Grassier, Emile: Male nurse at Glen Canyon Spa.

Hansen, Spencer: Bilagáana ["non-Indian"]. Community college student, protégé of Dr. Deschene. Spencer was a member of a scout troop until he was judged too irreverent, and was disfellowshipped. He joined with others who shared his beliefs and who had formed the E'e'aahjigo Kiva (Westward Kiva) with both Navajo and Hopituh Shi-nu-mu members, in defiance of both nations' beliefs. As a Nordic blond, Spencer stands out from the aboriginal members of the kiva. Nineteen years old when the story begins.

Hilflinger, Mr. Karl: Owner of the Peaceful Rest Mortuary and Crematorium, Folio, Arizona.

Ivanovich, Dmitry: Head of Kuznetzov's guards and assistants.

Krafft, Carlotta: Astrologer and Tarot Card Reader for Ivan Kuznetzov, q.v.

Kraznachey, Gospoden: "Mr. Paymaster," a pseudonym of Ivan Kuznetzov, below.

Kuznetzov, Ivan: Bratva (Russian Mafia) figure behind the broader organ harvesting operation. Superstitious. Has a resident Tarot Card reader he consults before every encounter or decision.

Little Cloud, Benny: Navajo boy arrested, charged, and died in prison.

Little Crow, Sam: Navajo. Retired US Air Force Senior Master Sergeant. Friend of Bidziil "Johnny" Two-Horses. Inveterate airplane watcher, Folio Municipal Airport.

Long Tree, Jessie: Navajo, victim of organ harvesting.

Martin, Hector: Son of a Nicaraguan crime family.

Mikhailov, Yury: Russian name of Gerald Michelson, head of the California Bratva.

Moenkopi Reapers: Scavenger team. Individual names not known at present. They may take direction from the Lay Council of the Ignatius Catholic Church.

One-feather, Johnny: Navajo. Carhop in Tuba City.

Petrov, Ivan: Original Russian name of Isaac Peterson, head of the Arizona Bratva.

POTUS: President of the United States.

Red Horse, Jimmy ("Pony Boy"): Pony Boy is Sam Red Horse's disparaging nickname for his nephew, Jimmy Red Horse, leader of the Tonaleah Reapers.

Red Horse, Sam: Navajo. Warden of Unified Prison System, Facility Nine (Prison Nine or U.P.S. #9) west of Folio, Arizona. Former US Army military policeman – interrogator and water-boarder in Afghanistan and Iraq. Assigned to Abu Ghraib prison in Iraq at the time of human rights violations. Received a mail-order degree in Criminal Justice and got the warden's job through political connections.

Running Deer, Kyle: Auxiliary Officer, Navajo Nation Police. Handler of trained cadaver dog.

Semi, Major USAF, MD: US Air Force surgeon, Luke AFB, Arizona hospital.

Schultz, Chris: Guard at U.P.S. #9.

Sokolov, _____: Member of Bratva in US, responsible for recruiting and paying politicians and judges for "protection."

Sontag, Father: Priest at St. Ignatius Catholic Church, Teec Nos Pos.

Standart, Todd MD: Medical Director and Chief of Surgery at the Glen Canyon Medical Spa.

Tabahaa, Doli: Navajo lawyer and advocate for children. Office in Fairfax, Virginia.

Smith, Thurmond: Navajo. Name taken by helicopter pilot operating from the Folio Municipal Airport. Provides helicopter tours of Glen Canyon, runs drugs, and ultimately is involved in both moving organ "donors" from other Arizona prisons to U.P.S #9 near Folio and disposing of bodies. Original name, Anáá, "one with eyes wide open."

Tonaleah Reapers: Scavenger team. Leader is Jimmy Red Horse, the nephew of Sam Red Horse (q.v.). Individual names not known at present. Operate around the bus station in Gallup, NM.

Two Horses, Bidziil: ("Strong") Navajo. Nickname, Johnny. Retired US Air Force Chief Master Sergeant. Friend of Sam Little Crow. Inveterate airplane watcher, Folio Municipal Airport, Arizona. Maternal Uncle of Hok'ee.

White Eagle, Joseph: Chief of Navajo Nation Police. Uncle of Tommy Chee. Shiehe'e ("Father")

Winder, Gabby: FBI agent associated with Chief Joseph's task force.

Glossary

@RealUSPOTUS: Twitter identification of the President of the United States in this fictitious reality.

128 Gig: One hundred twenty eight gigabytes, as in the capacity of a computer flash drive.

Aboriginal: Meaning "from before the beginning." It is used herein to define the first people to "discover" the American continents and specifically those who were the first inhabitants of what is now the Four Corners area of the United States. See also "Athabascan."

Adá'í: A boy's mother's brother (uncle).

Al Arabia: A real newsgathering and dissemination organization. Headquartered in Saudi Arabia.

Al Jazeera: A real newsgathering and dissemination organization. Headquartered in Qatar.

Antigen: Any foreign substance that causes an immune system response.

AP: Associated Press. A real newsgathering and dissemination organization.

Apalachin: Town in New York at which some 60 "American-Italian-Sicilian Mafia" crime bosses were arrested in the early 20th century, and location of more recent meeting of the Bratva (q.v.).

Aryan: Technically, Aryan was the name given to themselves by speakers of a particular language who invaded northern India and Iran in roughly 2,000 BCE. The notion of Aryans as a "pure, white" race came from Arthur De Gobineau in the 19th Century. It was adopted by Hitler and other racists, but is not generally accepted by scientists and academics.

As-salāmu ʿalaykum: "Peace be upon you."

ATF: (Bureau of) Alcohol, Tobacco, and Firearms. A real agency of the US Government.

Athabascan: Alaskan and Northern Canadian natives and others descended from those who spoke the Athabascan ethnolinguistic group of languages. It is loosely used to describe all "Native Americans" including those on the Pacific coast of California, Oregon, and Washington as well as those in and around the Four Corners area of the Southwestern US.

B&B: Bed and breakfast. A facility, often a private home, offering overnight accommodations and breakfast.

BBC: British Broadcasting Company. A real newsgathering and dissemination organization.

Bilagáana (bill-la-GAH-na): Navajo name for white people or people of Caucasian descent. Sometimes, but not always, used in a derogatory way.

Bratva: Russian, "brotherhood." A coalition of criminal elements originating in Russia, often referred to as the "Russian Mafia."

Cannula: A tube inserted in the body intravenously or as a peripherally inserted catheter line, a power port, or similar. Used to inject or remove fluid from the body.

244

cc: Cubic centimeters. Same as milliliters (ml).

Cell Block 11: Location at Prison Nine in the for-profit Arizona prison system where clean prisoners (those who passed drug, bacterial, HIV/AIDS, and other screening) are kept isolated as candidates for organ transplantation.

CGI: Computer-Generated Imagery.

Chindi: A ghost, the spirit of a dead person. Chindi are believed by some to linger around the person's body or possessions and to cause illness.

CIA: Central Intelligence Agency. A real agency of the US Government.

Ciborium: Container at some Christian churches used to hold the Eucharist.

Connected: Said of members or associates of the US Mafia.

Diné: In the Navajo language, Diné means "the people" and is the Navajos' preferred name for themselves. The name, 'Navajo' grew out of a Tewa-puebloan word, "nava hu" which means "place of large planted fields." [See the Hubble Trading Post/National Park Service web site.]

Dobryo utro: Good morning. (Russian)

Emolument: From Latin, *molere*, to grind. The emolument is the portion of the flour the miller keeps as payment for grinding grain. The word has come to mean also a stipend or payment made, for example, by a congregation to a Cleric.

EMT Team: Emergency Medical Technician team, often part of a municipal fire department.

EPA: Environmental Protection Agency. A real agency of the US Government.

ESL: English as a Second Language.

Eternal Lemnescate: See "Lemnescate," below.

Finochietto Retractors: Tools used in chest surgery to hold open the bones.

FOIA: Freedom of Information Act.

Folio, Arizona: Fictitious town abutting the western edge of the Navajo territory.

Forensic: As used here, means the application of science to criminal investigation.

Foxprop: Disparaging term for political propaganda. From the *kitsune,* a fox of Japanese legend – a shape shifter – and the legends of the Quechua, a fox of the Andes – a scoundrel.

FQO: Full-quill Ostrich. A kind of leather used for boots and belts, among other things.

Ghutra: Traditional headdress in Saudi society.

Glen Canyon Country Club: Fictitious, exclusive, membership-only, golf and tennis club. Guest privileges available, for a large price, for guests at some lodges, hotels, and resorts.

Glen Canyon Medical Spa: Fictitious spa for the ultra-ultra-rich and famous. Licensed for liposuction and plastic surgery. Conducts other, more extensive surgeries, including organ transplantation. Located on the river north of Folio.

Gluteus Maximus: The large muscles of the buttocks.

246

GPS: Global Positioning System.

Hazmat: Hazardous Material.

HIV/AIDS: Human Immunodeficiency Virus/Acquired Immunodeficiency Syndrome.

Homeland: Short for "Homeland Security," an agency of the US Government.

Hogan: A traditional Navajo home.

Hopituh Shi-nu-mu: A more complete name of those often called Hopi.

H-1B Visa: Visa issued to persons allowing them into the US to work in "hard to fill" jobs, usually in high-tech industries.

ICE: Immigration and Customs Enforcement. A real agency of the US Government.

James Holomon University: Fictitious school whose forensic anthropology department pioneered the recreation of faces using information gleaned from partial remains.

JV: Junior Varsity school sports teams.

Kaibito: Settlement in the Navajo Nation with a population of about 1,500. Home of one school, one gas station, and three churches.

LAX: designation for Los Angeles International Airport.

Lemnescate: A figure eight usually lying on its side. A symbol for infinity or eternity.

Naestan: Earth Goddess.

Navajo: See Diné, above.

Navajo Western Regional Hospital: Fictitious hospital east of Folio, AZ, on the Navajo "reservation," which is operated by the Navajo Nation, and at which Dr. Nastas Deschene is the pathologist.

NSA: National Security Agency. A real agency of the US Government.

Occam's Razor: A statement in logic, which suggests the simplest explanation, the one requiring the fewest assumptions, is often the best explanation.

OPTN: "Organ Procurement and Transplantation Network." A real organization. Accessed through a US Department of Health and Human Services web site. Maintains lists of people waiting organ transplants.

OTCC: One True Christian Church. Cult whose beliefs include the factual accuracy and inerrancy of the King James version of the bible. Goals include converting the US into a theocracy.

Overlook Resort: One of many fictitious resorts in or near Folio, Arizona.

Reaper: Someone whose livelihood involves finding and securing candidates for illegal organ harvesting and drug testing.

Reuters: A real newsgathering and dissemination organization.

RFID, RFID Chip: Radio-frequency Identification. Small chips that get energy from a "reader device" and report to the reader. Little bigger than a grain of rice, chips are implanted in pets, for example. They are also used to track consumer products. The

Unified Prison System locks anklets that hold RFID chips onto their prisoners in order to track prisoners' locations.

Rohypnol: Brand-name of a "sleeping pill," which acts nearly instantly and has been abused as a "date-rape drug" with the nickname, "roofies."

Rough Rock County: Fictitious county in Arizona. County seat: Jake's Lake.

RT: A real newsgathering and dissemination organization. Headquartered in Russia.

Sallie: Nickname for the Salvation Army or a Salvation Army shelter.

Shizhé'é Yázhí: Maternal Uncle.

Skin-walker: Navajo medicine man or shaman who has achieved great power and can transform into an animal, usually for some evil purpose (murder, e.g.). Popular Bilagáana culture often incorrectly equates "skin-walker" to "ghost" or "zombie."

SOL: Somewhat Out of Luck.

Sputnik: A real newsgathering and dissemination organization. Headquartered in Russia.

STD: Sexually-Transmitted Disease.

T-cell: Cells of the immune system that recognize specific antigens. "Killer" T-cells attack body cells infected with pathogens including viruses. "Inflammatory" T-cells attack microphages. "Helper" T-cells help other cells produce antibodies.

Taphonomy: The process of decay; what happens to human remains exposed to animals, insects, and the elements after death.

United Press Universal (UPU): Fictitious newsgathering and distribution organization headquartered in London.

UNOS: The United Network for Organ Sharing. This is a real organization, recognized by governments throughout the world. Their "... mission is to advance organ availability and transplantation to support patients through education, technology, and policy development." Their web site is https://unos.org.

U.P.S.: (Arizona) Unified Prison System. U.P.S. #9 designates the prison, located in Rough Rock County, across the river from Folio.

Wa'alaykumu as-salām: "And upon you, peace."

Yá'át'ééh: Navajo. "Hello" or "goodbye."

Yadilyil: Sky god.

References

In addition to the internet links, below, I recommend <u>Stiff: The Curious Lives of Human Cadavers</u>, by Mary Roach. Available on Amazon.com.

Internet links were correct when accessed.

Abu Ghraib Prison https://en.wikipedia.org/wiki/Abu_Ghraib_torture_and_prisoner_abuse

Adaptation (Eye) https://en.wikipedia.org/wiki/Adaptation_(eye)

Aircraft, Bombardier http://us.bombardier.com/us/home.htm

Antigen https://en.wikipedia.org/wiki/Antigen

Arab Headdress http://www.arabnews.com/fashion/news/769871

Aryan (1) https://en.wikipedia.org/wiki/Aryan

Aryan (2) https://www.merriam-webster.com/dictionary/Aryan

Aryan (3) https://www.britannica.com/topic/Aryan

As-salamu alaykum https://en.wikipedia.org/wiki/As-salamu_alaykum

Athabascan (1) https://en.wikipedia.org/wiki/Alaskan_Athabaskans

Athabascan (2) https://en.wikipedia.org/wiki/Athabaskan_languages

Athabascan (3) http://www.bbc.com/news/science-environment-42555577

Auschwitz, Staff https://www.jta.org/2017/01/30/news-opinion/world/list-of-auschwitz-commanders-and-guards-posted-online [and links contained therein]

251

Autopsy, Definitions https://www.medicinenet.com/autopsy/article.htm

Autopsy, Toxicology Tests https://www.webmd.com/mental-health/addiction/features/the-truth-about-toxicology-tests#1

Autopsy, Videos:
https://www.youtube.com/watch?v=iBdVroBI4M0&index=29&list=WL and numerous others on YouTube.

Beckett Farm Airport NM28 https://www.airnav.com/airport/NM28

Blessing Way (1) https://www.britannica.com/topic/Blessingway

Blessing Way (2)
https://en.wikipedia.org/wiki/Navajo_song_ceremonial_complex

Blessing Way (3)
http://www.hanksville.org/voyage/navajo/BlessingWay.php3

Blood Donation, Disqualifying Factors
https://www.theregister.co.uk/2006/08/25/the_odd_body_donating_blood/

Blood Products http://www.bloodbook.com/

Body Farm, Australia https://www.youtube.com/watch?v=8fqF6_HKtaU

Body Farm, National Geographic
https://www.youtube.com/watch?v=rDDl71d3CIM

Body Farm, Video https://www.youtube.com/watch?v=8wDJINtov6U

Bug-out Bag https://en.wikipedia.org/wiki/Bug-out_bag

Cannula https://en.wikipedia.org/wiki/Cannula

Catholic Lay Leaders
http://www.patheos.com/blogs/billykangas/2011/10/what-are-lay-leaders.html

Christianity and original sin
http://www.bbc.co.uk/religion/religions/christianity/beliefs/originalsin_1.shtml;
https://www.desiringgod.org/articles/what-is-the-biblical-evidence-for-original-
sin

Clergy House https://en.wikipedia.org/wiki/Clergy_house

Concentration Camp, Arbeitsjuden
https://www.sobiborinterviews.nl/en/extermination-camp/arbeitsjuden

Concentration Camp, Block 11 https://en.wikipedia.org/wiki/Block_11

Cremation (1) https://ask.metafilter.com/58485/No-smoke-or-smell-from-crematoriums

Cremation Equipment https://www.cremsys.com/

Cremation Equipment (2) https://www.uscremationequipment.com/

Cremation Equipment (3) https://www.affordablefuneralsupply.com/

Cremation Equipment (4) http://www.americanincinerators.com/

Cremation Q&A https://www.chipmanfuneralhome.ca/questions-and-answers-about-cremation/

Crematory https://en.wikipedia.org/wiki/Crematory

Desert Pavement https://en.wikipedia.org/wiki/Desert_pavement

Desert Varnish https://en.wikipedia.org/wiki/Desert_varnish

DNA Sequencer (1) https://en.wikipedia.org/wiki/DNA_sequencer

DNA Sequencer (2)
https://en.wikipedia.org/wiki/DNA_sequencer#/media/File:DNA-Sequencers_from_Flickr_57080968.jpg

DNA Sequencer (3) https://www.youtube.com/watch?v=K-d6PDZTVO8, https://www.youtube.com/watch?v=8n2LvJ-m0n0

Edmonds, Master Sergeant: https://www.csmonitor.com/World/Middle-East/2015/1202/Holocaust-hero-US-soldier-told-Nazi-captors-We-are-all-Jews

Enemy Way http://www.manataka.org/page1671.html

Estonia https://en.wikipedia.org/wiki/Estonia

Estonia Islands https://www.visitestonia.com/en/where-to-go/islands

Estonia Passport, Visa Requirements
https://en.wikipedia.org/wiki/Visa_requirements_for_Estonian_citizens

Extradition Treaties http://www.wlox.com/story/22665099/countries-with-no-extradition-treaty-with-us

GPS accuracy https://www.gps.gov/systems/gps/performance/accuracy/

Golf, Draw and Fade http://golftips.golfweek.com/difference-between-draw-fade-golf-20621.html

Göth, Amon https://en.wikipedia.org/wiki/Amon_G%C3%B6th

Grese, Irma https://en.wikipedia.org/wiki/Irma_Grese

H-1B Visa NPR https://www.npr.org/2017/03/06/518743020/h-1b-visa-debate-are-foreign-tech-workers-hired-over-americans

H-1B Visa NYT https://www.nytimes.com/2017/02/05/business/h-1b-visa-tech-cheers-for-foreign-workers.html?_r=1

Hacking, Malware NSA https://www.thedailybeast.com/stolen-nsa-tech-shuts-downhospitals

Heart Attacks - Harvard Health
https://www.health.harvard.edu/newsletter_article/heart-attacks-come-in-all-kinds-sizes

Heart Transplant (First): http://time.com/5050803/1967-heart-transplant/

Helicopter, Bell 206B III
https://www.avbuyer.com/aircraft/helicopter/turbine/bell-helicopters/206b-iii

HIV/AIDS (1) https://www.webmd.com/hiv-aids/guide/hiv-aids-difference#1

HIV/AIDS (2) https://dhhr.wv.gov/oeps/std-hiv-hep/HIV_AIDS/Pages/HIVAIDSInformation.aspx

HIV/AIDS (3)
https://www.isentress.com/raltegravir/isentress/consumer/about_hiv1/?gclid=EA
IaIQobChMIv9-
tyYPp1wIVC7jACh37LQdsEAAYASAAEgKsN_D_BwE&gclsrc=aw.ds&dclid
=CI2QvcuD6dcCFccvgQodgNIL_w

Holocaust:
https://en.wikipedia.org/wiki/The_Holocaust#Victims_and_death_toll

Holocaust Heroines http://historylists.org/people/5-heroines-of-the-
holocaust.html

Hubbell Trading Post FAQ https://www.nps.gov/hutr/faqs.htm

Immunity from Prosecution
https://en.wikipedia.org/wiki/Witness_immunity

Islam and original sin https://www.islamreligion.com/articles/1776/original-
sin/

Jaundice http://www.merckmanuals.com/

Jicarilla Apache https://en.wikipedia.org/wiki/Jicarilla_Apache

Kidney Disease, End Stage https://www.verywell.com/dying-of-kidney-
failure-what-to-expect-1132509

Kiva https://en.wikipedia.org/wiki/Kiva

Knights Templar Drug Cartel
https://www.ted.com/talks/rodrigo_canales_the_deadly_genius_of_drug_cartels

Krafft, Karl Ernst https://en.wikipedia.org/wiki/Karl_Ernst_Krafft

Luke Air Force Base https://en.wikipedia.org/wiki/Luke_Air_Force_Base

Mafia, Apalachin Meeting 1957
http://www.nydailynews.com/news/crime/62-mafia-members-seized-upstate-ny-
1957-article-1.2428519

Mafia, Arrests https://www.csmonitor.com/USA/2011/0120/Mafia-arrests-Four-of-the-most-famous-mob-busts-in-history/Charlie-Lucky-Luciano-1896-1962

Mass, Text http://www.catholicbridge.com/catholic/catholic_mass_full_text.php

Medical Examiner, GA https://gbi.georgia.gov/medical-examiners-office

Meningitis https://www.mayoclinic.org/diseases-conditions/meningitis/symptoms-causes/syc-20350508

Methylprednisolone https://en.wikipedia.org/wiki/Methylprednisolone

Morgue https://en.wikipedia.org/wiki/Morgue

Mormon DNA https://en.wikipedia.org/wiki/Genetics_and_the_Book_of_Mormon#Statements_regarding_the_Hebrew_ancestry_of_Book_of_Mormon_people

Mormon, DNA Evidence http://articles.latimes.com/2006/feb/16/local/me-mormon16

Mormons and original sin http://eom.byu.edu/index.php/Original_Sin

Mossad https://www.britannica.com/topic/Mossad

Names, Aboriginal Americans https://names.mongabay.com/data/indians.html

Native Americans, Genetic Component for Substance Dependence https://www.ncbi.nlm.nih.gov/pmc/articles/PMC3603686/

Navajo Chants.docx https://nhmu.utah.edu/sites/default/files/attachments/Navajo%20Chants.pdf

Navajo Culture http://www.discovernavajo.com/navajo-culture.aspx

Navajo Dictionary (English-Navajo) https://glosbe.com/en/nv

Navajo Gods and Goddesses https://navajocodetalkers.org/navajo-gods-and-goddesses/

Navajo Hogans http://navajopeople.org/navajo-hogans.htm

Navajo Language Ak'éí (Diné Bizaad) http://navajowotd.com/word/akei/

Navajo Taco https://www.cookingclassy.com/moms-navajo-tacos-and-indian-fry-bread/

Navajo-English Dictionary
https://glosbe.com/nv/en/e%CA%BCe%CA%BCaahjigo

Navajo, Four Sacred Colors and Stones http://navajopeople.org/blog/the-navajo-four-sacred-colors/

Navajo, Ghosts https://en.wikipedia.org/wiki/Chindi

Navajo Mentorship http://n-nurse.org/mentorship.html

Nazi Concentration Camps http://en.truthaboutcamps.eu/ [and links therein]

Nazi, Sonderkommando https://en.wikipedia.org/wiki/Sonderkommando

Ninth Fort Massacres November 1941
https://en.wikipedia.org/wiki/Ninth_Fort_massacres_of_November_1941

Offshore Banking https://hfsoffshore.com/

Operating Room Equipment and Supplies
https://www.dremed.com/catalog/index.php/cPath/45

OPTN Organ Procurement and Transplantation Network
https://optn.transplant.hrsa.gov/

Organ Harvesting, China http://www.cnn.com/2016/06/23/asia/china-organ-harvesting/index.html, http://www.newsweek.com/despite-zero-tolerance-organ-harvesting-prisoners-continues-553986

Organ Harvesting, Illegal http://affinitymagazine.us/2017/03/15/the-illegal-harvesting-of-black-mens-organs-is-going-unnoticed/

Organ Harvesting, NAPTIP https://www.premiumtimesng.com/news/top-news/247609-naptip-investigates-organ-harvesting-ritual-killing.html

Organ Harvesting, Parasitic Infections
http://onlinelibrary.wiley.com/store/10.1111/j.1600-
6143.2009.02915.x/asset/j.1600-
6143.2009.02915.x.pdf;jsessionid=F44A9B9D90B99093C4C4AAB354D2E75
D.f02t04?v=1&t=jasccz5m&s=309c033eb085e5f2b600bbb5f11847a1cf9be63c

Organ Procurement https://en.wikipedia.org/wiki/Organ_procurement

Organ Trafficking, Illegal (1) http://bigthink.com/philip-perry/what-you-
need-to-know-about-human-organ-trafficking

Organ Trafficking, Illegal (2) http://cofs.org/home/wp-
content/uploads/2012/06/Budiani_and_Delmonico-AJT_April_20081.pdf

Organ Trafficking, Illegal (3)
http://digitalcommons.wcl.american.edu/cgi/viewcontent.cgi?article=1311&cont
ext=hrbrief

Organ Trafficking, Illegal (4) http://www.ajkd.org/article/S0272-
6386(09)01177-9/fulltext

Organ Trafficking, Illegal (5) http://www.liver4you.org/ [The "reality" of
this web site is in question, but it's a frightening experience to view it and
follow a few links.]

Organ Trafficking, Illegal (6) *New York Times*: "Kidney Thefts Shock
India" http://www.nytimes.com/2008/01/30/world/asia/30kidney.html

Organ Trafficking, Illegal (7) *Newsweek*, 1 September 2009
http://www.newsweek.com/organ-trafficking-no-myth-78079?GT1=43002

Organ Transplants, Cost https://www.transplantliving.org/before-the-
transplant/financing-a-transplant/the-costs/

Organ Transplants, Immunosuppresants https://transplantliving.org/after-
the-transplant/medications/types-of-immunosuppressants/

Organ Transplants, Trends https://unos.org/data/transplant-
trends/#waitlists_by_organ

Pinyon Nuts https://en.wikipedia.org/wiki/Pinyon_pine

Pneumonia Symptoms, Causes, Treatments & More
https://www.webmd.com/lung/tc/pneumonia-topic-overview#1

Possession With Intent To Sell Or Deliver
https://www.jgcrimlaw.com/possession-with-intent-to-sell-or-deliver.html

Priapism https://en.wikipedia.org/wiki/Priapism

Prisons, California https://ww2.kqed.org/lowdown/2012/08/22/interactive-map-of-californias-33-state-prisons/

Prisons, Private http://www.motherjones.com/politics/2016/06/cca-private-prisons-corrections-corporation-inmates-investigation-bauer/

Prison Industries Scam https://www.huffingtonpost.com/john-w-whitehead/prison-privatization_b_1414467.html

Prison Industries Scam (2) http://projects.seattletimes.com/2014/prison-labor/1/

Prison Industries , Federal
https://en.wikipedia.org/wiki/Federal_Prison_Industries

Property Forfeiture in Drug Busts
https://www.criminaldefenselawyer.com/resources/criminal-defense/white-collar-crime/defenses-civil-asset-forfeiture.htm

Property Forfeiture in Drug Busts (2)
https://www.criminaldefenselawyer.com/resources/criminal-defense/white-collar-crime/defenses-civil-asset-forfeiture.htm

Propofol (1) https://www.health.harvard.edu/blog/propofol-the-drug-that-killed-michael-jackson-201111073772

Radio-frequency Identification https://en.wikipedia.org/wiki/Radio-frequency_identification

Refractory Bricks https://en.wikipedia.org/wiki/Fire_brick

Refractory Bricks, Crematory
https://www.blcremationsystems.com/FAQRefractory.html

Rib Spreader https://en.wikipedia.org/wiki/Rib_spreader

RICO
https://en.wikipedia.org/wiki/Racketeer_Influenced_and_Corrupt_Organizations_Act

Rohypnol (1) http://www.drug-testing-kits.com/how-long-does-rohypnol-roofies-stay-in-your-system.asp

Rohypnol (2) https://www.drug-rehabs.org/research/rohypnol-drug-testing.htm

Romani https://en.wikipedia.org/wiki/Romani_people

Russian Mafia https://en.wikipedia.org/wiki/Russian_mafia

Silver Coins, British Mint
https://www.royalmintbullion.com/Products/Britannia/Silver/UKB17SSA

Skin-walker (1) https://en.wikipedia.org/wiki/Skin-walker

Skin-walker (2) http://www.navajolegends.org/navajo-skinwalker-legend/

Sky Burial https://en.wikipedia.org/wiki/Excarnation

Snowden, Edward (1)
https://www.theguardian.com/world/2013/jun/09/edward-snowden-nsa-whistleblower-surveillance

Snowden, Edward (2) https://en.wikipedia.org/wiki/Edward_Snowden

Spanish Missions in the Americas
https://en.wikipedia.org/wiki/Spanish_missions_in_the_Americas

Taphonomy & Body Farms
https://www.forbes.com/forbes/welcome/?toURL=https://www.forbes.com/sites/kristinakillgrove/2015/06/10/these-six-body-farms-help-forensic-anthropologists-learn-to-solve-crimes/&refURL=&referrer=#67edd882489f

Taphonomy & Preservation
http://paleo.cortland.edu/tutorial/Taphonomy%26Pres/taphonomy.htm

Taphonomy, Human Decomposition
https://www.youtube.com/watch?v=OFJrow7yaec

Tarot Card Meanings https://www.trustedtarot.com/card-meanings/

Tarot Career Spread https://labyrinthos.co/blogs/learn-tarot-with-labyrinthos-academy/three-career-tarot-spreads-for-finding-your-path-and-calling

Tarot Spreads (1) http://tarotprophet.com/6-most-common-tarot-spreads-and-their-uses/

Tarot Spreads (3) https://science.howstuffworks.com/science-vs-myth/extrasensory-perceptions/tarot-card2.htm

[Two spreads are illustrated following the references.]

Tarot, Biddy https://www.biddytarot.com/

Tarot, Five Card Spread http://www.angelpaths.com/spreads.html

Titanium Medical Pins http://www.supraalloys.com/medical-titanium.php

Transplants, Immunosuppressants
https://www.kidney.org/atoz/content/immuno

Transplants, Liver (1) https://www.mayoclinic.org/tests-procedures/liver-transplant/details/what-you-can-expect/rec-20211848

United States Attorney, AZ https://www.justice.gov/usao-az

United States District Court, AZ http://www.azd.uscourts.gov/

United States (Federal) Grand Juries http://corporate.findlaw.com/litigation-disputes/federal-grand-jury-crash-course.html

Valium (diazepam) Uses, Dosage, Side Effects
https://www.drugs.com/valium.html

Vatican, Nazi Ties https://www.vanityfair.com/style/1999/10/pope-pius-xii-199910

VFR flight altitudes by direction http://www.lapeeraviation.com/odd-north-east/

Wirth, Christian https://en.wikipedia.org/wiki/Christian_Wirth

Yázhí http://navajowotd.com/word/yazhi/

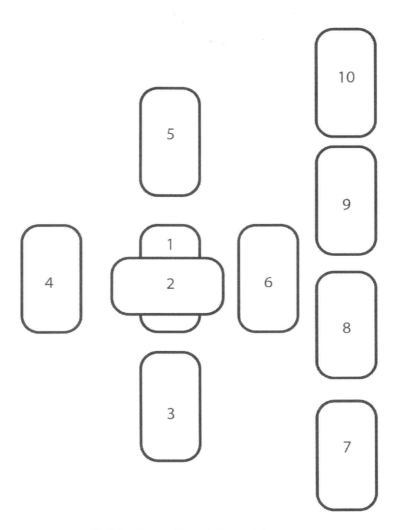

Celtic Cross Tarot Spread
1. Where you are
2. Challenges
3. Where to focus
4. Past
5. Strengths
6. Immediate future
7. Approach
8. What needs to be discovered
9. Hopes, fears
10. Long-term future

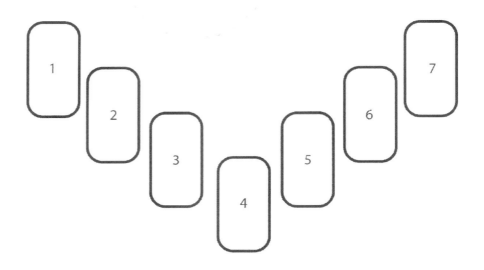

Ellipse Tarot Spread
1. Past
2. Present
3. Future
4. Path to take
5. Outside forces
6. Goals and fears
7. Ultimate outcome

Fable Elements in "The Cry of the Innocents"

This novel is intended to be a fable, with elements and characters representing and reflecting the real world. Most are related to the Holocaust, especially Nazis responsible for the imprisonment, torture, starvation, and murder of some of the eight million (or more) Jews, Soviet Prisoners of War, Ethnic Poles, Roma (Gypsies), Disabled Persons, Jehovah's Witnesses, Homosexuals, and others they labeled "Undesirables."

93526, the identification number of an inmate whose organs were harvested, is the zip code of Manzanar National Historic Site, a "Relocation Camp" for American citizens of Japanese heritage and ancestry during World War II.

Reductions created by Jesuits and Franciscans (Page 32) represent Concentration Camps.

Suite Nine at the spa, and **Unified Prison System Number Nine** after Fort 9 and the Ninth Fort Massacres, Lithuania; first systematic mass killings of German Jews during the Holocaust.

19330130, the NSA case file on Carlotta Kraft, is the date Hitler became Chancellor of Germany. It would take fewer than 2 months before he achieved absolute power.

Cell Block 11, where candidates for organ harvesting were kept in solitary confinement at Unified Prison System #9, after Block 11, a brick building at Auschwitz concentration camp, where prisoners were tortured, and where the first tests of Zyklon B were conducted.

Cooperation will make you free (several places) told to prisoners selected for medical experiments and as unknowing transplant donors, reflects the words, "Arbeit Macht Frei" (Work

Sets You Free) which appeared on the entrance of Auschwitz and other Nazi concentration camps.

Bass, Roseanne: Forensic anthropologist at the Grand Junction "body farm." After the Anthropologist who created the first such facility.

Falco, Francis: Assistant United States Attorney, Flagstaff, AZ. After a prosecutor, at the Nuremburg Trials.

"Final Solution", on Page 214. The "Final solution to the Jewish Question," discussed at the Wannsee Conference, Berlin, January 1942.

Goth, Mona: Guard at U.P.S. #9. After Amon Göth, Commandant of the Kraków-Plaszów Concentration Camp. Tried and convicted of ordering the deaths of camp inmates and of personally killing an unspecified number of people.

Grassier, Emile: Male nurse at Glen Canyon Spa. After Irma Ida Ilse Grese, female guard and nurse at Ravensbrück and Auschwitz, and warden of the women's section of Bergen-Belsen Concentration Camp. Nickname, "Hyena of Auschwitz." Hanged for crimes against humanity.

Hilflinger, Mr. Karl: Owner of the Peaceful Rest Mortuary and Crematorium, Folio, Arizona. After *Hilfinge*, meaning "Helper," Nazi euphemism for the Sonderkommandos – Jews forced by threat of death to load bodies into the crematoria at concentration camps.

"Just following orders" on Page 225. A "defense" cited by some Nazis when tried for crimes and atrocities.

Krafft, Carlotta: Astrologer and Tarot Card Reader for Gospoden Kraznachey. After Karl Ernst Krafft, astrologer and graphologist to Hitler, Rudolf Hess, Heinrich Himmler, and others.

Red Horse, Sam: Warden of Unified Prison System U.P.S. #9 near Folio, Arizona. After the first commandant of Auschwitz Concentration Camp, Rudolf Höss.

Schultz, Chris: Guard at U.P.S. #9. After Schutzstaffel member Christian Wirth, SS officer who was key in creating the program to exterminate Polish Jews.

Sheriff Edmonds, Tularosa County: After Master Sergeant Roddie Edmonds, the highest-ranking noncommissioned officer in a German POW camp. When told that Jewish soldiers would be separated and sent to an uncertain fate, he proclaimed, "We are all Jews." He did not waver, and eventually his captors backed down.

Standart, Todd MD, FACS: Medical Director and Chief of Surgery at the Glen Canyon Medical Spa. After Joseph Mengele, who was Standortartz, or garrison physician, at Auschwitz. Nickname, Todesengel, Angel of Death.

Winder, Gabby: FBI agent associated with Chief Joseph's task force. After Gabrielle Weidner, heroine of the Holocaust who died in a concentration camp after helping more than 900 people evade the Nazis.

RFID on prisoners after tattoos on concentration camp inmates.

Made in the USA
Columbia, SC
01 February 2020